Peter A. Flannery lives .... wife and two sons. After leaving .... college before changing tack to work in forestry and horticulture. After several years of working with plants he switched again, setting himself up as a sculptor for the toy and hobby industry. It was while working for a design studio in Edinburgh that he moved from sculpting to writing, producing background stories for the company's models and games. He is now a self-published author working entirely on his own material.

Peter's Books

First and Only - 2011

Battle Mage - 2017

Decimus Fate and the Talisman of Dreams - 2020

Decimus Fate and the Butcher of Guile – 2021

Contact:

Twitter: @TheFlanston

Website: www.peterflannery.co.uk

Decimus Fate

and the
Butcher of Guile

Peter A. Flannery

BLACKHEART BOOKS

Decimus Fate
and the
Butcher of Guile

ISBN: 978-1-7399341-0-1

First published by Blackheart Books in 2021

To Julie with love

Decimus Fate

and the

Butcher of Guile

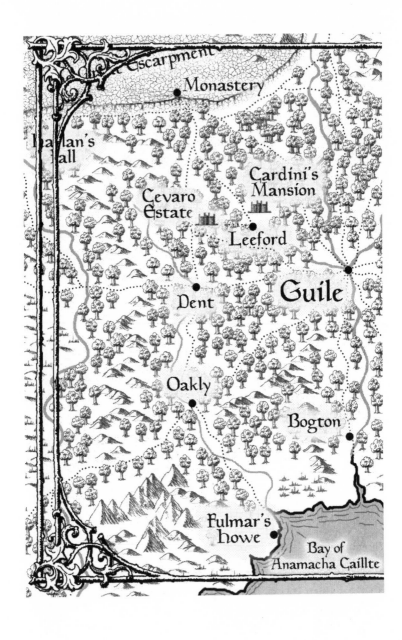

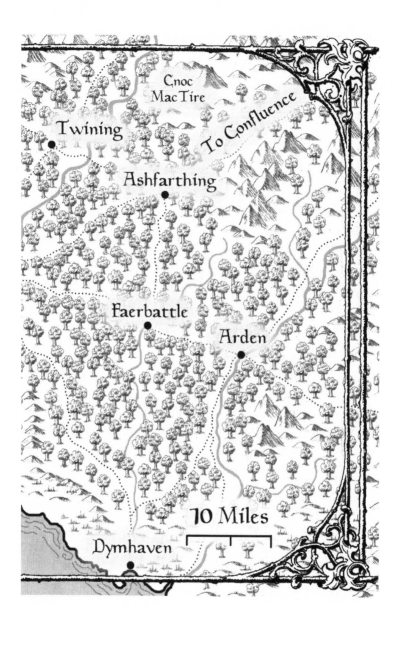

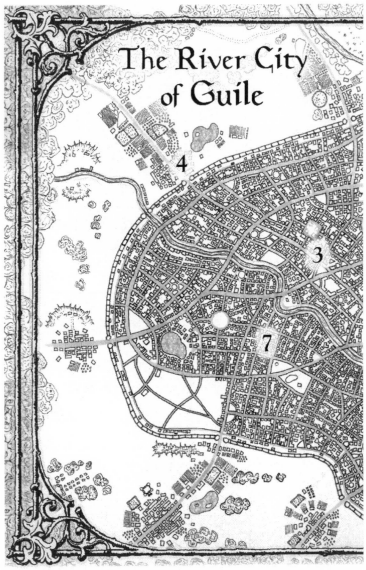

The River City of Guile

4

3

7

1. Blackfell House
2. Fool's Hope Inn
3. The Temple of Abnoba
4. The Northwest Gate

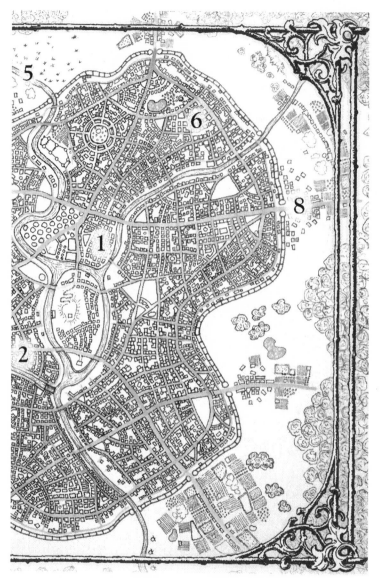

5. The River Scéal   7. Fleshmarket Close
6. Medici Mansion   8. The East Gate

Prologue

The Butcher

The sewers of Guile were a labyrinth of pipes, drains and brick-lined aqueducts, all weaving between a series of natural tunnels carved out before guile was even a word. They were a place of fear and urban myths with none so disturbing as the so-called Butcher of Guile. Many had heard the stories of how he chopped up his victims before disposing of their bodies in the river. However, what nobody knew was that the Butcher did not work alone.

It was deep in the night when the hunched form of a troglodyte emerged from a storm drain in the northern part of the city. Looking almost like a man, the cave-dweller was dressed in knee-length trousers with a plain linen shirt, and its pale skin shone with a faint silvery light.

Pausing at the mouth of the storm drain, the troglodyte checked to make sure the coast was clear before venturing into the street that led down to the river. The pale figure was slender at the waist with broad shoulders, short legs and long arms. Over one shoulder he carried a sack and it was clear from his hunched posture that the sack was heavy.

Keeping to the deepest pockets of shadow, the troglodyte moved quickly towards the river. His route took him through the black buildings of the caulking yard where the river boats of Guile were made watertight. The air grew thick with acrid smells and he failed to notice an area of pine pitch that had spilled across the road. The normally tacky substance was made slippery by a layer of moisture and the troglodyte made a cursing sound as he slipped and fell. He lost his grip on the sack and something tumbled out.

There was just enough light to reveal that the 'something' was an arm, cleanly severed at the shoulder and tied with a short length of rope to other shapes in the sack.

Coming quickly to his feet, the troglodyte grabbed the arm and stuffed it back into the sack. As he closed up the sack he saw the dark silhouette of a tattoo on the back of the arm's hand. Even in the darkness he could make out the shape of a harp, the mark of an apprentice musician. Unfortunately, this young man had yearned for excitement which led to him making some bad decisions. Those bad decisions led to a price on his head from one of the most dangerous gangs in the city, and that price had brought him to the tender mercy of the Butcher.

Quickly, the troglodyte gathered up his sack and continued down to the dark expanse of the River Scéal. Pausing once again to make sure the coast was clear, he tipped the grizzly contents of the sack into the river. The pale shapes tumbled into the water with a series of noisy splashes, but within a matter of seconds all was quiet as the river carried away the remains of a teenage boy. The various parts were tied together and so they did not drift far from each other. Unlike a killer who might seek to hide a body, the Butcher wanted his handiwork to be found.

For just a moment the troglodyte lingered at the water's edge, then he threw the empty sack into the river and turned back towards the storm drain and the maze of tunnels and sewers that he called home, a home he shared with a man known as the Butcher of Guile.

1
Of Murder and Marriage

Three nights later, in a large and luxurious mansion, a young man called Luca choked back a cry of shock as he peered through an interior doorway. There, on a bloodstained carpet, lay the seventeen-year-old niece of his employer, stabbed... strangled... dead.

Knowing *he* would be dead if anyone saw him, Luca backed away from the horrific scene and walked towards the patio doors of the drawing-room. In his trouser pocket he had a letter from the dead girl, a plea for help that he had promised to deliver to her father. But now it was too late.

Suddenly he heard voices from the adjacent room.

'I know!' cried a strident voice that he knew all too well. 'I know this is different. I know this is family!' There was a pause. 'Oh, don't worry,' the voice continued as if in answer to a question. 'We'll... we'll blame it on the new footman. The boy always had an eye for Eliza. Now *he* can hang for the death of my dear cousin.'

Luca knew that the 'new footman' meant him. Filled with terror he fumbled with the key in the patio doors. He had to tell someone what happened. He had to show someone the letter. If he showed them the letter then that would prove his innocence.

Finally the door opened, but Luca paused. No, the letter was not enough. He needed the potion too. Turning back into the room he dashed over to a drinks cabinet that was wreathed in what looked like steam. In the adjacent room, the voices continued.

'No, you fool.' said the strident voice. 'Bring the wash bowl *here*! I can't go dripping blood through the house.' Then... 'Right, now go and find the boy!'

Luca's time was up. Opening the drinks cabinet he felt a blast of cold as a chill mist blew into his face. With no time to spare he caught a quick glimpse of a small silver flask and reached out to grab it. Then, before anyone even knew he was there, he slipped out of the patio doors, sprinted across the lawn and scrambled over the boundary wall before disappearing into the night-time streets of Guile.

In the space of an hour, Luca had seen a young woman murdered, lost his job and was now on the run for his life. He had taken this job despite his mother's objections because they needed the money and he hated being poor. But, as it turned out, his mother was right.

There are worse things in life than simply being poor.

*

In another part of the city, a young woman called Jane wept tears of despair as she argued with *her* mother.

'I don't care what you say,' said the girl. 'I'm going to marry Inganno and there's nothing you can do about it.'

'Jane, please!' said the mother. 'Please just let us talk about it.'

'There's nothing to say,' insisted the girl.

'But it's all so quick,' said the mother. 'Please. Just speak to this man before you do something that you might regret.'

'I'm not speaking to any *man*,' cried Jane. 'Nothing he can say will change my mind.'

'But he might be able to help,' said the mother. 'His name is Fate, but they call him the Sage of Blackfell House.'

'I don't need help,' snapped Jane, 'and I don't need any so-called 'sage' telling me who I should love! I'm going to marry Inganno and that's that!'

'Please,' begged the mother. 'He said he would call on us tomorrow. Just one more day, that's all I'm asking. Just one more day, and if you still want to marry Inganno then I won't stand in your way.'

For a moment Jane's conviction appeared to waver, but then her pretty face became fixed with determination.

'No,' she said. 'My mind is made up. I will be leaving for Inganno's house in the morning.'

*

And, just a mile away in the basement of an expensive townhouse, a potion maker called Inganno smiled in anticipation as he waited for his beloved Jane to arrive.

2
Tormented by Demons

The river city of Guile lies in a region of forests and hills known as the Seven Vales. Half a day's journey west of the city two men were riding along the forested road as the autumn sun filtered through a canopy of green and russet gold.

One of the men was a tall man with long black hair, blue eyes and the dark skin of those who hailed from the Southern Isles. Dressed in black leather, he had a band of throwing stars across his chest and plates of hard leather armour covering his right arm and shoulder. The sword hanging at his waist was curved with a long handle and a white gemstone encased in the pommel. It was a Hadean Blade, a weapon capable of channelling the essential life-force of the wielder, and the man carrying it was once a demon hunter. His name was Alexander Teuton, but most people knew him only as the Tutor.

The other man wore the charcoal grey robes of a sorcerer, the dark fabric edged with arcane designs that shimmered with a touch of silver. He wore a bracelet of dark metal charms on his wrist and two daggers hung from his belt, the handles of which were carved in the form of dragons, one white, one black. This man was also tall with long dark hair and the paler skin of those who lived in the cooler climes of the Seven Vales. The man's features had a hawkish quality and his deep brown eyes were shot through with flecks of gold. His name was Decimus Fate, a once-notorious sorcerer who renounced his power to avoid becoming a slave to magic.

In recent years, both men had earned a reputation for helping people, but it was only in the last few weeks that they had found themselves working together. Now they were on their way to see the countess of a country estate.

The estate in question was owned by Count Leopold Cévaro, a cruel man who had recently hired two demonic sorcerers, known as the Kane Twins, to kill Fate and the Tutor. However, after learning of her husband's nefarious plot, the countess had risked her own safety and ridden through the night to warn them. She had managed to get back home before her absence was noticed, but now she was dealing with the consequences of her husband's foolish plans.

During their time at the mansion, the Kane Twins had used one of the serving girls in their spells, trading her body and soul for power from the demonic realm.

'Do you think we'll be able to help her?' asked the Tutor as he and Fate drew closer to the Cévaro estate.

'I don't know,' said Fate. 'Apparently the girl has some unique physical characteristics, but it all depends on the nature of the link that's been established with the Daemonaria.'

'I could go through to see if it's a specific entity,' said the Tutor. 'If I could kill the demon that's trying to claim her...'

Fate shook his head.

'It doesn't sound like an individual demon. Besides... opening a rift to the Daemonaria requires magic, and...'

'...you no longer do magic,' finished the Tutor.

'No,' said Fate.

'Well, there must be something we can do to help,' said the Tutor. 'It's not fair that the countess should pay for the mistakes of her murderous husband.'

'No it's not,' said Fate. 'It's not fair at all.'

Fate glanced at the demon hunter as they continued on their way. The Tutor and the countess had something of a history. Their first meeting had resulted in a feeling of mutual animosity. However, more recent events had caused those feelings to evolve into something closer to mutual respect, something that neither of them would choose to admit.

The Tutor tried to hide it but Fate could sense the nervous tension in the air.

'What?' said the Tutor as he caught Fate looking at him.

'Nothing,' said Fate, and he smiled as they turned into the main driveway of the Cévaro estate.

*

Countess Cévaro was dozing in a chair beside the window of her bed-chamber. She was exhausted. For days now she had been caring for one of the serving girls who had been traumatised by the two demonic sorcerers that her husband had hired. The two sorcerers were now dead, but the link they had forged with the realm of demons continued to torment the girl and she was haunted by nightmares of being lost to creatures of the Daemonaria.

For the first few nights the countess had tried to comfort her, insisting that the threat was all in her dreams, but the evil of those dreams had begun to seep into the real world. Objects would fly across the room and patches of the floorboards and the walls had been scorched as if they had been exposed to fire. Disturbing noises could be heard and foul smells permeated the room as the poor girl wrestled with dreams that could easily drive her mad.

And so the countess was exhausted. She was just trying to take an hour's rest when one of her maids entered the room.

'Pardon, my lady,' whispered the maid, clearly reluctant to disturb her mistress's rest. 'But there are two men to see you.'

The countess blinked and adjusted her long dark hair as she struggled into a more upright position in her chair.

'Can the count not see to them?'

'The count has gone into town for a flogging,' said the maid. 'And the men asked for you in particular.'

'They did?' said the countess stifling a yawn.

'Yes, my lady. Polite as you like, but scary too... one of them looks like some dark assassin, while the other one looks like...'

'A sorcerer,' finished the countess.

'You know him, my Lady?'

'Yes,' said the countess. 'His name is Fate.'

*

Fate and the Tutor watched as Countess Cévaro entered the reception room of the Cévaro mansion. The autumn sun shone through the windows and the two men were struck once more by the woman's beauty. With high cheekbones, a full mouth and a strong jaw line, she was not pretty as some women were, but there was an appealing dignity to this woman's appearance, softened only by a sadness that lay behind the surface of her deep brown eyes.

'Good morning, my lady,' said Fate.

'Good morning, Lord Fate,' said the countess before her gaze moved over to the demon hunter. 'Lord Teuton,' she said, clasping her hands together as she lowered her eyes.

9

'My lady,' said the Tutor with a slight bow of the head.

'My housekeeper passed on your letter. I believe that one of your servants is bedevilled by visions of the demonic realm.'

'More than visions,' said the countess as the tension and the worry returned to her face.

'The manifestations have become physical?' asked the Tutor.

'Oh, yes,' said the countess and the gold streaks in Fate's eyes glowed with a dangerous light.

'Take us to her,' he said.

*

Even before they entered the room they could feel the taint of the Daemonaria, like a foul stench, a shadow of fear, or the whispered promise of unspeakable pain.

'She might be asleep,' said the countess as her maid opened the door. 'It was a difficult night.'

Fate gave a nod of understanding as they entered the room where a young woman was lying on a freshly made bed. The woman appeared to be neither awake nor asleep, but rather somewhere in-between. She moaned and shifted, scrunching up her eyes before opening them wide as if startled by something *they* could not see.

'My lady!' cried the countess's maid, pointing to a corner of the room where the floorboards and skirting board had begun to glow.

Moving quickly, the countess filled a jug from a basin of water at the foot of the bed. She handed it to the maid who flung it over the glowing corner of the room. A foul sulphurous smell filled the air but the steaming floorboards continued to glow.

'That used to work!' said the countess with a touch of panic in her voice. 'The water used to work.'

Striding past the maid, the Tutor drew his sword and reversed his grip before driving the point of the blade into the oak boards that had now begun to smoke. Gripping the handle, he closed his eyes and the white stone in the pommel suddenly flared with light. Almost instantly, the fiery glow faded from the corner of the room and the sulphurous stench gave way to the earthly smell of scorched wood.

Removing his sword from the floorboards, the Tutor turned to the maid.

'Salt is more effective than water for quenching the demonic contusions.'

The maid had no idea what a contusion was, but she gave a frightened nod and the Tutor rose to his feet.

'It used to happen only at night,' said the countess as Fate moved to stand over the afflicted woman. 'But now the harassment continues through the day.'

The frown on Fate's face grew deeper as he sat on the bed and placed his hand on the young woman's brow.

'Can you hear me?' he asked.

'Please,' breathed the woman. 'Please don't let them take me. I made no promise... I did not agree.'

'Open your eyes,' Fate told the woman and slowly she did.

Her gaze flitted for a moment as if she was searching for the deep voice that offered some comfort. Finally, her frightened eyes settled on Fate's face.

'Can you feel them in your mind?' he asked and the young woman's terrified expression made it clear that she could. 'Look into my eyes,' Fate continued. 'Focus only on my eyes.'

Looking down at the woman, Fate was struck by the jewel-like brightness of *her* eyes, one bright blue, the other an equally bright and vivid green. Her hair and eyebrows also differed in colour from one side of her head to the other. Such individuals were lusted after by creatures of the underworld. No wonder the demonic forces refused to let her go. He waited until the girl's eyes were fixed on his; until he could see the gold streaks in *his* eyes reflected in hers.

'Good,' said Fate as the woman grew calmer. 'Now... let them see what you see... Let them see me.'

The woman's gaze seemed to grow more intense and her eyes widened as she stared into Fate's dark eyes. The demonic whispers in the room suddenly stopped as if they had been interrupted. Continuing now, they stuttered uncertainly then rose quickly to a spiteful pitch before pinching out into silence.

At the same instant, the young woman closed her eyes and slumped back on the bed; her face relaxed and her breathing calmed as she fell into a peaceful sleep. Still sitting on the bed, Fate let out a breath while the countess looked down at him in awe. What kind of man was this; that the demons of the underworld would flee from him in fear?

'She should be alright for a while now,' said Fate as he stood up from the bed and raised the dark metal charm bracelet that he wore on his left wrist.

The countess caught a quick glimpse of a firefly beetle and a tiny hourglass before Fate removed a particular charm and reached out to place the metal object in her hand. The countess looked down to see the small figurine of a cat.

'No one knows why,' said Fate, 'but demons have an aversion to cats and this charm has been enchanted to keep them at bay.'

The countess frowned with uncertainty. She did not see how a tiny charm could protect them from the supernatural forces that were plaguing her home. Nevertheless, she placed it on the bedside table as she turned back to Fate.

'Will it stop?' she asked.

'I don't know,' said Fate. 'It all depends on what was promised, and to whom.'

The countess would have preferred a more definite answer, but still she breathed a sigh of relief, grateful for even a brief respite.

'The charm and the salt might help,' said Fate as he and the Tutor prepared to leave. 'But if it gets worse, I would suggest that you take her to Abbess Shimitsu. The Shīku monks have powers that can guard against the forces of darkness.'

Abbess Shimitsu was the leader of a monastery about a day's ride to the north. Fate and the Tutor had recently helped the abbess with a mysterious malady that was making the monks ill.

'I will remember that,' said the countess. 'Thank you.'

'Not at all,' said Fate.

Together they left the room, leaving the maid to make the sleeping woman more comfortable in her bed.

'Would you care for something to eat or drink?' asked the countess as they returned to the reception room. 'The count will be away for some time.'

'Thank you, but no,' said Fate. 'I'm afraid we need to get back to Guile.'

'Then allow me to…' began the countess, but Fate raised a hand.

'It's the least we could do, after what you did to help us.'

The countess inclined her head while Fate and the Tutor offered shallow bows as they turned to leave the room.

*

The Tutor appeared unusually pensive as they headed back to Guile and Fate stole a sideways glance at the man riding beside him. He could not be certain, but he could make a reasonable guess at the thoughts running through his mind.

The Tutor had rebelled against the demon hunters when the unit was turned into a political weapon, and this rebellion had resulted in the death of his family. Fate knew he could never let go of the love he felt for his Faerie wife and his beautiful half-Faerie child, but life is a river that refuses to be still, and the Tutor was likely confused by the way his thoughts kept returning to the Countess Cévaro.

Riding beside him, Fate's hawkish features were softened by a poignant smile.

'It's all right,' he said in a surprisingly gentle tone.

'What's all right?"

'To like the Countess,' replied Fate. 'She is, after all, a very attractive woman. Strong and brave too.'

The Tutor seemed annoyed by this topic of conversation.

'She's also married,' he snapped.

'Not for long, I suspect' said Fate and the Tutor shot him an accusing look.

'What have you done?'

'Me? Nothing,' said Fate. He paused. 'Although some of the count's enemies might have recently decided that life might be better if their cruel neighbour was no longer in the picture.'

'I wonder what gave them that idea,' said the Tutor.

'I can't imagine,' said Fate and the Tutor shook his head as they headed back to Guile where they had agreed to meet the mother of a young woman called Jane who was suddenly consumed by the desire to marry a man she barely knew.

3
The Tincture of Fixation

The following day Fate and the Tutor went to visit Jane's mother to see if there was anything unusual about her daughter's sudden change of heart. They arrived late in the afternoon only to find that Jane had already left the house so her mother led them to the home of the potion-maker she intended to marry.

The potion-maker was called Inganno, but when they called at *his* home the young man refused to let them in. The Tutor tried to reason with him, leaning in close until the potion-maker slammed the door shut trapping a lock of the demon hunter's long hair, which was yanked from his scalp as he recoiled.

The Tutor gave a curse and was about to kick in the door when Fate stepped forward.

'Allow me,' said the sorcerer and, reaching to the bracelet on his wrist, he removed a small charm in the form of a skeleton.

'Oh, you've got to be kidding!' said the Tutor and Fate smiled.

Holding the skeleton by the skull, he inserted the body into the lock and the bones of the enchanted charm began to rearrange themselves as they matched the various tumblers of the lock. A moment later Fate turned the skeleton key and the door opened onto a large hallway where they found Jane standing beside another door leading down to the cellar.

'What's going on?' she asked in an anxious tone, her eyes shifting to the open cellar door.

'These men are here to help,' said her mother as Fate and the Tutor headed down to the cellar where they found Inganno in a basement room filled with all the paraphernalia required for creating potions. A series of cast iron cauldrons sat near a stove pit in the centre of the floor and the walls were lined with a huge array of ingredients along with glass coils, bottles, flasks and books… lots and lots of books.

'We just want to talk,' said Fate as he and the Tutor passed through a heavy steel door.

'No you don't,' said Inganno. 'You want to take her away from me.'

The potion-maker was a narrow-chested man with dark oily hair and a plump cherubic face. In his hand he held a small potion bottle, which he had just lowered from his wet and fleshy lips. Reaching to a bench, Inganno put the potion bottle down and picked up a large glass beaker which he then threw directly at Fate.

The sorcerer instinctively raised an arm to protect himself, then winced as the beaker shattered, cutting his hand. At the same moment, Inganno darted forward with a surprising burst of speed, barging past the Tutor as he surged through the doorway and raced up the stairs.

Back in the hallway, Jane's mother was trying to calm her daughter. They were blocking the front door which was now closed and Inganno spat out a curse before heading for a door at the back of the house. The route took him through the dinner-service room and several porcelain plates tumbled to the floor, smashing noisily as he hurried past with the Tutor hot on his heels.

'Stop him!' cried Fate as he emerged from the cellar. 'We need to talk to him.'

Charging into the kitchen, the Tutor threw himself across the kitchen table just as Inganno was reaching for the latch on the back door.

'Got you!' he cried, grabbing the young man's waistcoat before he could open the door. But Inganno was not so easily caught. With a strength that belied his soft physique, he struck at the Tutor with his fists before wrenching open the door.

'Have you got him?' Fate called out from the hall.

'No!' snapped the Tutor as he tried to prevent the young man from escaping through the half-open door. 'The damnable wretch... is surprisingly... strong.'

'I think he took something before we came in,' replied Fate holding up the empty potion bottle that Inganno had put down. 'Something to enhance his speed and strength.' His lip curled in distaste as he noticed that the bottle was still wet with the young man's saliva.

'Well... it seems... to be working,' said the Tutor. With a final grunt he got a better grip on Inganno and pulled the young man to the floor where they continued to wrestle for control.

Back in the hall, Fate held up the potion bottle and wondered what it might have contained. Wrapping the small bottle in a silk handkerchief he tucked it into a pocket in his robes as the Tutor's voice rose up from the kitchen.

'Calm down!' said the demon hunter as Inganno struggled to break free.

'Don't hurt him!' cried Jane from the hall. 'Don't you dare hurt my beloved!'

Satisfied that the potion maker was now contained, Fate turned to look at the young woman who was having her own wrestling match with her mother.

'Don't touch me!' the young woman cried. 'You never approved of our love and now you've ruined everything!' She was clearly distraught and her pale cheeks were streaked with tears.

'Dearest Jane,' said her mother. 'Surely you can see that he's not the one for you. I thought Fidanza was your love.'

'Fidanza is in my past, mama,' said the young woman. 'Inganno is my future. He is the one I truly love.'

Jane's mother gave a sigh of exasperation and Fate rolled his eyes as he heard a scuffle and a squeal coming from the kitchen. The Tutor had finally subdued his man. Suffering a tirade of complaints, the demon hunter hauled Inganno to his feet and propelled him out of the kitchen and into the hall where the others were waiting. Glancing down, he saw blood dripping from Fate's hand.

'Are you all right?' he asked.

'I'm fine,' said Fate. 'Just a cut from the glass beaker he threw at me.'

'And no less than you deserve,' said Jane who had now broken away from her mother. She rushed towards her 'beloved' then stopped as the Tutor fixed her with a cold blue stare.

'Get your hands off me, you brute!' cried Inganno. He continued to struggle in the Tutor's grasp, but the effects of his 'strength potion' were wearing off and the Tutor had no problem restraining him.

'Hold him still,' said Fate as he stepped forward to search Inganno's pockets. He frowned as he found a roll of snakeskin, a small bottle of silvery metal fragments and the desiccated eye of a rabbit, all ingredients that were commonly used in the creation of potions.

'You can't do this!' spluttered Inganno. 'You have no right to go searching through my...'

'Aha!' said Fate holding up a small vial filled with a distinctive purple liquid.

The mother looked horrified, the Tutor looked furious, while Jane was beside herself with distress.

'Let him go!' she wailed. 'He's done no harm. Let him go!'

Again she started towards Inganno, but then Fate gave the mother a nod and she stepped forward to catch her daughter's arms.

'What are you doing?' cried Jane. 'Let me go!'

But the mother held onto her as Fate took a small packet of white powder from a pouch at his waist. Laying the packet on a nearby table he opened the vial he had taken from Inganno and poured two drops of the purple liquid onto the powder. The combined ingredients fizzed until the purple liquid was absorbed by the powder at which point Fate lifted the small packet, brought it over to Jane, and blew it into her face. She drew a startled breath, coughed several times, and slowly the distressed expression faded from her eyes to be replaced by a look of confusion and fear.

'What... Why... Where is Fidanza?' she began.

'No!' insisted Inganno. 'She loves me, not him!'

'What are you talking about?' said Jane in a tone of bewilderment. 'I love Fidanza. I have never loved you. I don't even like you.' Eyes filling with tears, she turned to her mother. 'What is going on?' she asked. 'Where is Fidanza?'

'We don't know,' replied her mother. 'Fidanza went missing two days ago.'

'What do you mean, missing?' asked Jane, an edge of hysteria creeping into her voice. 'And why are we here in Inganno's house?'

Her mother was clearly overwrought so Fate stepped forward to answer.

'You have been the victim of deception,' he said, holding up the vial of purple liquid.

'What do you mean?' asked Jane. 'What is that?'

'It's a tincture of fixation,' replied Fate. 'Otherwise known as a love potion.'

'What!' exclaimed Jane.

'Two days ago, this young man slipped some into your drink and from that moment you have been fixated on him. The brain confuses this fixation with the emotion of love.'

Jane just stared at him, her eyes narrowing as if she was trying to recall the details of a dream.

'I remember,' she breathed in a horrified tone as her eyes shifted to Inganno. 'I remember feeling...' Her mouth twisted in a gesture of fury and she lunged forward. Her foot lashed out towards Inganno's groin, and it was only the restriction of her dress that saved him from a painful kick.

'I did it because I love you,' said Inganno.

'No,' said Fate. 'You did it because you wanted her, and now you will spend the next five years in jail reflecting on your crime.'

'No!' cried Inganno, beginning to struggle once more. 'I did her no harm. Now let me go!' He twisted and kicked, but the Tutor grabbed him by the scruff of the neck and pressed his face into the wall.

'Will he really be imprisoned?' asked Jane.

'We'll take him to the local sheriff's office,' said Fate. 'But he is wealthy so he might escape the punishment he deserves.'

'I don't care,' said Jane's mother. 'So long as he is gone from my daughter's life.'

'But what about Fidanza?' asked Jane.

'He's not at his home,' said her mother. 'His coachman said he left the house looking confused and that was two days ago.'

A look of suspicion tightened Fate's face as he turned back to Inganno.

'What did you do to this other man?' he asked, but Inganno refused to answer until the Tutor's grip tightened on his neck.

'I didn't hurt him!' squealed the cherub-faced man. 'I just gave him something to make him forget.'

'Didn't hurt him,' repeated Fate with a dangerous glint in his eye. 'You wiped a young man's memory and sent him out into the murky streets of Guile.'

There was no remorse in Inganno's eyes, but he lowered his gaze in fear.

'You had better pray that he's found safe and well,' said Fate. 'The use of a love potion carries a heavy sentence, but if anything happens to this young man then you could be locked up for good.'

'You can't prove anything!' spat Inganno, but Fate just smiled.

'Oh, but I can,' he said as he held up the vial containing the purple liquid. 'And even if I couldn't, my housekeeper makes a truth potion that will make you sing like a blackbird at midnight.'

With that, Fate gave the Tutor a nod and the potion-maker was dragged from the house and out onto the street. They descended the short flight of steps and had just reached the pavement when a richly dressed man stepped out of a coach bearing the gold motif of the letter M.

'What's going on here?' asked the man in a lofty tone.

Somewhere in his mid-twenties, the man was tall and slender with fine cheekbones, dark eyes and a full mouth that seemed permanently cast in an expression of scorn.

'Oh, thank goodness...' began Inganno, stepping forward until the Tutor yanked him away.

'And who are you?' asked Fate.

'That is none of your concern,' said the man. 'I have business with this man and you will tell me why he is being apprehended.'

Fate arched an eyebrow. 'He is accused of potion crimes,' he said. 'We are escorting him to the sheriff's office to be formally charged.'

The man's eyes narrowed with displeasure.

'You are welcome to join us at the sheriff's office, if you wish,' added Fate.

The young man hesitated as his eyes moved from Fate to the intimidating figure of the Tutor. Behind him, there was a shadow of movement from inside the coach as a large figure edged closer to the door. Fate and the Tutor caught a brief glimpse of crimson robes, but the young man made a halting gesture and the mysterious figure held back. He seemed reluctant to get involved so, ignoring Fate and the Tutor, he spoke to Inganno.

'I will have my lawyer attend you,' he said before climbing back into the coach. 'Ride on,' he called out, and Fate frowned as the carriage disappeared up the street.

'Did you sense that?' he asked.

'The shadowy figure inside the carriage,' said the Tutor.

'Yes,' said Fate. 'That young man has a person of power in his employ.'

The two men stared after the disappearing coach as Jane and her mother joined them on the pavement. Together they marched Inganno down to the local sheriff's office and handed him over to the officer on duty.

'Is that it?' asked Jane. 'What about Fidanza?'

'Don't worry,' said the Tutor. 'We'll help you find him.'

'Thank you,' said Jane's mother.

'Don't thank us yet,' said Fate. 'If Inganno's potions are *that* powerful then Fidanza might never recall that he knew your daughter at all.'

With nothing else to be done, they escorted the two women back to their townhouse before heading for home.

'We need to find this Fidanza quickly,' said the Tutor as they turned onto one of the main streets.

'Yes,' said Fate. 'A rich youth won't last long on the streets of this city.'

They continued along until they saw two grubby girls running along the street. The two girls were wayfinders, street urchins who earned a crust by guiding people through the twisting streets of Guile.

'Weasel might be able to help,' suggested the Tutor and Fate gave a nod as he raised a hand to stop the children.

Weasel was also a wayfinder and, even though they had not known him long, the young boy had proved himself to be quick-witted and brave. He seemed to know every wayfinder in the city so, when it came to finding things in the city, Weasel was a useful person to know.

'Do you know Weasel on the northwest gate?' Fate asked the two girls.

'Might do,' said one of the girls warily.

Fate smiled and fished out two copper coins from a pouch at his waist.

'Yeah, we know him,' said the other girl.

'Good,' said Fate, tossing each of them a coin. 'Well, tell Weasel we've a job for him. Tell him to come to Blackfell House if he's interested.'

The two girls pocketed their coins muttering to each other as they walked away.

'Bloomin' Weasel!' said one of the girls. 'He always gets the cushy jobs.'

'Aye,' replied the other girl. 'And I bet that housekeeper gives him something from the kitchen.'

Fate and the Tutor smiled. The wayfinders thought Weasel was just lucky, but *they* knew that there was more to it than that. No... he might be cheeky and mischievous, but the wayfinder called Weasel had earned his good luck.

4
Blackfell House

It was early evening when Fate and the Tutor arrived back at Fate's home, a large grey-stone property known as Blackfell House.

For the last few years, the Tutor had been renting a room at the Fool's Hope Inn. However, he and Fate had recently been the focus of a fight that had caused considerable damage to the inn, not to mention the injuries suffered by several patrons and staff. After causing so much trouble, the Tutor did not feel comfortable staying at the inn and was now living in one of the guest rooms of Blackfell House, an arrangement that both men agreed was purely temporary.

The house itself sat in modest grounds with a square perimeter fence and a gravel driveway leading from the main gate to the front door.

Flanking the driveway was an avenue of gnarled trees, their leafless branches fanning out like something from a dark fairytale. But these were no ordinary trees. These were Arborio Custos, dendroid sentinels from the hidden realm of Faerie. Just a small amount of magic would bring these trees to life, but they were just one of the measures protecting the home of Decimus Fate. Even the perimeter fence was charged with magic to burn those who tried to enter with malicious intent.

Passing through the gate, they followed the driveway to the house. The delicious smell of chicken stew and home-baking greeted them as they entered the kitchen where a small hunchbacked woman was tending a large cast-iron range. A loaf of freshly baked bread sat on the table and the Tutor was just reaching for a knife when the woman spoke.

'Hands!'

The Tutor pulled back his arm and turned to the sink where Fate wore a slight smile as he washed his own hands. The woman at the stove was Varna Motina, Fate's housekeeper, who also happened to be an exiled witch from the distant region of Karuthia.

'So, was it a love potion?' she asked as she added a pinch of herbs to a pot of stew.

'Yes it was,' said Fate and Motina muttered a heartfelt curse in her native tongue.

'And did you catch him!' she asked.

'We did,' said Fate. 'We took him along to the sheriff's office, although he might wheedle his way out of any charges.'

Motina shook her head in disgust while Fate took a seat, glancing down to look at the shallow cut on his hand.

'Let me see that,' said Motina.

Putting the pot of stew on the table, she brushed back a few strands of her black hair as she took Fate's hand and brought it closer to her wrinkled face. 'Did the potion-maker do this?'

'It's fine,' said Fate.

'Hmm…' murmured Motina as she passed him a clean cloth to press against the cut. 'And what about the young woman?' she asked. 'Were you able to reverse the effects of the love potion?'

'Yes,' said Fate. 'The antidote worked, but the potion-maker wiped her fiancé's memory, and now he's missing.'

'Well, at least you broke the spell,' said Motina. 'So now you can turn your attention to finding him.'

'Indeed,' said the Tutor as he also took a seat. 'We saw a couple of wayfinders on the way back here. They're going to ask Weasel to call at the house.'

The housekeeper gave a nod of approval. She was particularly fond of Weasel after the young wayfinder had risked his own life to help her when she was being attacked by the Kane Twins. Coming back to the table, she laid out three bowls for the stew. 'What have you got there?' she asked as Fate took out the small potion bottle he had taken from Inganno's cellar.

'It's the strength potion he swallowed as we arrived.'

Motina could see the curiosity in Fate's eyes and she wondered how long it would be before he disappeared to test it. Putting down the bottle Fate ate a few mouthfuls of stew, but it was only a matter of seconds before he pushed away his bowl and got to his feet.

'I'm just going to analyse this before it starts to degrade,' he said as he made his way out of the kitchen.

Motina and the Tutor exchanged a glance as Fate left the room.

'He just can't help himself,' said the housekeeper. 'Even food has to wait when the master has a mystery to solve.'

'And is he?' asked the Tutor. 'Is he your master?' His tone suggested that he meant no offence and Motina laughed.

'Not in the way you're thinking,' she said. 'He does not own or control me, but he is the master of this house.'

'And you don't mind waiting on him?'

'Why should I?' replied Motina and the small witch smiled. 'In Karuthia we have a saying... garbė yra tarnauti, the honour is to serve.'

'So you honour him?' said the Tutor, and Motina bowed her head.

'How else do you repay a man who saved your life, even after you tried to kill him?'

'You tried to kill Fate?' asked the Tutor and Motina positively beamed with pride.

'Hit him squarely in the chest with a powerful spell.'

'And what did he do?'

'He snarled like a scalded wolf, then he hit me with a pulse of energy that put me to sleep for a day and a half.'

The Tutor raised his eyebrows in surprise as the housekeeper continued.

'When I came to, I was free from my prison, my tormentors were dead, and we had escaped from the country that I called home.'

'The Karuthian Purge,' said the Tutor and Motina nodded.

'Most of the magic-users that I knew were killed.' A shadow of sadness passed over her face. 'Put to death by one of the *two* powerful sorcerers that had come into Karuthia from the outside world. One saw magic-users as a force of natural wonder, the other saw them as a threat, and so he turned the authorities against us.'

'Oruthian Bohr,' said the Tutor and Motina gave a sigh.

'Oruthian Bohr went on to become the Emperor's personal sorcerer, while Fate gave me a home in the river city of Guile.'

'The honour is to serve,' said the Tutor and Motina's small black eyes glistened as she dipped bread in her stew.

They sat in silence for a few minutes until the jangle of a bell sounded from outside.

'That's the gate bell,' she said and, rising from her seat, she left the room to see who was calling at the house this evening.

Munching on a piece of bread, the Tutor thought about Fate and how the man he had come to know did not match the reputation of the ruthless sorcerer he had heard about over the years. He was still lost in reverie when Motina came back into the room supporting a woman who was clearly in some distress.

The Tutor rose to his feet as Motina guided the woman to a chair.

'Here,' said the housekeeper. 'Sit here and tell us what's happened.'

As she sat down, the Tutor could see that she was a woman of substance even if her dress was a little faded and worn. Her hands were soft, and she would have been considered beautiful were it not for the extensive burns covering the left side of her face and neck. But even with this disfigurement, there was something about her that seemed vaguely familiar.

'He's gone,' said the woman.

'Who's gone?' asked Motina.

'My son,' said the woman, holding up a locket that contained a tiny portrait of a young man with a mole at the base of his jaw. 'He's disappeared. He went to work for a wealthy family, but then something happened and now he's disappeared.'

'Do you know why your son might've gone?' asked Motina.

'They say he killed a girl, but my son would never do such a thing.'

'Who did he work for?' asked the Tutor. 'Do you know the name of the family?'

'Medici,' said the woman, and the Tutor frowned as a thought occurred to him. The Medici's were a notorious family... aristocratic, wealthy, and well known for their ruthless pursuit of power. But what gave the Tutor pause, was that their family motif was the stylised design of the letter 'M'.

The Tutor tried to hide his concern as the woman turned back to Motina.

'Can you help me?' she asked. 'A friend of mine went to look for him. He was a sergeant in the city guard, but now he has also disappeared. Then someone told me that the Sage of Blackfell House might help me.'

'I'm sure he will try,' said Motina.

'We have to find him,' said the woman. 'The Medici family has put a price on his head and that could make him a target for the Butcher.'

'I'm sure that won't happen,' said Motina as she exchanged a worried glance with the Tutor.

'He took the Harper's boy,' said the woman. 'What if my son is also taken? What if my boy is chopped into pieces by the Butcher of Guile?'

The woman's distress had risen to new heights, and Motina reached out a hand to calm her. 'What's your name, my dear?'

'Reyna,' said the woman. 'Reyna de Lorni.'

'And your son?'

'His name is Luca.'

'We'll help you,' said Motina. 'Just start from the beginning.'

It took only a few minutes for the woman to tell them what had happened and by the time she had finished she was breathless with anxiety. Moving to the stove, Motina poured a cup of chamomile tea and added a pinch of finely ground herbs from a pouch at her waist. The agitated woman took only a few sips of the tea before her breathing calmed and she began to look drowsy. Leaning on the table, she folded her arms, laid her head down, and fell asleep.

'Well,' said Motina, glancing at the Tutor as she leaned down to checked the woman's pulse. 'Now it looks like there are *two* young men you need to find.'

5

Witches of the Black Pact

Up in his study, Fate finished analysing Inganno's potion. It turned out to be a simple strength potion, and yet he was surprised by the purity of the concoction, yet more evidence of the young potion-maker's skill. Returning downstairs he found the kitchen empty and went through to the parlour where Motina and the Tutor were watching over a woman who was now asleep on a soft upholstered couch. Crossing the room, Fate looked down at the sleeping woman.

'She's an actress,' said Motina.

'Reyna de Lorni,' said Fate, for even with the extensive scarring he had recognised her face. 'I saw her perform at the Beehive.'

Seated nearby, the Tutor was surprised by the note of respect in Fate's voice. He glanced at the sorcerer as Fate continued.

'She played Queen Vilandra in The Fall of Tarse... one of the finest performances I have ever seen.'

'Well, now she's lost her son,' said Motina handing Fate Madam de Lorni's locket. 'This is what he looks like, and he also has burn scars on his hands.'

'Did you give her something to make her sleep?' asked Fate as he looked down at the young man's portrait.

'Just a little psilo and valerian,' replied Motina.

Fate nodded. Herbs and fungi could be dangerous in the wrong hands, but Motina was extremely skilled in such things. Moving away from the sleeping woman, Fate also took a seat as they spoke in lowered tones.

'So what happened?' he asked as he handed the locket to the Tutor.

'A typical story of an actress falling on hard times,' began Motina. 'The acting dried up after the fire that scarred her face. Her son went out to work, but they were barely scraping by so he started taking jobs of a more dubious kind. He ended up in a wealthy household, but something went wrong and the house owner's niece was killed.'

'The boy killed her?'

'Madam de Lorni is adamant that he didn't,' said Motina. 'But we really have no way of knowing for sure.'

'And the name of the family he was working for?'

'The Medicis,' said the Tutor and Motina was unsettled by the look of concern on Fate's face as he turned to look at the Tutor.

'That rich brat outside the potion-maker's house,' said Fate. 'The gold 'M' on the black livery of the coach.'

'Yes,' said the Tutor. 'It was the Medici crest.'

Fate put a hand to his face as if this was the worst possible news.

'Are they really that bad?' asked Motina.

'If the boy killed a relative, then yes,' said Fate. 'They're about as bad as it gets.' He glanced at Motina as if he were trying to decide how much he should say. 'Lord Medici is a member of the Juoda Pakta.'

'What?!' exclaimed Motina, and the Tutor was shocked by the sudden force of her tone.

'The Black Pact,' said Fate turning to the Tutor. 'It's like an elite club that offers magical protection to its members.'

'I know what it is,' said the Tutor. 'It's a coven of dark witches that trade with the Daemonaria.'

'But do you know what they trade?'

'Magic items,' said the Tutor.

34

'Yes,' said Fate. 'But they also trade people with magical abilities, and faeries too.'

'Ah,' said the Tutor, glancing at Motina.

The dark sisters of the Juoda Pakta hailed from Motina's home country of Karuthia. And now the Tutor recalled how Oruthian Bohr had used them to hunt down magic-users during the Karuthian purge.

'The treacherous sows!' cursed Motina who now looked like she was ready to take on Medici by herself.

'This is worse than I thought,' the Tutor went on. 'Even if we find the boy, he won't be safe in the city.'

'Then you'll need to get him *out* of the city,' said Motina.

'That won't help,' said Fate. 'The Medicis have connections in every town and city from here to Confluence.'

'Does that mean you're not going to help?' asked Motina.

'Of course not,' said Fate. 'It just means it won't be easy.'

'And what about the Butcher?' asked the Tutor. 'Madam de Lorni is right... The Butcher often takes people with a bounty on their heads.'

'That's true,' said Fate. He was about to continue when the dark shape of a raven appeared at the window. The bird looked directly at Motina before giving a distinctive croak.

'It's Weasel,' said Motina. 'The birds have taken a liking to the boy.'

Hardly had she finished speaking before the jangling chimes of the gate bell sounded once more.

'He does know it's safe for him to come to the front door?' queried Fate.

'Oh, he knows,' said Motina. 'He's just a little wary after I told him what could happen to an intruder who tried to cross the fence.'

The hint of a smile softened Fate's stern features as Motina went to meet Weasel at the gate. The Tutor stood up while Fate took a quilted blanket from the back of a nearby chair.

'Tragic how life can be turned upside down in an instant,' said the Tutor.

'Isn't it just,' replied Fate as he laid the blanket over the sleeping form of Madam de Lorni.

Quietly, the two men left the room and made their way through to the kitchen to speak with the young street urchin called Weasel.

'Would you like some soup?' asked Motina as Weasel took a seat at the large kitchen table.

'Soup and a piece of pie would be wonderful,' replied Weasel with a twinkle in his blue-grey eyes.

Motina arched an eyebrow then turned away before he could see the smile on her face.

At about thirteen years old, Weasel was a small and skinny boy with bright eyes and a mass of dark unruly hair. Most wayfinders were nervous and withdrawn, but Weasel was different. He was quick-witted and resourceful, and he was also part of a community that saw things in the city that normal people tried to ignore.

'So, what's this about a job?' he said, slurping a spoonful of soup as Fate and the Tutor sat down at the table.

'Two people have gone missing,' said Fate. 'I wondered if you and your friends might help us find them.'

'It'll cost you,' said Weasel as he dunked a piece of bread in his soup.

'How does twenty copper sound?' asked Fate and Weasel almost choked on his food. 'And twenty more if you find the people we're looking for.'

'And who would that be?' asked Weasel.

'Two young men in their early twenties,' said the Tutor. 'One called Fidanza, a wealthy young man with sandy hair and green eyes.'

'And the other?'

'A man of about the same age called Luca,' said Fate. 'A young man of modest means, with dark hair, scarred hands and a mole at the base of his jaw.'

'And where would we start looking?' asked Weasel as the Tutor showed Weasel the portrait in the locket.

'They both went missing in the First Quarter, but they could be anywhere,' said the Tutor.

'Luca is probably hiding,' said Fate. 'While Fidanza might just be wandering around looking lost.'

'Then he should be easy to find,' said Weasel. 'A rich toff, wandering around like he's lost... He's gonna stand out a mile!'

'Good,' said Fate. 'But you mustn't approach either man. If you *do* find them, just send word and then watch them until we arrive.'

'As you say, Master Fate,' said Weasel as he finished his soup and started on a piece of apple pie. 'Find'em and watch'em... No problem.'

Weasel appeared to understand, but Fate was not so sure. The young wayfinder was clever, but he could also be impulsive. And when it came to a dangerous family like the Medicis, then Weasel's boldness could easily get him into trouble.

'Well, it's too late to start looking for anyone tonight,' said the Tutor.

'Agreed,' said Fate. 'We shall begin our search tomorrow.'

6
The Sergeant

Night was setting in as Madam de Lorni's 'friend' moved slowly towards a large storm drain near the banks of the River Scéal. In truth, he was less of a friend and more of an adoring fan. He had followed the actress for years, never missing a production despite his duties as a sergeant in the city guard. He had been heartbroken when the fire ended her career, and even though her face was now marred by scars, she remained beautiful to him.

The sergeant knew he was late in reporting back to Madam de Lorni, but he was following a lead from a reed-cutter who worked on the river. The man had reported seeing someone hiding in a storm drain and so the sergeant had come to take a look. The storm drain itself was like the mouth of a cave with a stone arch curving six feet over a paved spillway. And there, hiding in the mouth of the drain, was Luca, Madam de Lorni's son.

The storm drain was surrounded by a fringe of blackthorn bushes and, being careful not to alarm the young man, the sergeant picked his way slowly through the surrounding bushes.

'Luca,' he called out in low voice. 'Is that you?'

Clearly startled, the young man shrank back into the shadows and the sergeant stopped. The last thing he wanted was for the boy to flee into the sewers.

'Wait!' he hissed. 'I'm a friend of your mother.' He held up a silk scarf that Madam de Lorni had given him.

Luca stopped as he recognised the scarf, but he was still frightened and confused.

'I didn't kill her,' he cried.

'I'm not here to judge you,' said the sergeant, and he raised his hands away from the sword hanging from his belt. 'I was only asked to find you.'

Still moving slowly, he crouched in the storm drain as an agitated Luca tried to explain what had happened.

'I wanted to prove that I didn't kill her,' said Luca, holding up a crumpled letter and a small silver bottle. 'But I took the wrong flask.'

'What do you mean - the wrong flask?'

'There were two flasks, just like this one,' said Luca. 'But the potion was in the other one.' He looked down at the flask in his hand. 'If I could get the other flask, I could prove I didn't do it.'

'And where is this other flask?' asked the sergeant.

'It's in a drinks cabinet... in the apartment of Lord Medici's son. I thought about going back for it,' said Luca. 'The cabinet is just inside the drawing-room, but the patio doors are locked from the inside and breaking the glass would alert the guards.'

'And this flask would prove your innocence?'

'Yes,' said Luca. 'With this letter and the potion in the flask, I could prove what really happened.'

'Then I suppose we need to get that flask,' said the sergeant. He knew that breaking into a rich household could be dangerous. However, before becoming a soldier he had been a fairly accomplished burglar. It was risky, but the sergeant had been in love with Madam de Lorni for years, and if it meant clearing her son of the charge of murder, then he was willing to take the risk.

'Why don't you tell me where to find this drawing-room?' said the sergeant.

'But the doors are locked,' said Luca.

'Don't worry,' said the sergeant with a smile. 'I know a thing or two about picking locks.'

7

Vulpyrac's Hound

Inganno the potion maker was red-faced with fury when he finally returned to his expensive townhouse. Not only had he been forced to pay an extortionate bribe, but his patron's lawyer had been unable to quash the charges.

'You should be fine,' the useless nib-scratcher had said. 'So long as they don't have any proof.'

'*Proof*,' thought Inganno.

The man called Fate was confident that he could prove Inganno's crimes. He and that accursed demon hunter were going to get him locked up, and that simply would not do. Inganno's mother had once tried to curtail his freedom, threatening to send him away to a stuffy old magic school in Confluence. She had paid for that mistake, and even the doctors could not tell the difference between a natural stroke and the lethal poison with which he had killed her.

Now it was time to take similar steps.

Lighting a candle, he made his way down to the basement. Passing through the wine cellar, he unlocked the steel door that led to his workshop. Once inside he lit several lamps before moving to a shelf filled with rare and expensive books. He ran a limp finger over the spines of the books, reading the titles as he thought about the two men who had ruined his plans.

'Poisons for Animals and Humans of a Strong Constitution,' read one of the titles.

'*No*,' thought Inganno. Fate and the demon hunter might have protection against such crude concoctions.

'For Treachery, Chaos and Mayhem,' read the spine of another book.

'*Too unpredictable.*' There was no way he could be sure that the two men would turn against each other.

'On the Conjuration and Control of Manitus and Effigies.'

Inganno remembered being impressed by the dangerous creatures in this book, but in order for them to find their prey, the manitus needed some physical trace of the intended victim.

Inganno's finger stopped and a wicked smile stretched his fleshy lips. He remembered spots of the sorcerer's blood on the floorboards of the hall, and a small clump of the demon hunter's hair caught on the frame of his front door. That would surely be enough.

Removing the book from the shelf he began to turn the ancient pages. All of the conjurations required potion lore and some carefully spoken incantations, but most were within the limits of his skill. He read about effigies that could move through a building like smoke to throttle the intended victim. And others that were little more than sounds, disembodied voices that could drive a person insane by whispering words of madness to haunt them in their sleep.

And then he came to a page with the title…

Vulpyrac's Hound

Inganno smiled as he read the main ingredients: mercury, sulphur, powdered diamond and tar. He had everything that was required; indeed he kept a large barrel of tar in the corner of his workshop. It might take some time to perfect the incantations, but he was sure he could do it.

Vulpyrac's Hound…. A creature of mercury and tar with teeth and claws as hard as diamonds.

Yes, that would do nicely.

'It creeps like a shadow across the ground,' Inganno read. 'Seeping through keyholes and under doors until it finds its prey, whereupon it will rise up, taking on the form of a great and ravenous hound. Steel cannot harm it, armour cannot stop it. The hound will keep on attacking until the intended targets are dead.'

'No wonder this book was outlawed,' breathed Inganno with delight.

For a moment longer he looked at the terrifying sketch of the sleek and terrible hound, then he went in search of a demon hunter's hair and the dried blood of a sorcerer called Fate.

8

A Butcher's Cleaver and the Sewers of Guile

It was now fully dark. The moon shone through a veil of low cloud, and the sergeant was running for his life.

Breaking into the Medici mansion had been easy. The sergeant merely climbed over the perimeter wall and crossed the gardens to the patio doors that Luca had described. A quick bit of lock-smithery and the doors were opened.

The cold drinks cabinet was exactly where Luca had said it would be, and it should have been a simple thing to retrieve the potion flask and disappear into the night. However, he was just closing the patio doors when an interior door opened and a man entered the room. The man was tall, and it appeared that he could see in the dark because his head immediately turned in the direction of the sergeant.

However, it was not until two armed guards entered the room with lanterns that the sergeant got a good look at the tall figure that seemed to be looking directly at him.

Dressed in the crimson robes of a desert nomad, he wore a curved sword on his hip. His head was covered by a headscarf that obscured half his face, including his eyes and nose. The lower part of his face was branded with arcane symbols, but it was not the livid brands that filled the sergeant with fear; it was the fact that the nomad's lips were stitched together with thick silver thread. The sergeant turned and fled, throwing himself over the perimeter wall as the Medici guards chased him into the night.

Now he was running through the narrow streets of Guile, desperately trying to outrun the guards and the nomad in the crimson desert robes. The mysterious figure appeared to be blindfolded, but the sergeant was now convinced that the terrifying man could see through walls.

Trying to catch his breath, the sergeant ducked into a narrow wynd as the Medici guards carried on past on the main road. Hugging the damp stone wall, he waited in the shadows, listening as the sound of running feet faded into the distance.

Face dripping with sweat, the sergeant breathed a sigh of relief. He had lost them. Peering out from his hiding place he waited another minute before leaving the shadows of the narrow wynd. He now knew that breaking into the Medici mansion had been a foolish mistake. Madam de Lorni's only chance of helping her son was to tell the authorities, and hope that the constables and magistrates were not in the pay of the Medicis.

Pausing to get his bearings, the sergeant turned in the direction of his home then skidded to a halt as a tall figure stepped out in front of him. It was the nomad.

Backing away he turned to flee but the nomad thrust out his arm and the sergeant felt an invisible hand grab the front of his leather tunic. Two of the Medici guards now appeared beside the nomad and one of them walked forward to stand before the captive man.

'Why did you break into the master's house?' The man's mouth moved but the voice that emerged from his lips was not his own. 'What were you looking for?'

The sergeant was terrified. He stared at the blindfolded figure of the nomad, even though it was the normal guard who spoke.

'I was just looking for money,' he lied. 'Silver or jewellery… anything I could sell.' The sergeant did not consider himself a brave man, but he would not betray Madam de Lorni's son if he could help it.

The nomad tilted his head slightly and his sewn lips curled up in a sneer.

'Please,' begged the sergeant. 'I didn't take anything.'

But the nomad was not listening. The direction of his 'blindfolded' gaze shifted to someone standing behind the sergeant.

'Take him,' said the guard whose voice was being used by the nomad, and before he could do anything else, the sergeant felt a strong hand close around his mouth as he was dragged backwards into a blind alley where another figure was waiting.

Cries of pain echoed around the alley and it did not take long before the sergeant gave up the location of Luca's hiding place. His description was babbling and incoherent, but the Medici guards now had a good idea of where to focus their search.

'Make sure the body is found,' commanded the nomad as the sergeant was forced to the ground.

The sergeant's eyes stretched wide as a figure loomed over him, and there was just enough light for him to see the object it was holding, an object that filled his mind with terror. It was a knife, a knife with a heavy rectangular blade, a knife commonly known as a butcher's cleaver.

The sergeant opened his mouth to scream, but the cleaver came chopping down and the scream never left his throat.

*

Back in the storm drain, Luca still held the crumpled letter in his hand as he waited for his mother's friend to return. It was now about two hours since the sergeant had gone to retrieve the potion flask from the Medici

46

mansion. A gibbous moon shone through a layer of cloud and Luca emerged from the cave-like entrance, peering through the surrounding bushes to see if there was any sign of the sergeant's return.

Feeling alone and hopeless, he was trying to decide what he should do when he heard a noise. Edging back towards his hiding place, he looked along the riverbank where the dark silhouettes of three men could now be seen against the moonlit sheen on the surface of the river.

They were looking for something…

They were looking for him.

The three figures came steadily closer and, even in the darkness, Luca could tell that the tallest of the men was different. Somehow this tall figure filled him with dread. Trembling with fear he backed into the storm drain, but then the tall figure turned in his direction as if it knew he was there.

Luca was just about to flee when a strong hand closed around his mouth and he was dragged backwards into darkness. Dropping the letter, he tried to break free, but it was no good. Whatever had grabbed him was far too strong and there was nothing he could do as he disappeared into the nightmare sewers of Guile.

9

The Search Begins

The following morning was overcast with low cloud and light rain. Moving around the kitchen of Blackfell House, Motina muttered to herself as she put together a basket of food for Madam de Lorni who had returned home in the early hours of the morning.

'You did tell her that she's welcome to stay here,' said Fate as he and the Tutor ate breakfast at the table.

'Of course,' said Motina. 'But she insisted on going home. She wants to be there in case Luca returns. And I told her that you will do everything possible to find her son.'

'We'll do our best,' said Fate as the Tutor gave him a furtive look of concern.

Sitting in silence the two men finished their breakfast before leaving Blackfell House to begin their search.

'So where shall we start?' said the Tutor as they passed through the gate in the perimeter fence.

'Well, Weasel is talking to the wayfinders,' said Fate. 'So, I think we should pay a visit to the Medicis.'

'Straight to the scene of the crime, eh?'

'Precisely.'

And so they made their way into the most affluent part of the city, to a white marble mansion set in extensive grounds. The main entrance featured two wrought iron gates, each emblazoned with an ornate golden 'M', leaving people in no doubt that this was the home of Lord Salvestro Medici, the head of a family that boasted connections to the emperor himself.

10
Sienna Blade

As Fate and the Tutor approached the gates of the Medici mansion, a young woman called Sienna Blade had just returned to the Port City of Dymhaven. Dressed like a man in breeches, boots and travel cloak, she rode into the stableyard of Amos Saddler, a great bear-of-a-man who had once been a friend of her father.

'So, how did it go?' asked Amos as he stroked the horse's nose. 'Or shouldn't I ask?'

'Actually,' said Sienna. 'The only thing I killed was a demon.'

Amos raised his eyebrows in surprise. Sienna, like her father, had chosen the life of a hired sword.

'And did you find who you were looking for?'

'I did,' said Sienna. 'But it turns out that he wasn't the man I thought he was.'

The man in question was Decimus Fate. Sienna had always believed that the sorcerer murdered her father. She had travelled to Guile seeking revenge only to learn that her father had *asked* Fate to kill him in order to save *her* life. With a sigh, she passed the reins to Amos and slid down from the saddle.

'You're hurt!' said Amos as Sienna winced with pain from a partially healed wound near her hip, a wound she had received during a fight with the Tutor.

'It's nothing,' said Sienna, and Amos frowned in concern as he handed her a small skin of wine. 'So, where's Isaac?' she asked. 'Don't tell me he's still in hiding.'

The frown on Amos's face grew deeper.

'Worse,' said the stable master. 'He's in jail.'

'What!'

'Turns out someone died in the fire he started. Our young friend could be charged with murder.'

Sienna let out a breath of frustration. A charge of murder was bad, but a charge of murder by the use of magic was considered to be even worse. Isaac might only be sixteen, but he *was* a gifted magic-user. Like Fate, Isaac was a feral mage. He was also the closest thing to a brother that Sienna had ever known.

11

Like Father, Like Son

Walking onto the gravelled driveway, Fate and the Tutor could see that the Medici mansion was decidedly palatial with white columns flanking a black lacquered door. Two armed guards challenged them at the main gate, but Fate put a hand in his pocket and took out a medallion like a large coin made from black jet and gold with thirteen arcane symbols encircling the design of a three-fingered hand.

He showed it to the guards.

'What's that?' asked the Tutor as the guards waved them through.

'It's a medal of membership to the Juoda Pakta.'

The Tutor looked at him in disbelief.

'You're a member of the Black Pact!?'

'Of course not,' said Fate. 'But I knew an earl who was.'

The Tutor shook his head at the extent of Fate's connections, and together they continued down the driveway to the black lacquered door.

'Decimus Fate to see Lord Medici,' said Fate when a liveried servant opened the heavy door.

'Your card?' said the man.

'Members of the Black Pact don't need a calling card,' said Fate holding up the medallion as he walked past the man into a marble-floored reception hall. 'And you should not be so insolent as to ask for one.'

The servant began to object, but a stern look from the Tutor made him think better of the idea.

'What's going on here?' asked another man as he descended a wide staircase leading down into the hall. It was Lord Medici's valet, a severe-looking man dressed in a black doublet with flared breeches and white knee-length socks.

'Decimus Fate. At your service,' said Fate.

'*The* Decimus Fate?' said the valet as he cast a wary eye over the intimidating figure of the Tutor.

A faint smile lifted the corner of Fate's mouth, but he said nothing. The flash of gold in his dark brown eyes was answer enough.

'Show them into the parlour,' said the valet, and the Tutor thought the man's pale skin had grown a shade paler as he turned to walk back up the stairs.

Clearly confused, the servant gave the valet a bow before leading Fate and the Tutor down a short gallery and into a large room with two other doors leading off to different parts of the house.

'Lord Medici will be with you shortly,' said the servant as he left the room with a bow.

'Impressive,' said Fate as the two men looked around the lavishly furnished room.

'A bit gaudy for my taste,' replied the Tutor, and Fate smiled as the door opened and the valet stepped into the room.

'Lord Salvestro Medici,' he announced.

A man of about fifty entered the room and, even though he was well-groomed and immaculately dressed, the Tutor frowned. The faint shadow of the Daemonaria lay upon this man's soul.

Lord Medici was a stern, grey-haired man dressed in rich blue doublet and hose. His gaze was hard and unyielding and he carried himself with the air of a man who knew he was untouchable.

The master of the house was accompanied by two armed footmen who eyed the visitors with open hostility, but Fate also noticed two areas of shimmering air that followed Lord Medici, like barely visible ghosts. Moving to a drinks table in the centre of the room, he cast a cursory glance over the imposing figure of the Tutor before his gaze settled on Fate.

'Decimus Fate,' he said as he poured himself a glass of amber spirit from a crystal cut decanter. He raised the glass and took a sip as if to reinforce the point that he had not offered his guests a drink. 'The man who killed the *demon of the vale...*'

Lord Medici raised his eyebrows as if to say *really*?

Fate said nothing although the Tutor noticed a faint suggestion of disquiet behind the sorcerer's hawkish frown. Like Fate, the demon hunter had also noticed the two areas of shimmering air and he wondered what kind of magical protection the head of this powerful family had employed. He watched now as Lord Medici took a few steps closer to Fate as if to prove that he was not afraid.

'Didn't you also kill the Earl of Haltsburg?' he asked.

'No,' said Fate.

'No?' echoed Medici, taking another sip of his drink. 'That's not what I heard.'

'I did not kill the earl,' said Fate. 'I merely let him die.'

'Oh?'

'The earl had been poisoned by one of his enemies,' said Fate. 'He hired me to find a cure, but he tried to cheat me out of the payment so I withheld the cure and allowed him to die.'

'Ha!' said Medici with wicked delight. 'Quite right,' he added. 'Nothing worse than a man who doesn't pay his debts.' He finished his drink and set down the empty glass with a 'clack'. 'Now,' he continued. 'What is it that I can do for you?'

'We're here about your niece,' said Fate. 'We'd like to find the man who killed her.'

'The actress's son,' said Medici, his gaze suddenly hardening. 'I believe my son is hunting the man down as we speak.'

'Would it be possible to speak with your son?' asked Fate. 'And to see where the murder took place, perhaps?'

Medici frowned. He did not like the idea of strangers poking around his home, but he was intrigued by Fate and arrogant enough to believe that *he* could handle a sorcerer that other people feared.

'I don't see why not,' he said with a dismissive wave of the hand as he turned to his valet. 'Have Alonso meet us in the drawing-room of his apartment.'

'Yes, my Lord,' said the valet dipping his head as he turned to leave the room.

'Shall we?' said Medici gesturing towards one of the other doors leading from the room.

Together they moved through the house until they reached the apartments of Lord Medici's son.

'I believe this is where the unfortunate event took place,' said Medici as Fate and the Tutor looked around the room. 'From what I hear, my poor niece was attacked in here and crawled through that door to the adjacent room, where she died.'

Fate was just moving towards the door when a man in his mid-twenties strode into the room.

'I don't care if he wasn't in the storm drain!' he snapped at someone behind him. 'Just find the accursed fool.'

The man had fine cheekbones, dark eyes and a sour sneering mouth. His angry expression vanished, and he came to an abrupt halt, as he saw Fate and the Tutor standing in his home. It was the wealthy young man who had emerged from the coach outside Inganno's house.

'Do you know each other?' asked Medici as his son moved to stand in front of an unusual drinks cabinet that exuded faint clouds of vapour that looked like steam.

'I think we passed each other in the street,' said Fate. 'But we haven't been formally introduced.'

'Then, allow me,' said Medici clearly intrigued by the tension he sensed in the air. 'This is my son, Alonso Medici... Alonso, this is Decimus Fate and...'

'They call me the Tutor,' said the Tutor.

Lord Medici looked surprised. 'And what is it you teach?' he asked, but the Tutor merely rolled his eyes and gave a soft snort of derision. 'Well,' continued Lord Medici, 'consider yourselves introduced. Now, what is it you would like to know?'

Lord Medici expected them to ask some questions of his son, but Fate and the Tutor were not looking at Alonso. They were looking at the man who followed after him; a tall and powerful man dressed in the crimson robes of a desert nomad. His skin looked to be almost as dark as the Tutor's, but it was difficult to tell because what little they could see was covered with arcane symbols that had been burned into the man's flesh. He wore a curved sword at his waist and a silver headscarf that came down over his face to cover his eyes and nose. But by far the man's most disturbing feature was his lips which had been stitched together with thick silver thread.

Fate and the Tutor shot each other a glance. So, *this* was the shadowy presence they had sensed in the Medici coach when they apprehended Inganno.

'Ah, yes,' said Medici as he noticed the direction of their gaze. 'My son's bodyguard. Quite the exotic brute, is he not?' Lord Medici moved closer to the bodyguard as if he were inspecting an expensive racehorse. 'He comes from the fractured deserts of Ash'nahari; a secret order of warrior mystics known as the Don'Sha'Vir.'

'The blind that see,' said Fate and Lord Medici inclined his head.

'It was a coming of age gift,' he continued. 'Most young noblemen are happy with a castle or some rich country estate. My son asks for a mystic bodyguard.'

'And I'll wager he cost you more than a castle,' said Fate.

'Indeed he did,' said Medici. 'But even the emperor employs Don'Sha'Vir as palace guards, and if it's good enough for the Emperor…'

He left the sentence unfinished.

Looking again at the bodyguard, Fate noticed how his blindfolded face was turned towards the Tutor as if he had identified the demon hunter as the most dangerous threat in the room. Fate smiled. There was a time when *he* would have held the full attention of a Don'Sha'Vir and he felt a vague sense of pique that such days were no more.

'So…' he said as the Tutor stared at the bodyguard with his deep blue eyes. 'This is where your niece was killed?'

'Well, just through there,' said Medici, indicating the adjacent room. 'But this is where we found the footman's jacket. It was covered in blood from the murder he had just committed.'

'And how was your niece killed?'

'Stabbed and strangled,' said Medici. 'And her clothes were dishevelled as if the fiend were in the act of ravaging her.'

'Any witnesses?'

'No.'

'And who found the body?'

'I'm afraid it was my son who discovered the murdered body of his cousin,' said Medici. 'He tried to revive her, but it was too late. The murderer had fled into the garden and disappeared.'

'And the girl's body?' asked Fate, but Alonso Medici forestalled any answer.

'This is grotesque,' he said, still standing in front of the mist-shrouded drinks cabinet. 'My cousin is dead and we stand around discussing the matter with strangers while the murderer continues to escape justice.'

'We're only trying to help,' said Fate.

'No you're not,' said Alonso. 'You're interfering with the search for a killer, and that simply will not do.'

'So, you've informed the authorities,' said Fate.

'Of course,' said Medici.'

'And the city guard is helping you with the search?'

'Certainly not,' said Alonso. 'This is a family matter and we shall handle it as such.'

The tension in the room suddenly increased and the Don'Sha'Vir took a menacing step forward, the entire set of his body changing as if he were readying himself for violence.

'Quite right,' said Fate with a sudden lightness of tone. 'A family like the Medicis has more than enough resources to handle a matter like this.'

'Indeed we do,' said Medici with absolute confidence.

'Then we shall leave you to it,' said Fate. Exchanging a look with the Tutor, the two men walked through to the main door of the house. 'And my condolences on the death of your niece,' added Fate as

57

they walked out of the mansion and descended the steps onto the fine gravel driveway.

'It has been... interesting to meet you,' said Medici with the smile of a man who felt total confidence in his wealth and power.

'And you,' said Fate. He gave a courteous bow and then he and the Tutor turned and walked away.

'Well, at least we know who killed the girl,' said the Tutor as they left the grounds of the Medici mansion.

'Indeed we do,' said Fate. 'But proving it is another matter entirely.'

'Madam de Lorni's son could well be a witness.'

'If he lives long enough to testify.'

'It's only a matter of time before Alonso finds him,' said the Tutor.

'I know,' said Fate. 'Especially if he has a Don'Sha'Vir at his beck and call.'

'An abomination,' said the Tutor and Fate was surprised by the strength of feeling in his voice. 'You know they draw their power from the Daemonaria?'

'Yes,' said Fate. 'And I've heard that they can stop a man's heart by sheer force of will, so we had better proceed with caution.'

The Tutor's blue eyes were hard as he gave a nod of agreement. 'And what about Alonso turning up at Inganno's house? Do you think that was just coincidence?'

'Possibly,' said Fate. 'But I'm always suspicious of coincidence. And the potion-maker's judgement is clearly flawed so I dread to think what concoctions he's been preparing for Alonso.' Fate paused as something else occurred to him. 'Did you notice the drinks cabinet?'

'It looked like it was steaming,' said the Tutor.

'It's known as sublimation,' said Fate, 'when vapour forms over ice. Magically chilled cabinets like that are a luxury that only rich people can afford, but they can also be used to store potions that need to be kept cold.'

'You think he was trying to hide something?' asked the Tutor and Fate pursed his lips.

'Perhaps,' said Fate. 'People with a guilty conscience often draw attention to the things they are trying to hide.'

'Maybe next time we should take a closer look.'

'I'm afraid there won't be a next time,' said Fate. 'Not unless we can find some proof of an *'alternative'* theory.'

'Then we had better find Madam de Lorni's son.'

'Yes, we had,' said Fate as they continued on their way.

*

Standing in the doorway of their enormous mansion, Lord Medici and his son watched as Fate and the Tutor disappeared from view. The Lord's expression was clouded with thought, while Alonso appeared anxious and agitated.

'So, you've heard of this Fate?' he asked, without looking directly at his father.

'A little,' said Medici. 'Just rumours and stories really.'

'And what do the stories say?'

'They say that he's a notorious sorcerer, ruthless and driven.'

'Not to mention impertinent,' said Alonso.

'Indeed.'

'Does he have connections to any of the major families?'

'Not that I know of.'

'Then perhaps we should teach him not to meddle in the affairs of his betters.'

Lord Medici looked mildly surprised as he turned to look at his son.

'Perhaps we should,' he said with an approving smile. 'But be careful,' he added. 'The little I *have* heard suggests that he is not a man to be taken lightly so proceed with caution. For all we know, he might have dropped the matter as soon as he passed through the gate. No point creating trouble where no trouble exists.'

'I'll watch him, of course,' said Alonso. 'But would you have any objections to me dealing with the matter if he *did* start to meddle?'

'No,' said Medici. 'Not so long as it doesn't harm the family.'

'Of course,' said Alonso.

'And try to be discrete... Your Don'Sha'Vir is effective but he is also very conspicuous.'

'What would you suggest?'

'Oh, use your imagination,' said Medici with some irritation. 'Hire a third party, or blackmail one of his associates. You need to learn subtlety if you're to start playing the game.'

Alonso heard the note of scorn in his father's voice. He knew his father considered him rash and immature. He bristled slightly at the unspoken criticism, but then a thought occurred to him and he smiled. Inganno's potions could make respectable girls do things that even a gutter whore would decline. Such potions were expensive, but Alonso wondered just how powerful such a potion could be if there was no limit to the price.

It was time to pay another visit to his pet potion-maker.

'Now,' said Medici turning away from the door. 'I have business to attend to.'

As he disappeared into the house, Alonso turned to his Don'Sha'Vir bodyguard.

'This sorcerer and his blue-eyed sword could be a problem,' he told the mystical warrior. 'Take four men and follow them. If they start poking their noses into the boy's disappearance, I want to know about it.'

The Don'Sha'Vir bowed his head and the mystical brands on his dark brown skin glowed with the orange light of a fire.

12
The Divine Spirit

Sienna Blade felt a disturbing sense of oppression as she and Amos entered the prison where Isaac was being held. Built into the foundations of the city's keep, this particular jail had been taken over by a religious order known as Lo Spirito Divino, The Divine Spirit. What was once an obscure order had now become a force to be reckoned with and the ordinary people of Dymhaven had come to fear the priests of the Divine Spirit.

However, Sienna Blade was not an ordinary person, and she was not about to be told what to do by the cassock-wearing boy who blocked her way.

'I don't care what your high priest says,' she told the young priest. 'I am going to see my friend and I am going to see him now!'

Dressed in a long black cassock, the priest appeared supremely confident, but then he made the mistake of trying to put a hand on Sienna who quickly grabbed his arm and threw him over her shoulder. The priest gave a grunting cry as he hit the stone-flagged floor, but Sienna ignored him as she strode towards the cells.

'Isaac!' she called out. 'Isaac! Are you there?'

'Sienna?' came a voice from around the corner of the stone-lined corridor. 'Sienna, here!'

Sienna increased her pace and Amos gave the priest an apologetic grimace as he moved to follow her.

'Amos, he's here,' said Sienna as she approached the cell at the end of the corridor.

When Amos arrived he found her looking through the barred window of a steel-bound door.

'What the hell have you been doing?' said Sienna in an angry tone that betrayed her anxiety.

'Hello Amos,' said Isaac as the big man came into view.

'Hello Isaac,' said Amos. 'More trouble, I see.'

Isaac's shoulders sagged as if he had let the stable master down. He was a slender youth with shoulder-length sandy hair that was now dirty and unkempt. He had bold features with a square jaw and green eyes that were shot through with streaks of gold.

'It wasn't my fault,' said Isaac, and Sienna arched a doubtful brow. Things were never Isaac's fault. 'All right, I did lose control for a minute,' he admitted, 'but my flames barely touched the building. Somehow it just ignited.'

'Just like that,' said Sienna, and Isaac gave a sigh.

'Can you get me out?' he asked.

'Can't you get yourself out?' challenged Sienna, but Isaac held up his arms, the wrists of which were encircled by silver-grey cuffs. The cuffs were not chained together, but they were engraved with Puritan symbols that inhibited the use of magic.

'Please,' said Isaac gesturing towards the barred window of his cell. 'That window is level with the street and when it rains all the mud and horse-dung just comes pouring in.'

'We'll try,' said Sienna who had to admit that the stench from the cell was overpowering.

'Stand away from the door,' said a voice of authority and Sienna turned to see a more senior priest standing in the corridor. The man had adopted a fighting stance. His elbows were raised to shoulder height while between his hands there burned a pure white ball of flame.

'My name is Divine Servant Arden,' said the priest. 'Now, move away from the accused.'

Stepping away from the door, Sienna adopted her own stance, one hand drifting to a throwing dagger hidden in her belt.

'I thought Puritans didn't use magic,' she said as she raised her chin.

'This isn't magic,' said Arden. 'This is the holy power of the Divine. It burns only the faithless, so if you don't want to test the purity of *your* soul then I suggest you leave this place immediately.'

'And those shackles,' said Sienna, nodding towards Isaac's cell. 'I suppose they're not magic either.'

'Imbued with Divine power,' said the priest.

'Of course they are,' said Sienna and the tension in the corridor increased as two more priests came striding around the corner.

'I think we should go,' said Amos stepping forward to place himself between Sienna and the priest.

'A man of wisdom,' said Arden. He did not dismiss the writhing sphere of energy, but it shrank down to become a ball of white fire in the palm of one hand.

'I assume Isaac will be given a fair trial,' said Amos.

'Of course.' said Arden. 'We are not tyrants. The accused will go to trial before he is transferred to the capital.'

'The capital?' said Sienna with a distinct note of concern.

'Yes,' said Arden. 'A unit of demon hunters will be arriving soon to escort the prisoner to the capital.'

'And why would demon hunters be required for a local case of arson?' asked Amos.

'It's no longer just arson,' said Arden. 'Now the Emperor's Divine Servant Bohr has shown an interest in the case.'

'Bohr?' said Sienna. 'Oruthian Bohr has shown an interest in Isaac?'

'Of course,' said Arden. 'Your friend is a feral mage and such people are a danger to us all.'

'But Bohr is a sorcerer,' said Sienna. 'He uses magic.'

'He did,' said the priest. 'But now he wields the pure power of the Divine.'

Sienna shook her head at this blatant hypocrisy.

'So, Isaac's guilt has already been decided,' she said.

'Not at all,' said Arden. 'His trial will take place a few days from now. If he is found innocent, he will be set free. If not, he will be sent to the capital for cleansing.'

'Cleansing?' queried Amos.

'Divine Servant Bohr has a chamber that can relieve criminals of their blasphemous powers,' said the priest. 'If your friend survives the cleansing, he will be set free.'

'This is bullshi...' began Sienna, but Amos quickly grabbed her elbow and steered her towards the exit as he asked a final question.

'The trial's in a few days?'

'Correct,' said Arden.

'Then we'll return when we have a lawyer,' said Amos as he propelled Sienna up the stairs and out onto the street.

'Trial, my arse!' cursed Sienna as she shook herself free of Amos's grip 'Do you even *know* any lawyers?'

'As it happens, I do,' said Amos, ignoring her anger. 'I tend the horses of a man who specialises in magical law.'

'Well, I hope he's good,' said Sienna. 'Because if he's not, then Isaac's as good as dead.'

13
The Storm Drain

Fate and the Tutor were barely half a mile from the Medici mansion when a man emerged onto the street ahead of them. Sitting astride a beautiful black stallion, the man was exquisitely dressed in a green velvet doublet with a double row of gold buttons, and even the metal fittings of his horse's tack appeared to be made from gold. The man was flanked by four armed guards wearing blue shirts and black leather waistcoats.

It was Master Veleno, one of Guile's most powerful crime lords. Silver-haired and with a goatee beard, the aristocratic crime boss was colloquially known as 'the Lord of the City'.

'Lord Fate!' said Veleno in a tone of mock surprise. 'We don't often see you in the finer parts of the city.'

'Veleno,' replied Fate in a weary tone.

'And our new friend the demon hunter,' said Veleno turning to look at the Tutor. 'Good morning Alexander.'

The Tutor merely dipped his head.

'So what brings our intrepid duo to the First Quarter?' asked Veleno. 'I would hate to think you'd started working for a wealthy client when you turned down the opportunity to work for me.'

Fate gave a small laugh. 'Have you been following me, Veleno?'

Veleno suddenly found a point of interest in the leather of his fine black gloves.

'I'm flattered,' said Fate. 'But no. I am not working for a wealthy client.'

'Not even a client as wealthy as the Medicis?' said Veleno and Fate's smile grew broader still.

'Not even them.'

'Well then,' said Veleno with a dazzling smile. 'The world can settle back on its axis, and *I* can proceed to discipline a troublesome landlord who refuses to pay his bill.'

'Goodbye, Veleno,' said Fate.

'Good day, Lord Fate,' replied Veleno. 'And you really must call on me some time,' he added as he led his small retinue off the main street. 'That 'statue' you acquired for me really does look splendid in my house.'

'I think he's obsessed with you,' said the Tutor with a teasing smile as they continued on their way.

'Don't be fooled by his garrulous charm,' said Fate. 'Veleno still hopes I will go to work for him, but he would happily kill me if he thought I was pledging my services to someone else.'

The Tutor pursed his lips in thought.

'And don't think he's forgotten about your tattoo either.' Fate nodded towards the Tutor's chest, where the enchanted tattoo of a demon hunter offered the bearer some protection from magical harm. 'Veleno might smile and wish you good morning but, if it suited his purpose, he would still skin you alive by the afternoon.'

The Tutor accepted the cautionary note with a nod. Together they turned onto the main road heading back towards Blackfell House. They had not gone much further when a young girl ran into the street. Her name was Daisy, and she was one of Weasel's wayfinder friends. Seeing them walking towards her, she put two fingers into her mouth and gave a surprisingly loud whistle.

'Weasel!' she cried in a high pitched voice. 'He's here.'

A few seconds later the wayfinder called Weasel skidded onto the street. He caught his balance and ran up the street to meet them.

'You have news?' asked Fate and Weasel nodded, taking a minute to catch his breath.

'The kids on the east gate say a posh toff was beaten up in Flesh Market Close.'

'You think it was Fidanza?' said Fate.

'It sounds like him,' replied Weasel.

'Is he badly hurt?' asked the Tutor.

'I don't know,' said Weasel. 'The eastgaters say he was beat up pretty bad, but then some women helped him... women dressed in green.'

'We should check it out,' said the Tutor, but Fate narrowed his eyes in thought.

'It's all right,' he said after a moment. 'I think I know where he'll be.' He turned his attention back to Weasel. 'And the other man, Luca de Lorni... any news on him.'

'Possibly,' said Weasel. 'Apparently, a street girl saw someone hiding in a storm drain near the river.'

Fate and the Tutor exchanged a look... Alonso Medici had mentioned something about a storm drain when he entered the room.

'Take us to it,' said Fate.

They followed Weasel and Daisy for about twenty minutes before climbing down an embankment and crossing an area of grass before picking their way through a thicket of blackthorn bushes that grew along the river.

'It's just along here,' said Weasel as they eased their way through the thorny bushes. 'The street girl was picking sloe berries when she saw someone hiding. Just there,' he added as he pointed to the cave-like mouth of a storm drain.

'Wait here,' said the Tutor as he moved out from the cover of the bushes.

He advanced slowly. If there was someone hiding here then they might be dangerous, and if it was Luca then he did not want to scare him. The storm drains of Guile formed a warren of tunnels large enough for a man to walk down. He did not want a frightened young man fleeing into the dark maze that ran beneath the city.

'Hello,' he said as he moved a little closer. 'Is anyone there?'

No answer came and the Tutor advanced until he could see into the shadowed mouth of the drain.

'I think it's clear,' he called back. 'But someone's definitely been here.'

Fate and Weasel came to join him, while Daisy held back.

'Yes,' said Fate as he studied the overlapping footprints in the layer of muddy silt that covered the floor of the drain, 'and recently too.'

The footprints were too muddled to make much sense, but he did notice a double set of drag marks leading back into the cave.

'We need light,' said Fate. He reached to the charm bracelet on his wrist, but then Weasel spoke up.

'Here,' he said as he lit a small lamp that all wayfinders carried in a sling draped over their shoulders.

'Looks like someone was dragged here,' said the Tutor as Weasel held the small lantern aloft.

They followed the drag marks a little way in and were surprised to see that the storm drain opened into a small cave of natural stone. The cave was about ten feet high and twenty feet across with a pool of clear water lying against the right-hand wall. To the left, a brick-lined drainage tunnel led away into darkness, while to the right there was a hole in the natural wall of the cave.

Putting his hand on the smooth stone wall, the Tutor looked into the hole which was barely a foot in diameter. 'It goes through to another chamber,' he said.

'How can you tell?' asked Fate.

'Because there's something glowing on the walls.'

Fate motioned for Weasel to bring his light closer as he moved to stand beside the Tutor. The hole was actually a narrow crawl space about two feet long.

'Too small for a man to get through,' said the Tutor, but Fate was not listening.

He was looking at the faint glow of light that seemed to be coming from a silvery white fungus growing on the walls of the adjoining cave.

'If these drag marks are Luca's,' continued the Tutor, 'then he might have been dragged into the sewers.'

Still lost in thought, Fate drew his attention away from the glowing fungus. 'I don't think so,' he said. 'Look here... the drag marks lead to the water.'

In the light of Weasel's lantern, they could see that Fate was right. The drag marks ended at the edge of the clear, still pool. As the Tutor looked for more clues, Fate returned to the hole in the wall. He was just reaching for the charm bracelet on his wrist when Daisy shouted from outside the cave.

'Weasel!' she shouted and Fate and the Tutor followed as Weasel dashed out of the cave.

'What is it?' asked Fate as he and the Tutor emerged.

'They've found another body,' said Weasel. 'Chopped up... and dumped... in the river.'

'The Butcher,' said Daisy in a voice filled with fear.

'Do you think it's Luca?' asked the Tutor.

'It could be,' said Fate. 'But we won't know until we see the body. Fortunately, I know the man who's likely to have it.'

'Of course you do,' said the Tutor.

They began to walk away from the storm drain then they stopped as Weasel moved to follow them.

'No,' said Fate. 'Where we're going is no place for children.'

And of course, this made Weasel even more curious.

'You wait here,' Fate told him. 'If Luca was hiding here then there's a chance he might return, and we need to know if he does.'

Weasel looked a bit put out. He gave a little humph, but he made no further move to follow them.

'But make sure you stay hidden,' said Fate.

'And stay away from that storm drain,' said the Tutor.

'Of course,' said Weasel with a disdainful scowl. 'I'm not bloomin' stupid!'

Fate and the Tutor exchanged a dubious look as they went to speak with a person who spent his life in the company of the dead.

Unfortunately, they had not spent much time searching the mouth of the storm drain. If they had they might have noticed a folded letter trodden into the muddy silt on the floor.

It was the letter that Luca had dropped when he was dragged back into darkness. That letter could prove that Alonso Medici was guilty of murder. And even now, as Weasel and Daisy waited in the nearby bushes, the pale figure of a troglodyte was coming back to retrieve it.

'Can we go?' asked Daisy who was getting bored with waiting. 'It'll be getting dark soon.'

'No,' said Weasel. 'We've been given a job to do and we're going to...'

'What was that?' hissed Daisy and the two wayfinders watched as a pale and broad-shouldered figure appeared in the mouth of the storm drain.

14

Curiosity Killed the Cat

It took Fate and the Tutor about fifteen minutes to reach their destination. Coming to the end of a blind alley, they approached two armed men who were guarding a set of stone steps that curved down into the ground.

'He's in the cutting room,' said one of the guards, and Fate gave the man a nod of thanks.

'What is this place?' asked the Tutor as they started down the steps.

'This,' said Fate, 'is one of the most fascinating places in the city.'

The Tutor's expression made it clear that he was yet to be convinced. Fate was clearly well known to the guards, but the Tutor's misgivings only increased as they passed through a room lined with shelves of large glass jars containing the pickled remains of various body parts and malformed organisms.

The room was illuminated by several white gems set into the walls and the air was filled with the acrid smell of embalming fluids. There were doors leading off to either side of the room, but Fate walked straight across to an archway where another set of steps led down to another wooden door. He lifted the latch and the door opened onto a vaulted cellar lit by more of the white crystals set into the walls and ceiling.

In the centre of the room, a round-shouldered man in a leather apron was leaning over a white marble slab on which were laid out the dismembered parts of a man's body. The man continued studying the body as Fate and the Tutor entered the room.

'I wondered how long it would take you to get here,' he said without looking up.

'Vivienne,' said Fate, by way of a greeting.

Somewhere in his late fifties, Vivienne was tall with a narrow mouth and long grey hair tied back from his face. Finally, he stood up from the body on the slab. Turning towards them, he cast a keen eye over the Tutor, taking in the dark skin, the blue eyes, the physical bearing and the exotic sword.

'A Vantu assassin?'

'A demon hunter,' replied Fate and Vivienne pursed his lips before giving the Tutor a quick nod of greeting.

'So, what's the latest news from the world of the dead?' asked Fate.

'Well, another body has disappeared from Aldo's morgue in the second quarter,' replied Vivienne. 'Maybe we *do* have a necromancer at work in the city.'

'A necromancer?' asked the Tutor.

'A magic-user who makes use of the dead,' said Fate.

'I know what it is,' replied the Tutor. 'But what makes you think there's one at work in the city?'

'Bodies missing from morgues and mortuaries,' said Vivienne. 'Whisked away in the dead of night.' He cocked his head in Fate's direction. 'Lord Fate believes there's some kind of pattern.'

'And you?' asked the Tutor, and Vivienne gave a shrug.

'There are other reasons for a body to go missing... relatives who can't pay the undertaker's fees... people selling body parts for use in dark magic spells.'

The mortician's tone suggested that he and Fate had discussed this matter before, but the sorcerer refused to be drawn.

'What have we got here?' asked Fate as he stepped forward to look at the body that Vivienne had been examining. The body's limbs had been cut off, but Vivienne had laid them beside the body.

Even though he was curious, the Tutor held back. It did not feel right to be examining the body of a dead person this way, but as Fate and Vivienne moved around the body, he noticed a distinctive tattoo on the man's upper arm. It was the portcullis tattoo of the castle guard.

'Is it the same as the others?' asked Fate.

'He's older than the previous victims,' said Vivienne. 'But apart from that, yes.' He moved to a nearby bench and held up a bundle of wet, knotted rope. 'The body parts were tied together and the cuts were made with the same kind of heavy blade. It certainly looks like the work of the Butcher.'

'But?' said Fate, for he could tell that there was something else.

'Well,' said Vivienne, moving back to the body. 'He's been in the water for several hours so it's difficult to say for certain, but I think some of these cuts were made while he was still alive.'

'Oh?' said Fate.

'Yes, see here,' said Vivienne. 'Some of the cuts have taken several attempts, and there are defensive injuries that suggest he might have been struggling.'

'Hmm,' said Fate. 'And the others were dismembered after death?'

'I believe so,' replied Vivienne and the Tutor frowned in distaste.

The demon hunter had seen plenty of corpses in his time, but he had never heard people discuss them in such a matter of fact kind of way.

'And there's something else,' added the mortician.

'What?' asked Fate, and Vivienne seemed amused that he had not noticed.

74

'Look at the skin.'

Fate's eyes moved over the man's deathly white skin. For a moment he frowned in confusion, but then he gave a soft sniff. 'No sheen,' he said and Vivienne smiled.

'No sheen?' queried the Tutor as if they were talking nonsense.

'The bodies of the other victims were covered with a faint metallic sheen,' Fate explained. 'As if someone had rubbed a silvery lotion into the skin.'

'It actually glows in the dark,' said Vivienne. 'Would you care to see?'

'You've got other victims here?' exclaimed the Tutor. 'How many?'

'Only two,' said the mortician. 'I've examined eight, but most of them had family who wanted to bury the body.' He turned to Fate. 'I can show you if you like.'

'Not just now,' said Fate. 'We're currently looking for someone and we thought this might be him.'

'It's not?' said Vivienne.

'No,' said Fate. 'But I think we know who this is.'

'Madam de Lorni's friend,' said the Tutor.

'Yes,' said Fate. 'This is the sergeant who tried to help her.'

'So... if this isn't the work of the Butcher,' began the Tutor, 'then this man was killed because he was looking for Luca.'

'And if the Medicis are willing to kill people for simply poking around...'

The two men exchanged a look of concern.

'We should get back to Weasel,' said the Tutor and Fate nodded.

Offering Vivienne a quick goodbye, they left the mortician's cutting room and headed back to the storm drain beside the river.

*

Weasel and Daisy had watched in frightened silence as the pale figure appeared in the storm drain and began pacing back and forth as if he was looking for something.

'He looks like a ghost,' whispered Daisy.

Weasel waved her to be quiet, but it was true. In the shadowed 'cave' of the storm drain the strange figure was shining with a faint silvery glow. It continued searching the ground then stopped to pick something up. It was now too dark to see what it was, but Weasel saw the figure tuck it into some kind of pouch at its waist. Then the figure disappeared into the cave and they heard a faint splash.

Hardly had the sound ceased when Weasel rushed out of the bushes and ran towards the storm drain.

'Weasel, wait!' hissed Daisy as she reluctantly moved to follow him. 'What are you doing?' she whispered as she hovered at the mouth of the storm drain, unwilling to proceed into the dark cave-like space.

Inside the cave, Weasel was peering through the hole in the wall.

'I can see him,' he whispered. 'He must have gone through the water into the cave on the other side of this hole.'

'You're not going to...'

'Follow him, yes,' said Weasel as he quickly lit his wayfinder lantern.

'You're mad!' said Daisy.

'I'll just go a little way,' said Weasel. 'Just so I have something to tell Master Fate.'

Daisy's face was pale with fear.

'It's alright,' said Weasel. 'I can outrun a big fella like that. And *I* can get through this hole while he has to swim under the water.'

The terrified girl looked from the hole in the wall to the dark pool of water lying against the wall of the cave. The thought of going into either place horrified her but, even as she watched, Weasel wormed his way through the hole until he was standing on the other side, his face illuminated by the faint glow of his lantern.

'I'll be back in a trice,' he said with a nervous but excited smile and Daisy could only watch as the light of his lantern began to move away. In its faint light, she could now see that the pool of water continued for quite some way into the adjoining chamber, running alongside a natural passage that disappeared into darkness.

'Weasel!' hissed Daisy in a final entreaty.

'Back in a trice,' came the faint reply.

And with that, the light of Weasel's lantern disappeared beyond a bend in the tunnel.

The young wayfinder felt terribly alone as she slowly backed her way out of the storm drain. She knew that she could not leave while Weasel was still in there, but just being near the sewers made her feel sick with fear, and she could not *believe* that Weasel could be so foolish.

'Weasel, you idiot,' she breathed to herself. 'Why did you have to do that?'

'Do what?' said a rough voice behind her and Daisy turned to see two armed men standing in the gloom.

Daisy made to run, but one of the men reached out and grabbed her skinny wrist.

'Hold on a minute, missy,' said the man, his lips parted in an unpleasant smile revealing a gold tooth that glinted in the darkness. 'You ain't goin nowhere till you tell us what you're doing here.'

Daisy struggled and kicked, and then the man gave a cry of pain as she sank her teeth into his hand.

'You little bitch!' cursed the man and Daisy felt the world tilt as he smacked her to the ground with a heavy-handed slap. 'Now,' said the man as he grabbed hold of Daisy's hair and hauled her to her knees. 'Why don't we start again?'

15
The Curse of a Feral Mage

Sienna and Amos were in the sitting room of the lawyer that Amos had mentioned, but things were not going well. Sienna frowned as the lawyer shifted nervously, refusing to look at them as he poured himself a glass of brandy.

'I'm sorry,' said the grey-haired man. 'I'm afraid I cannot take the case.'

'But you said you would,' said Amos. 'You said you'd be happy to take it.'

'I know,' said the lawyer. 'But that was before I knew who was prosecuting.' He held up his hands to forestall their objections. 'I'm sorry,' he said, 'but I need to protect my family.'

'Protect them from what?' said Sienna.

'Lo Spirito Divino,' said the lawyer as if it were obvious. 'Your friend isn't the only magic-user to be threatened by the priests of the Divine Spirit.'

'You've dealt with them before?' asked Amos and the lawyer's shoulders sagged.

'My niece,' he said with a shake of his head. 'A gifted magic-user, forced to leave the city because she refused to acknowledge the "one true power" of the Divine.'

'I'm sorry,' said Amos.

'And she wasn't dangerous like your friend,' continued the lawyer. 'If he's losing control of his powers then he might be going through the Scourge.'

'The what?' asked Sienna and the lawyer gave a sigh.

'There are four stages in the life of a feral mage,' he began. 'It begins when a child is about four with a stage they call the Spark. Next, comes the Flame when the young mage learns to control their power. This continues until they reach their teenage years when their powers become unstable during a stage known as the Scourge, a dangerous period that only a few feral mages survive. And even if they survive the Scourge, most feral mages are destroyed by a process known as Consumption, they become consumed by power, ego and ambition. There's a reason why feral mages are so rare and so feared.'

'Some must manage to control it,' said Sienna.

'True, said the lawyer. 'And that is why we know their names. They become figures of myth and legend. Arcenlade... Montadimus... Torvonius the Black... mages so powerful as to make a mark on history itself.'

'So you think Isaac could survive the Scourge?'

The lawyer shrugged.

'I think your friend is beginning to realise that the gift of being a feral mage is actually a curse.'

'But Oruthian Bohr is a feral mage,' said Sienna.

'Indeed he is,' said the lawyer. 'But he has formed an alliance with the priests of the Divine Spirit, and now he's using them to hunt down anyone who could challenge his power.'

'Then Isaac doesn't stand a chance.'

'I'm sorry,' said the lawyer. 'But if he killed a priest of the Divine Spirit then I'm afraid your friend is doomed.'

Once again Sienna tried to object, but Amos knew there was no point arguing. With a half-hearted word of thanks, he bade the lawyer goodnight and led Sienna out onto the street where she rounded on him once more.

'We have to get Isaac out!' she cried.

'How?' said Amos. 'Any trial is sure to be a sham and the prison is guarded by priests who wield a magical burning fire.'

Sienna chewed her nails in thought.

'The window of his cell is level with the street…'

'Yes…' said Amos warily.

'So we just need to cut through the bars and pull him out.'

Amos gave a sigh. 'It would take hours to cut through those bars.'

'But he'll die if we don't get him out!'

'I know,' said Amos. His face was tight with frustration until something occurred to him. 'There might be another way.'

'What other way?' demanded Sienna, but Amos just smiled.

'I think it's time I introduced you to Hector and Starke.'

16
The Sump

Fate and the Tutor were just a few minutes from the mortician's when the Tutor spoke.

'We're being followed,' he said as they hurried through the streets on the way back to the storm drain.

'I know,' said Fate. 'It's the Don'Sha'Vir.'

'Strange that we didn't notice him earlier.'

'He must have been concealing his presence,' said Fate. 'Not so easy now that we're moving more quickly.'

'Well, maybe we should move even faster,' said the Tutor and, stepping into the street, he leapt onto a passing hire carriage.

'Woah!' cried the driver as the Tutor grabbed the reins and drew the horses to a halt. 'What the 'ell...' he began, but the Tutor cut him off.

'Time for a detour, my friend,' he said as Fate climbed onto the light carriage.

'I'm on my way to a client,' protested the driver.

'They can wait,' said the Tutor, holding out a handful of silver coins.

The driver's eyes widened at the sight of the money.

'Yes they can,' he said, and the horse gave a whinny of protest as he drew it sharply about. 'Eeyup!' cried the driver and the light carriage lurched forward.

'Look,' said Fate, pointing behind them as they sped off.

The Tutor looked back down the street where three men had now emerged from the corner of a building. Two were ordinary house guards, but the third was dressed in the crimson robes of a nomad. Even now, standing in the open, his form seemed to shimmer slightly as if he were partially obscured by shifting clouds of shadow.

A few minutes later Fate and the Tutor alighted from the carriage.

'Maybe Medici's men were just following us,' said the Tutor as they hurried down the bank towards the river. 'Maybe they didn't go to the storm drain.'

'Let's hope so,' said Fate.

They began making their way through the blackthorn bushes then stopped as they heard a young girl cry out in pain. It was almost dark now but the scene was lit by the faint glow of a wayfinder's lantern. There, just in front of the storm drain, two of the Medici guards were standing over the sobbing form of Daisy. The girl gave a muffled cry and the Tutor reached for one of the throwing stars from the bandoleer across his chest.

'Please,' mumbled Daisy, her mouth swollen and filled with blood. 'I've told you everything.'

'I know,' said one of the men and a gold tooth glinted in the darkness as his lips drew back in a smile. 'We're just entertaining ourselves until the desert freak gets here.'

The guard with the gold tooth raised his arm to strike the girl once more then cried out as a pointed disk of steel stabbed into the flesh of his shoulder. The second man looked up in alarm then grunted as another throwing star struck him in the chest.

Barely did they have time to realise what was happening before the Tutor was upon them. Charging forward, he winded the first guard with a kick to the stomach. However, 'Gold Tooth' managed to draw his sword and the Tutor was forced to recoil as the shortsword slashed towards him. The man was clearly a trained fighter, but he was no match for a demon hunter. Drawing his own sword, the Tutor parried a series of attacks before disarming the man with a sweep of his

Hadean blade. He pressed forward until the point of his sword was resting against the man's chest and then he stopped as the first guard spoke up.

'Cut him and the girl dies.'

The Tutor looked round to see the first guard standing over Daisy with a knife pressed to her throat.

'The sword,' said the man. 'Why don't you put down the sword?'

'Easy there,' said the Tutor.

Raising a hand to calm the man he placed his sword on the ground as Gold Tooth now stepped forward to place his own dagger against the Tutor's throat.

'Pathetic!' he breathed into the Tutor's ear. 'Giving up your sword to save a worthless street rat. Now you're both going to die.'

The guard holding Daisy laughed, but the humour died on his lips as he felt the cold steel of a dragon-handled dagger press against *his* throat.

'Let the girl go,' said Fate.

With an angry snort the man shoved Daisy away before turning to slash at Fate, but the sorcerer had been ready for such a move and he avoided the man's attack before stabbing him quickly in the gut.

In the same instant, the Tutor twisted quickly raising a hand to block Gold Tooth's dagger before hammering his fist into the man's jaw. Taken by surprise, the man staggered back. Once again, he struck out with his dagger, but the Tutor grabbed his wrist and flipped him onto his back before relieving him of his knife.

'You're dead,' said Gold Tooth as he scrambled back to his feet.

'No, we're not,' said Fate. 'But your friend soon will be if you don't tend to that wound.'

With a baleful glare, Gold Tooth crossed the clearing to his injured companion.

'Lord Medici'll kill you for interfering in his business.'

'Perhaps,' said Fate as he moved to stand beside Daisy while the Tutor retrieved his sword. 'And perhaps he will want to know what *really* happened to his niece.'

Uncertainty crept into Gold Tooth's gaze as he stared into Fate's dark eyes.

'Come on,' gasped the guard that Fate had stabbed. 'We have to tell the boss.' With final hate-filled looks, the two men staggered off through the bushes. Gold Tooth's injuries were purely superficial, but the other guard would be lucky to make it back to the Medici mansion alive.

As the two men disappeared, Fate bent down to Daisy. 'Are you all right?' he asked, and the girl gave a dazed nod as he wiped away some of the blood from her mouth. 'Where's Weasel?'

Clearly in pain, Daisy pointed back towards the storm drain. 'He... went... through the hole in the wall,' she managed. 'He wanted... to follow the... bogeyman.'

'Bogeyman?' queried the Tutor.

'Big man,' said Daisy in a strained and drowsy voice. 'Pale skin... glowing... like a ghost.'

With great care, they lifted the girl and carried her into the mouth of the storm drain where they sat her down on a dry mound of earth. Taking a small bottle from a pouch at his waist, Fate poured a couple of drops of brown liquid into Daisy's swollen mouth.

'We'll never fit through there,' said the Tutor as he examined the hole in the wall.

'The water,' mumbled Daisy. 'The Bogeyman... went through the water.'

The Tutor frowned as he looked at the pool of water lying against the wall of the cave.

'It's a sump,' said Fate. 'The pool leads through into the other chamber.'

The Tutor nodded as Fate looked back at the hole in the wall where a faint glow of light had suddenly appeared.

'Someone's coming,' said the sorcerer as he watched the glow of light shining off the slick walls of the adjoining passage. A moment later, a lantern came into view and Fate could just make out the vague shape of a boy's slender body. 'It's Weasel.'

'Is he all right?' asked the Tutor as he also tried to peer through the hole.

'I don't know.'

Peering through the hole, they could see the boy's lantern swaying wildly. Weasel was obviously hurrying, but it was not easy because the wet rock sloped towards the long pool of water that ran down one side of the passage. He was about twenty yards away when he slipped. There was a sudden cry, followed by a splash as he dropped his lantern and fell into the water. The meagre light wavered and went out, but even as it died, Fate saw the vague outline of a second figure, a large figure with pale skin that shone with a weak silvery light.

As Fate stared into the darkness they heard the echoing sounds of Weasel splashing about and struggling in water.

'Help!' came a gurgling cry.

As the tunnel went black, Fate looked down at the charm bracelet on his wrist. In the cave it was now too dark to see the bracelet clearly, but then Fate closed his eyes and one of the charms began to glow. The small charm was in the form of a firefly. Reaching to his wrist,

Fate quickly removed the charm as another bubbling cry reverberated down the stone passage towards them.

'He's drowning!' said the Tutor. 'We have to get to him.'

'But Weasel's a good swimmer,' murmured Daisy from the mouth of the cave.

'The sump,' said Fate as the glowing firefly now hovered over his hand. 'You'll have to go through the sump.'

'Can that thing go underwater?' asked the Tutor but Fate shook his head.

'I need to maintain eye contact.'

'Then I'll have to feel my way.'

The Tutor's tone was resolute, but the idea of swimming through a submerged passage in total darkness, with only a vague idea of where he might emerge, was terrifying.

'No,' said Fate. 'We can see where the sump leads, and I can send the light into the passage. If I keep it close to the water you might be able to see the glow.'

The Tutor gave a nod and quickly removed his sword and anything else that might snag on the rock. He pulled off his boots, slipped into the cold water and was just about to go under when Weasel's frantic splashing and cries for help were suddenly cut off.

'Weasel!' cried Daisy, but Fate was not listening.

Frowning in concentration, he sent the firefly charm flying through the hole in the wall and along the adjoining passage, keeping it close to the water as the Tutor ducked his head beneath the surface of the pool.

'I can see it,' he said. 'Keep it there.' Then, taking a deep breath he plunged into the pool and began to swim towards the faint glow of light that he could see through the surprisingly clear water.

Fate was controlling the firefly charm with his mind and could only take his eyes off it for brief periods of time. Flicking his gaze away from the firefly, he looked for any sign of Weasel, but all he saw was the large figure with the faintly glowing skin. The glimpse was fleeting, but it looked like the figure was pulling something out of the water.

Forcing himself to remain calm, Fate checked to make sure the firefly was still hovering over the water, but this time, when he glanced away from the glowing charm, the pale figure was gone. Clenching his jaw in frustration, he waited for the Tutor to emerge, but there was no sign of the demon hunter.

There was no sign of him because down there, in the cold dark water of the sump, the Tutor was fighting for his life.

*

The water seemed to drag at his clothes as the Tutor swam through the submerged passage towards the faint glow of light from Fate's charm. He knew it was only about twenty feet, but it felt like much longer and he tried not to think about getting trapped as one of his feet struck a hidden outcrop of rock.

As he got closer the glow of light grew stronger, but then he saw something pass in front of it... a dark sinuous shape, like a short snake or an eel. Taking another stroke, he dismissed the creature until something cold and slimy brushed against his hand. Another undulating shape passed between him and the light, and another, and then the Tutor let out a bubbling groan as something bit into the bony flesh of his ankle.

He twisted around, but it was too dark to see anything and then he grunted again as something bit into the back of his neck. He tried to quell a sudden sense of panic as he realized he was under attack. Reaching a hand behind his head, he felt the smooth leathery skin of something attached to his neck. He grabbed the creature and tried to pull it off, but it was firmly attached and the pain was too great. A third creature now clamped onto his hand, while another bit into the muscle of his thigh. More creatures brushed past him in the water and he realized that, far from going to help Weasel, he would be lucky to get out of the water alive.

Knowing he could not continue, he tried to turn back. Now desperate for air, he instinctively went up only to feel the sense of panic grow stronger as his head bumped against the hard ceiling of stone. Suddenly disorientated, he stared into the darkness, but there was no glow of light to guide him back. Fate's light was on the other side of the sump and now he was filled with the horrific idea that he might not find his way out.

Another creature bit him and his head scraped against the roof as he scrabbled his way forward. His lungs burned and his throat convulsed with the urge to breathe and then, finally, the rock was gone and his head broke the surface. He gulped in a mouthful of air and reached for the side of the pool, although he barely had the strength to pull himself out.

As soon as the Tutor reappeared in the cave, Fate recalled the firefly charm and rushed to the edge of the pool to help him out.

'Eels!' gasped the Tutor. 'Been attacked by eels.'

'Not eels,' grunted Fate as he hauled the demon hunter onto the floor of the storm drain. 'Subterranean lamprey... No!' he cried. 'Don't try to pull them off!'

Drawing the white dragon-handled dagger from his belt, Fate took hold of the eel-like creature attached to the Tutor's neck. The slick, leathery body was strong and the

Tutor gasped as the creature's circular maw of teeth sank deeper into his flesh.

'You have to cut them off,' said Fate as he severed the first of the lampreys close to its eyeless head.

The urge to rip the creatures from his body was incredibly strong, but the Tutor tried to remain still as Fate moved from one writhing creature to the next.

'Weasel?' he asked through gritted teeth, but Fate just shook his head.

'I think he was also attacked by the lampreys.'

'You think he drowned?'

'I don't know,' said Fate, 'I saw a figure pulling something from the water, but I couldn't see if it was Weasel.'

'Then he could be alive,' said the Tutor. 'We have to go after him.'

'And we will,' said Fate. 'But not now.'

The Tutor began to object then he winced as Fate cut another of the lampreys free.

'No,' Fate continued. 'This girl needs help and these lamprey bites won't stop bleeding until we can remove the heads.'

The Tutor hated the thought of abandoning Weasel, but Fate was right. Daisy had been badly beaten and there was no way he could swim back through the sump. They would have to find another way.

'Then we need to be quick,' said the Tutor and, even as Fate cut the last of the lampreys from his body he pulled on his boots, buckled on his sword and stumbled over to Daisy who seemed to be hovering on the edge of sleep. The Tutor's body trembled with pain and pent up adrenaline, but still he knelt down and gathered the girl into his arms.

'Hush now,' he said as she gave a low moan of pain.

He looked down at her bruised face and felt his heart convulse with grief. This girl could not have been much more than ten, just a few years older than his daughter had been when her life was brutally cut short.

'What kind of men would beat a child?' he murmured.

'The kind of men who think they're above the law,' said Fate as he reattached the firefly charm to the bracelet on his wrist. 'Now, come on. We need to get back to Blackfell House.'

It was dark when they emerged from the storm drain. They pushed their way through the blackthorn bushes then stopped as Fate took a moment to get his bearings.

'Look,' said the Tutor, nodding up along the bank where the shadowy outline of three men was now visible. The three men were heading towards them and they did not need to see his desert robes to know that one of them was the Don'Sha'Vir.

Despite his injuries, Fate could almost feel the demon hunter's desire to face them.

'Now is not the time,' he said. 'We need to get you back to the house before you lose too much blood.'

With obvious effort, the Tutor drew his eyes away as Fate headed along the bank in the other direction. The Medicis might be one of the most powerful families in the city, but if Weasel, or this young girl, died then the Medicis would learn that there were limits to the kind of protection that money could buy.

Reaching the lamp-lit streets of the city, the two men headed back towards Blackfell House and Fate's housekeeper, who also happened to be a gifted healer.

*

As Fate and the Tutor headed for home, Weasel was waking up to a world of dim light and pain.

The young wayfinder was lying on his back on a flat surface that felt as hard as stone. The horrific memory of drowning in darkness suddenly surged in his mind and he tried to sit up, only to find himself pressed back down by hands of incredible strength. The memory was like something from a nightmare... the darkness... the cold water... and then something biting into his flesh. The sense of panic and terror came rushing back and Weasel began to struggle.

'Hold him,' said a deep voice and Weasel looked up.

He was in some kind of cave, a cave that glowed with a ghostly green light. Strong hands were holding him down, but there was someone else in the room and Weasel's heart almost stopped as a figure loomed over him. The figure was pale and fleshy and bald, but what terrified Weasel most was the object in the figure's hand. It was a large, almost rectangular knife; the kind of knife used in a meat factory or slaughterhouse.

And now the terrifying truth dawned... the reckless young wayfinder had been taken by the Butcher of Guile.

The sharp knife gleamed in the ghostly green light.

And Weasel screamed.

17
Unleashed

As Fate and the Tutor returned to Blackfell House, the potion-maker Inganno was muttering the words of an enchantment in the lamp-lit gloom of his workshop. His mind burned with an anger that seemed disproportionate to the actions taken against him, but he had always been this way. Even as a child he had refused to acknowledge any boundaries or limits on his freedom. When his mother had threatened to send him away, Inganno had simply killed her.

Now that same murderous rage was focussed on Fate and the Tutor. Not only had they ruined his plans to have a beautiful and doting wife, they had also tried to rob him of his liberty, and that was inexcusable.

So now Inganno spoke magical words of power over a large cauldron of hot tar. For hours now he had been rehearsing this enchantment and now he could see that it was beginning to work. The glutinous black substance had begun to thicken and writhe. Smooth canine shapes rose up from the surface as if a liquid wolf were drowning in darkness.

Without ceasing the enchantment, Inganno picked up a dish containing a mound of powdered diamond. This exotic ingredient was incredibly expensive but it was worth it, and the tar glistened like frost as Inganno sprinkled the powder onto the surface. To this he added a precise measure of mercury. The liquid metal sank quickly into the tar, but now, when the wolf's head rose from the surface, the teeth shone with a dark silvery light. Sulphur was the next ingredient and the room was filled with a noxious stench as the yellow powder was absorbed by the black viscous tar.

Inganno shook his head to clear his mind of the fumes. Then, glancing back at the book, he spoke the final enchantment. And as he did so the substance began to flow over the side of the pot. The fire below the pot was no longer lit, but the black substance did not simply drip into the charcoal brazier, it moved with purpose until it formed a wide puddle on the stone floor of the basement.

In nervous awe, Inganno watched as the puddle rose up assuming the shape of a sleek and powerful hound. Tall as a wolf and shining black, the manitu opened its eyes, eyes that glowed like coals in a fire. It curled a lip to reveal sharp silvery fangs and its claws now scraped against the flagstones like talons of steel.

The manitu's gaze suddenly seemed to focus on the potion-maker and Inganno drew back in alarm. It opened its mouth and a sound emerged, half growl and half shriek, like steam forcing its way through a crack in the Earth's crust. Trying to control his fear, Inganno reached for the two final ingredients... a small clump of the Tutor's hair and a few scrapings of Fate's dried blood.

Placing them in his hand, Inganno made a fist then took a nervous breath as he prepared himself for the last step in the conjuration. He needed to place these samples deep in the manitu's chest so that it would be able to home in on its targets, but the black tar was hot and he knew this step would be painful.

Still hesitant, he turned back to the book and read the relevant passage once more.

Before the manitu cools, the conjurer will add the target's sample as they speak the final enchantment. With each recitation

94

*the medium will grow hotter, but
the longer one persists, the more
powerful the manifestation will
become.*

Finally, he could put it off no longer and with a grimace of anticipation, he pushed his hand into the hound's black chest. Through gritted teeth, he muttered the final incantation and winced as he felt the tar growing hotter. Another repetition and he could take no more. His willpower crumbled and, with a gasp of pain, he withdrew his hand and plunged it into a pitcher of cool rapeseed oil that was standing nearby.

As the pain subsided, Inganno turned to look at the hound. Standing in the middle of his workshop, the terrifying creature raised its black muzzle as if it were scenting the air. Black lips curled back from silvery teeth then it turned towards the door and its glowing eyes flared. Wiping his scalded arm on a towel, Inganno moved to open the steel door, but there was no need.

With barely a sound, the powerful hound walked towards the door and then, even as Inganno watched, its form dissolved to form a black puddle on the floor. The puddle glistened with diamond dust and swirls of mercury before sliding forward to seep under the door.

Both fascinated and frightened, Inganno opened the door and watched as the shimmering puddle rose back up into the form of the hound. He tried to follow it up the cellar stairs but it was too quick for him and, by the time he had caught up to it, the hound had torn a hole in his front door which was only made of wood. Apparently, the hound found it easier to break through rather than melting under as it had with the metal door in the cellar.

Now it stood at the top of the steps leading down into the street. For a moment it looked like a nightmarish dog awaiting its night-time walk, but then it raised its head to sniff the air and its chest glowed as it sensed the direction of its quarry. For just a moment it turned to look at the man who had conjured it and Inganno's heart quailed at the murderous light in its glowing eyes, and then it sped off into the night and Inganno slumped back against the splintered remains of his front door.

The hellish creature loped like a wolf through the twisting streets of Guile. From a distance it looked like a large black dog and few people gave it a second glance, never looking closely enough to see that its skin was hairless and shining black, or that its eyes gleamed like furnace coals. Only when the hound ran into a pack of feral dogs did it encounter any kind of resistance.

The street dogs snarled at the intruder, but the normal process of intimidation had no effect. When the hound did not retreat, the pack surrounded it and the pack-leader lunged forward even as two of the other dogs attacked from the rear.

With the speed of a seasoned pitbull, the hound reared back, avoiding the pack leader's teeth and striking out with the talons of a front paw. The silvery talons were longer and sharper than any dog's claws and they tore into the pack-leader's face like blades, slicing through skin and bone with ease. Half its face was torn away and the unfortunate dog gave an agonised howl as it stumbled away, pawing at its lacerated head as if to rid itself of the pain.

At the same time, the other two dogs had attacked from the rear. One managed to make contact, sinking its teeth into the hound's back leg, but the hound's body had no bones to break, no tendons to sheer. Its black limb simply oozed through the dog's teeth and came away unharmed. The dog's mouth was filled with foul-tasting tar and it coughed and whimpered even as the hound spun round to kill it with another swipe of its lethal claws.

The other attacker now leapt back, but it was not quick enough and it gave a strangled yowl as the hound's jaws closed around its neck. For a moment, the poor animal struggled to break free until the manitu clenched its jaws and the dog's body went limp as the bones in its neck were crushed.

The lifeless body fell to the ground, the rest of the pack slunk away into the shadows, and Vulpyrac's Hound resumed its hunt.

Inganno the potion-maker, had done his work well.

18
Hector and Starke

Meanwhile, in the port city of Dymhaven, Sienna was standing in the stables of Amos Saddler. Reaching up, she stroked the neck of an enormous draft horse called Hector. In the adjacent stall was a horse of similar stature known as Starke. They both had the mottled grey coat of a breed known as Haysian Blue.

'You really think they can pull the bars from the window?' asked Sienna.

Amos just smiled patting Starke's rump as he adjusted the modified harness that he had made for the task.

'We might need to loosen the mortar with a steel spike or two,' said the stable master. 'But yes. These handsome fellows are so strong that I wouldn't be surprised if the entire keep shifted on its foundations.'

'But they're not fast,' said Sienna.

'No,' agreed Amos. 'That's why we'll have Sorrel and Kensie standing by. They're as fast as you could wish.'

'And what about you?' asked Sienna. 'Are you're sure *you'll* be all right?'

'Don't you worry about me,' said Amos. 'There's a disused coach house just across from the keep. Me and the boys will hide in there while you make your escape. You just focus on getting out of the city and then hope that your mysterious friend is willing to help.'

'He'll help,' said Sienna.

'How do you know?'

'Because he's also a feral mage.'

Amos raised his eyebrows. 'Are you sure you can trust him?'

'My father trusted him,' said Sienna. 'Right up to the moment of his death.'

19

The Fungus and the Fiend

Back in Guile, Motina had treated Daisy's injuries. She settled the wayfinder girl in one of the guest rooms before heading back to the kitchen where Fate was tending to the Tutor. The demon hunter winced as Fate removed another lamprey head from his body.

'We have to get going,' said the Tutor. 'Weasel could be dying while we sit here.'

'You'll be here even longer if you don't sit still,' said Motina as she entered the room.

'How's Daisy?' asked the Tutor.

'Sleeping,' said Motina.

'Good,' said Fate. Sitting in a chair, he leaned down over the Tutor's leg. 'Just two more,' he said as he used a pair of metal tongs to remove another of the blind heads.

'Hideous things!' said Motina. 'I didn't know we had those in the sewers.'

'Not the sewers,' said Fate. 'The lampreys live in the natural tunnels that run alongside them.' Washing his hands in the sink, he glanced at the Tutor. The lampreys had not had time to bore into his flesh so the bites were superficial but Fate was still surprised at how quickly the demon hunter had recovered from his brush with a watery death.

'You're sure you don't mind going back through the sump?'

'Not if you can keep those things off me,' replied the Tutor and Fate nodded.

It was when they first returned to the house that a possible solution had occurred to him.

To make the lamprey heads easier to remove, Fate had used a concoction of alcohol and valerian. He had been bathing each head with the solution when Motina came back into the kitchen for some hot water.

'That'll work even better if you add some powdered skullcap,' she said. 'The fungus will relax the jaw muscles, ' she added and Fate threw up his hands with a frustrated...

'Dah! Of course.'

'What?' said Motina.

'It's the fungus in the cave,' said Fate. 'The glowing fungus that was growing on the wall.'

'You think it's luciferin?' said Motina. 'I thought that only grew in the caves of Korolivka.'

'Some of the spores must have washed downstream and established themselves in the caves beneath Guile.'

'Can someone explain how this is going to help keep those things away from me?' the Tutor had said.

'Luciferin,' replied Fate. 'It's a fungus that grows in caves.'

'And?'

'Crushed into a paste it can be used to repel parasites and fish that hunt by scent.'

'And it will keep the lampreys away?'

'Hopefully,' said Fate. 'And think about it... the bogeyman got through the sump without being attacked and Daisy said his skin glowed like a ghost.'

The Tutor nodded his understanding. 'And your mortician friend said the sheen on the Butcher's victims glows in the dark. Maybe they were also killed in the caves.'

'Precisely,' said Fate, and with that he had proceeded to remove the last of the lamprey heads while Motina went back to check on the sleeping girl.

With both tasks completed, the two men now gathered up their things and prepared to head back to the storm drain. Fate was adding items to a leather shoulder bag when Motina handed him a bottle of tonic and several pieces of date and raisin flapjack wrapped in waxed paper.

'Weasel likes it,' said the housekeeper. 'And it'll help if you get too cold.' Her lips tightened into an anxious line. They were all working on the assumption that Weasel was still alive.

Along with the food, Fate had packed a length of slender rope, several pieces of charcoal and chalk, and two elongated crystals that glowed with a bright bluish light.

'They get brighter if you shake them,' he explained, but the Tutor also noticed that he checked the firefly charm on his wrist.

'I thought you no longer used magic.'

'I don't,' said Fate and, taking hold of the charm he held it against the Tutor's forehead.

'Think of the moon,' he said, and slowly the metal firefly began to glow.

'The charm is controlled by thought, not magic,' said Fate as he cinched up the top of his bag and slung it across his back. 'Now, let's go.'

'Find him,' said Motina as they got up to leave the kitchen.

'We will,' said the Tutor.

Walking quickly, they left the house and hurried along the driveway. Their thoughts were focussed on finding Weasel and so they did not notice the black shape of a dog lurking in the darkness beyond the railings of the perimeter fence.

*

Hidden in the shadows, Vulpyrac's Hound seethed with primal fury as it watched Fate and the Tutor move towards the gate in the fence that *it* had been unable to cross. Three times it had tried to enter the grounds of Blackfell House, and each time it had sensed the magical power that would burn it if it tried to proceed.

It was difficult to say if such a creature was alive, but it certainly possessed some degree of consciousness and that consciousness had the capacity for cunning. It crouched in the darkness as its prey approached the gate. Opening the gate they emerged from the protection of the fence and Vulpyrac's hound moved in for the kill.

*

'Do you think he's still alive?' asked the Tutor as they reached the end of the driveway.

'He'd better be,' said Fate and the Tutor glanced at the sorcerer.

'You like him, don't you?'

'I asked him to help,' said Fate, and now the Tutor understood. The great Decimus Fate felt guilty.

'It's strange,' Fate continued as the Tutor opened the gate and they emerged onto the street. 'I never used to think twice about using people like Weasel.'

'Inconvenient, isn't it?'

'What?'

'Growing a conscience.'

Fate gave him a sidelong look then his eyes widened as the Tutor suddenly charged into him, knocking him to the ground. At the same instant, a dark shape leapt through the space that Fate had just occupied and the sorcerer caught a fleeting glimpse of shining black skin and dark silvery teeth.

Fate hit the ground hard, but the Tutor was already coming back to his feet. Spinning around, he turned to see what had attacked them. His first thought was that it was some kind of rabid street dog, but this sleek monster had not been born of the street.

No, this hell hound was a creature of magic.

With shocking speed, the creature leapt for the Tutor's throat, and once again he was forced to twist out of its path, only this time he was not quite quick enough and the creature's talons scored three bloody lines on his shoulder. Barely had the hound landed before it was slashing at his stomach and the Tutor lurched back to avoid being disembowelled.

The hound lunged once more, but this time the Tutor was ready. Drawing his sword, he arced his body away from the scything claws and swung a downward blow, cutting deeply into the hound's shoulder. The creature let out a searing hiss, but the sharp blade merely sliced through the black body leaving a deep gash that quickly closed up and disappeared.

The Tutor frowned then stabbed his sword forward as the manitu came at him once more. This time, the point of the sword sank into the manitu's chest, but the conjuration had no heart to pierce, no lungs to burst. It merely absorbed the blade and pressed forward, its claws slashing at the Tutor's forearm as he tried to fend the creature off. It was like trying to hold back liquid tar. The blade sank deeper, the hound's jaws snapped closer, and it seemed that there was nothing the Tutor could do to stop it.

Then the hound's forward movement stopped as Fate stabbed it in its hindquarters with his white dragon-handled dagger. The blade of this dagger was imbued with magic that made it more deadly to creatures from the

Daemonaria, but the manitu was not from the demon realm and Fate's dagger slipped free of its body, the flesh sealing up like the surface of a dark pool.

However, Fate's attack gave the Tutor the opportunity he needed. Pulling his sword free of the creature's body, he began to channel something of himself into the frosted stone encased in the pommel.

'That's it!' Fate cried, backing away as the manitu now slashed at *him*. 'The power of a heart-stone might kill it.'

The Tutor's sword was a Hadean blade, a weapon forged to cut through the armoured skin of demons. The heart-stone allowed the wielder to channel their passion into the blade. The Tutor's greatest inspiration had always been his wife and daughter, but they had been taken from him, so now the only thing he had to draw on was his willpower.

Fortunately, the demon hunter's willpower was no trivial thing and the heart-stone began to glow as the Tutor struck at the hound just as it took another swipe at Fate. The manitu gave a howl of fury and whipped around. It leapt into the air, but the demon hunter stepped back, the blade of his sword glowing as he drew a deep cut across the creature's chest.

This time, the creature's howl spoke of real pain, and the cut in its chest did not immediately close up. It flapped open, a trail of silvery liquid running from the wound like blood. The hound attacked once more, but the Tutor sidestepped and struck it a second time as he drove it back towards the fence. The manitu gave another snarl of pain then it positively shrieked as the Tutor kicked it backwards into the fence which suddenly erupted in green and purple flames.

For a moment the manitu was caught in the magical flames, its black body stuck to the metal railing the way skin might stick to a red-hot iron. For two long seconds it thrashed in the flames before tearing itself free. Still burning, and cut in several places, the hellish hound gave up the attack and sped off into the night.

Still thrumming with tension, the Tutor watched it turn a corner and disappear.

'What the hell was that?' he asked as Fate came to stand beside him.

'Some kind of conjuration.'

'From Medici?'

'No,' said Fate. 'If I had to guess, I would say it was sent by Inganno.'

'The potion-maker! I thought he was just some love potion crackpot.'

'Love potions are not easy to make, and he must have some significant skills if he's working for Alonso Medici.'

Still watching to see if the creature might return, the Tutor raised a hand to the shallow cuts on his shoulder. The injuries would have been much worse were it not for the hardened leather armour that covered his sword arm and shoulder. The two men turned as they heard footsteps on the gravel driveway of Blackfell House.

'What on earth is going on here?' exclaimed Motina as she opened the gate. 'I thought you'd be long gone by now, but then the charm on the perimeter fence began to chime.'

'We were attacked,' said the Tutor.

'Some kind of conjured effigy,' said Fate.

The housekeeper appeared suitably shocked, then she noticed the fresh blood on the Tutor's shoulder.

'You're bleeding,' she exclaimed. 'Again!'

106

'It's all right,' said the Tutor. 'It can wait till we find Weasel.'

Motina's eyes narrowed, but he was right. The first priority just now was finding Weasel. The Tutor turned back to Fate and the two men scanned the streets for any sign of the black hound that had just attacked them.

'Do you think it's dead?' asked the Tutor.

'No,' said Fate. 'Your sword didn't cut deep enough to kill it. It might take a while to recover, but it will definitely be back.' He bowed his head in thought before turning to Motina. 'Do you know how to make a net?'

'Do I look like a fisherman?' said Motina and Fate raised an eyebrow until the housekeeper rolled her eyes. 'Yes,' she said. 'I know how to make a net.'

'Good,' said Fate. 'You'll find several skeins of strong cord in the storerooms. About ten-foot square should do.'

'Anything else?' asked Motina archly.

'Yes... You'll need to soak it in a solution of rosemary.'

'To constrain a creature of magic.'

'Precisely,' said Fate.

'Come on,' said the Tutor. 'We've wasted enough time as it is.'

And with that the two men hurried off down the street and back to the storm drain where Weasel had disappeared.

*

Motina gave a sigh as she turned back to the house.

'I don't know,' she muttered to herself as she walked along the driveway. 'First it was dark sorcerers and poisoned monks, now it's love potions, lost boys and magical creatures that attack in the night. Whatever happened to living a quiet life in a sleepy river city known as Guile?'

Walking back to the house, the small hunchbacked woman reached up to touch the bare branches of the trees that lined the driveway. With a rueful smile, she shook her head. Even the trees in Fate's garden were enchanted sentinels from the hinterlands of Faerie. Their presence gave her comfort. However, as she reached the last of the trees, a shiver ran through them and Motina stopped as she felt the distinctive presence of Faerie right here in the garden. She turned around as a single dandelion seed appeared in the air before her face.

Her eyes followed the glowing seed as it floated down to the ground where it remained upright like a tiny ballerina. Motina scanned the garden as if she expected to see someone.

'He's not here,' she called out, her eyes scanning the driveway. 'If you were hoping to speak to him, he's not here.'

Now she could definitely feel the presence of someone in the grounds, but she could see nothing. Then, from high in the trees, she heard a sound like the faint whisper of silk on sharpened steel.

'You can't frighten me,' she said with a defiant smile. 'I know your daughters would never harm me.'

She felt, more than heard, another sound like deep laughter and then, down on the ground, the dandelion seed chimed like a tiny bell before dissolving into a cloud of silvery dust that slowly disappeared.

Motina arched an eyebrow as the presence in the garden faded.

'Bloomin' faeries,' she sighed, adopting one of the words that Weasel often used.

And with that, Fate's housekeeper hobbled up the shallow steps of the porch and back into the safety of Blackfell House.

*

Across the city, Inganno's stomach was a knot of nervous excitement. Sitting in his basement workshop, he felt a conceited glow of satisfaction at being able to perform such a powerful conjuration. However, his success was tempered by a distinct sense of anxiety. He had no way of knowing if the manitu had killed its victims or not. But he knew that normal weapons could not harm it, and he knew it would never give up. He would wait a few days and then he would make enquiries about the demon hunter and the Sage of Blackfell House.

If everything went to plan then both men would soon be reported dead.

*

In the dark corner of a wheelwright's yard, Vulpyrac's Hound stood close to the lingering warmth of the blacksmith's forge. The workers had long since left for the night, but the forge retained its heat, and the heat would help to seal up the wounds that had threatened to end its existence.

Somewhere in its rudimentary mind, the manitu's murderous rage was growing once more. It would wait until its form was whole and then it would return to the purpose for which it had been summoned... to kill.

*

In the cave-like mouth of the storm drain, Fate and the Tutor slipped off their boots and their outer layers of clothing. They pushed them through the hole in the wall along with the Tutor's sword and the bag that Fate had

109

brought. Then Fate began to scrape the glowing fungus off the wall of the cave. He rubbed it between his hands until it turned into a glowing silvery paste and then he smeared it over the Tutor's body.

With this done, the Tutor moved back to the edge of the sump while Fate sent the firefly charm into the adjoining tunnel to light his way.

'Are you ready?' he asked and the Tutor gave a determined nod.

They did not know if the fungus would keep the lampreys away and the Tutor's mind was still full of the images from his previous attempt... the claustrophobia and the pain of the lamprey bites, all combined with the horrific fear of drowning.

Slipping into the cold water, the Tutor waited for the touch of a sinuous body or the searing pain of a bite, but there was nothing.

'What if Weasel's already dead?' he asked.

'Then we kill whoever took him,' said Fate.

They exchanged a final look and then the Tutor ducked beneath the surface and tried to suppress the thought of being eaten alive as he swam towards the light of Fate's firefly charm.

20

The Empty Slab

Weasel was dreaming. He was dreaming about drowning in darkness while unseen creatures bit into his body. Darkness engulfed him and then he was floating, carried along a twisting passage before being laid down on a cold slab of stone. Strong hands held him and he was too terrified to scream - until he saw the knife. The butcher's cleaver gleamed in the pale green light as a figure brought it down towards his body, and then...

Weasel woke to the same pale green light, but the figure and his butcher's cleaver were gone. He was lying on a padded blanket, a thick quilted blanket like those used by the ferrymen during the cold days of winter. He was in a cave with a domed ceiling and a smooth earthen floor. The rock walls of the cave were smooth and speckled with some kind of fungal growth that glowed with a faint emerald light.

It took Weasel a moment to come round and then he sat up with a start.

He remembered following the bogeyman into the caves. Being careful not to get too close, he had followed the pale figure until the passage merged with two others. Fearful of getting lost he turned round to check the route, but when he looked back the pale figure was no longer a distant glow, it was coming back towards him.

Weasel began to run, but in his panic he took the wrong passage. He had not gone far before he realised his mistake and now he needed to find somewhere to hide until he could go back. Spotting a narrow crevice, he snuffed out his lantern and hid for several minutes, listening carefully for any sound of pursuit.

Nothing.

Finally, he judged it safe and, relighting his lantern, he made his way back to the passage leading out to the storm drain. He felt a huge surge of relief as he recognised the way out, then he froze. What he had taken for an outcrop of rock was actually a large and powerful figure. It was the bogeyman, right there in front of him.

For a second they just stared at each other, and it was in that moment that Weasel realised the bogeyman was not human. The figure was big but hunched over, with broad shoulders, a narrow waist and arms so long that its hands hung down below its knees. Now so close, he could see that its glowing skin was smooth and grey, like a combination of human skin and mottled stone. But it was the bogeyman's eyes that froze Weasel to the spot. Like the fungus on the walls of the cave, those eyes glowed with a pale green light.

And then it 'spoke'.

The sound was like the echoing clack of pebbles, punctuated by the tuneful plop of water falling into a pool. Slowly the sounds merged into human words.

'No leave.' The sound was like millstones grinding together and Weasel turned to flee.

Almost dropping his lantern he fled down the tunnel, the makeshift lamp swaying wildly as he tried to keep his footing on the slippery rock. Behind him he heard the sound of footsteps and he realised the bogeyman was coming after him.

Slipping and stumbling, he rounded a bend and his heart leapt as he recognised the entrance passage leading to the hole in the wall. For a moment he thought he heard voices, and that was when he had fallen into the water and the nightmare had closed in around him.

Now Weasel was sitting in a cave.

His body felt stiff and he winced as he got to his feet. Looking down, he saw a small circular wound in the skin of his forearm, and there was another on the back of his right calf. Both wounds were bleeding slightly and he quickly became aware of similar wounds on other parts of his body. With a disturbing flashback, he realised that the biting creatures from his nightmare had been real. But that was in the past.

Like most street orphans, Weasel was no stranger to suffering and this had forged a resilience that allowed him to put unpleasant experiences behind him. He was a survivor and now his mind turned to escaping from this cave and somehow getting back to the surface.

Rising from the floor, he began to examine his surroundings and it took only a moment to realise that the entrance to the cave was blocked by a large stone. The arched entrance was about three feet high and there was a small gap at the top where the stone did not quite fit. Weasel could get his arm through the gap but there was no way his head would fit through.

Putting his shoulder to the stone he tried to push it away, but it was too heavy and his feet merely skidded in the loose earth on the floor. With a groan of frustration he thumped the stone and immediately regretted it as the pain of the impact shot through his hand. Peering through the gap, he could see that it led into a passage, but the light was not strong enough to see very far.

Stepping back from the gap, he began to search around the cave, looking for something he could use to lever the stone out of the way. However, apart from the blanket, the only other thing he found was a small copper bowl. He was about to throw it down when an idea occurred to him.

Kneeling down at the base of the stone, he scraped the edge of the bowl into the floor. The sandy earth was packed hard but the bowl gouged out a channel and his idea might just work. There was no way he could dig an escape tunnel *under* the stone because it would simply fall down and trap him. However, if he could dig a hole for the stone to fall *into* then it would widen the gap at the top. With a renewed sense of optimism, he set to work.

It was hard going, but slowly Weasel began hollowing out the space under the stone. His one fear was that it might slip and trap his arm. At one point the stone moved and he grazed his knuckles as he snatched his hand out of the hole.

A few more minutes and the sand at the side of the hole began to crumble as the stone sank down into the hole that Weasel had dug. It was still tight, but now there was just enough room at the top of the stone for him to squeeze through the gap.

Holding his breath, Weasel peered through the gap. Seeing the coast was clear, he put one arm through the hole and was about to continue when a thought occurred to him…

What if some of the tunnels were completely dark?

How would he find his way out?

Settling back into the cave, Weasel cursed the fact that he had lost his lantern then he glanced at the fungus on the walls. Quickly, he began to scrape it off until he had a mound of the glowing fungus in the palm of his hand. It was not exactly bright, but it would offer a faint source of light if the passages became completely dark. Now he was ready and, taking a deep breath, he squeezed through the gap until he fell through onto the other side.

Weasel felt a surge of joy at his escape but the area beyond the cave led into a branching passage and he had no idea which way to go. Fortunately, the walls were mottled with the same glowing fungus so he did not need to rely on the meagre light emanating from his hand. With no way of knowing, Weasel trusted to his wayfinder instincts and took the passage on the right.

Once again it was clear that this was a natural passage, but there was also evidence of deliberate excavation. Jutting outcrops had been smoothed away and there was even the occasional step carved into the floor. Weasel followed the passage until it came to a junction.

To one side there was a dark crevice running along the floor of the passage and he could hear the sound of running water coming from below. It made him feel uneasy and so he took the other route.

He passed several branching tunnels, but he kept to the main way until he came to one passage that did not seem quite so dark. He was just wondering whether to take it when he heard the faint sound of voices behind him, and they were getting louder.

With no time for hesitation, Weasel set off down this new passage. Glancing backwards, he stumbled as he reached another set of steps carved into the floor. The passage began to slope upwards and Weasel saw light up ahead. Maybe it was daylight.

Increasing his pace, Weasel hurried forward and the light grew brighter. His hopes rose until he burst into a larger cavern, at which point the young wayfinder skidded to a halt. This cavern was more brightly lit, but Weasel wished it was not. For there, lying on a stone slab in the centre of the cave was a body. It was the body of a young man with dark hair. The skin on his hands was puckered with burn scars. All that was missing was the mole at the base of his jaw.

The blood pounded in Weasel's ears as he recognised the young man from the picture that Fate had shown him in the locket. It was Madam de Lorni's son. It was clear that the young man was dead and the ghostly green light made him look even more deathly.

Lying close beside the young man was a second slab of stone, but this one was empty.

Too frightened to register any sadness, Weasel began to back out of the cave then he stopped as he heard a guttural sound behind him. It was the sound of pebbles rolling in a cave…

It was the sound of the bogeyman.

Weasel whipped round and what he saw filled him with confusion and fear. There was the bogeyman, broad-shouldered, long arms and glowing rock-flesh skin. Beside him was a large man whose skin was so pale as to be almost white. The man was bald, and the whites of his pink eyes shone with the same green light as the bogeyman's. Hanging from his belt was a large rectangular cleaver, and the front part of his body was covered by a discoloured leather apron. Weasel had seen aprons like that before and he knew he was looking at the Butcher.

'No,' said the butcher, replying to the bogeyman's rolling-pebble words. 'Now we definitely can't let him leave.'

Weasel felt his knees go weak, but it was not the bogeyman or the Butcher that unsettled him. It was the young man standing beside them that made him feel faint. On wobbly legs, Weasel started to back away, but his vision was beginning to fade and there was a strange ringing sound in his ears.

'Catch him!' said the Butcher and Weasel felt the ground tilt as the bogeyman lunged towards him.

21

The Butcher of Guile

Fate had been a child when he first learned how to master fear, but even for him, swimming through the sump was no small challenge. He could only imagine how the Tutor must have felt with the attack of the lampreys still fresh in his mind. His respect for the demon hunter grew even stronger as he finally emerged on the far side of the submerged passage.

The Tutor reached down a hand then winced as he helped Fate out of the water.

'Are you all right?' asked Fate.

'I'm fine.'

'No, you're not,' said Fate as the Tutor clasped a hand to his injured shoulder.

After swimming through the sump, the Tutor had taken Fate's firefly charm in his hand. He did not have the skill to control its flight so he simply held it over the water so that Fate could see its light as he also swam through. The sorcerer now reclaimed the charm and clipped it back on his bracelet before reaching into his bag for one of the glowing blue crystals.

Now he leaned in closer to have a look at the Tutor's injured shoulder. 'Hmm...' he murmured. 'The hound's talons cut more deeply than I thought.'

'I'm fine,' repeated the Tutor, gritting his teeth as he pulled on his dry leather doublet before easing his right arm into his hardened leather armour.

'We should have let Motina stitch you up.'

'No time,' said the Tutor as he buckled on his sword belt. 'Now, come on.' Retrieving the second blue crystal from Fate's bag, he gave it a shake before holding it up to illuminate the tunnel. 'Look,' he said. 'That's where Weasel fell in.'

'And where the bogeyman caught him,' replied Fate.

The sorcerer quickly donned his long-coat and pulled on his boots before moving to stand beside the Tutor.

'It looks like Weasel was also attacked by the lampreys,' said the Tutor, indicating a watery trail of blood on the rock floor of the passage. 'They went this way.'

Holding the blue crystals aloft, they began to make their way down the natural passageway.

'I had no idea these tunnels existed,' whispered the Tutor as the main passage merged with several others.

'They've been here for eons,' said Fate. 'Carved out by underground rivers that flow beneath the city.'

At every junction, the sorcerer insisted on marking the route with either charcoal or chalk so they could find their way out. They continued for about two hundred yards before the floor of the passage became covered in water and the trail of blood disappeared.

'Which way now?' said the Tutor as the passage branched off in two directions.

'Shield your light,' said Fate, and the passage was plunged into darkness as the two men tucked the glowing crystals under their clothes.

At this point, there was only a speckle of glowing fungus on the walls. As the Tutor peered into the gloom, Fate closed his eyes and waited until the glow of the crystals had faded before opening them again. For a moment all he could see was darkness, but then he slowly became aware that one of the passages looked a tad brighter than the other.

'This way,' he said in a low voice. 'There's a hint of light down this way.'

Fate drew a dagger and the Tutor drew his sword, but they kept their crystals partially shielded so as not to betray their presence.

'It's getting brighter,' whispered the Tutor and Fate gave a nod.

The way ahead was definitely getting lighter and the floor of the passage was no longer wet. In fact, it began to show signs of being worked. The light ahead of them was now unmistakable and they continued until they heard the echoing sound of voices. A deep voice was speaking, but it was too muffled and distant to make out the words. Then they heard another voice that sounded lighter and younger.

Moving more quickly they pressed on until the Tutor gestured for caution. Ahead of them the tunnel opened out into a cavern that was filled with a pale green light. Edging his way closer, the Tutor advanced until he could see into the open space, and then he stopped.

At the centre of the room were two slabs of stone and standing between them, with his back to the entrance, was a large man with a bald head, pale skin and a stained leather apron tied around his waist. It was the Butcher of Guile standing, bold as you like, in the cold light of his lair. On the nearest of the two slabs was the lifeless body of a young man. It was too far away to be certain, but the figure fitted the description of Madam de Lorni's son.

The Tutor could not make out the figure on the second slab, but he knew it must be alive because the Butcher was now speaking to it.

'Remember,' came the sound of that deep resonant voice. 'The pain will not last for long.'

The words turned the Tutor's heart to ice. He could see a rectangular cleaver hanging from the Butcher's waist, and he was too far away to intervene if the Butcher chose to use it. Being careful not to make a sound, the Tutor reached for one of the throwing stars from the bandoleer across his chest. It would be a long throw, but it was his only chance of causing a distraction that might allow him to close the distance. Turning slightly, he showed the throwing star to Fate and the sorcerer gave a nod of understanding.

As the Tutor adjusted his body for the throw, the Butcher reached out a hand to each of the slabs. The Tutor could only see the dead body on the near slab, but he saw the Butcher lay a hand on the dead youth's face. Then, with one arm stretched out to each of the figures, the Butcher's hands began to glow.

Fearing this was some kind of torture, the Tutor's arm whipped forward as he let fly with his throwing star. The spinning projectile struck the Butcher in his right shoulder and he gave a grunt of pain as he withdrew his hands. Clearly shocked, he reached a hand to his shoulder. He turned to see where the attack had come from and his glowing pink eyes grew wide as he saw the dark figure of the Tutor charging towards him.

The Tutor sprinted forward, his sword already beginning the attack that would end at the Butcher's throat. The bulky figure of the Butcher stumbled back against the far slab as the demon hunter closed the distance. The Tutor was almost in striking distance when a large figure barged into him from the side.

It was the bogeyman.

The figure seemed to have appeared from nowhere and the Tutor was taken by surprise as he was knocked to the floor. His sword arm was now restrained by a hand with incredible strength and there was no way he could break free so he dropped his sword and used his free hand to draw a dagger from his belt. The figure grappling him was extremely strong. However, it was also clear that it had never been trained to fight and the Tutor was able to regain the initiative.

Even though his right arm was still being held, he managed to get behind the figure, using his trapped arm to pull his attacker close as the blade of his dagger came up under the figure's chin.

At the same time, Fate rushed forward with his white-handled dagger, hoping to prevent the Butcher from causing any harm. He had also been taken by surprise by the figure that attacked the Tutor. Bursting from a side passage, the bogeyman had knocked the Tutor to the ground and in that split second Fate realised that the figure was not human. Long arms, short legs and pale skin that looked like rock... the sorcerer had seen such creatures before.

The bogeyman was a troglodyte.

Pushing aside his surprise, Fate finally reached his target. He raised his dagger to kill the Butcher even as the Tutor's own weapon was pressing against the bogeyman's throat. Both were about to die when a shout echoed around the cavern.

'NO!' came the cry, and so urgent was the tone that both Fate and the Tutor hesitated as they turned to see who had spoken.

It was Weasel.

'Stop!' said the young wayfinder. 'Don't hurt them.'

Suddenly appearing from the mouth of another passage, Weasel rushed forward and, even as he did so, the person on the far slab sat up.

It was Luca de Lorni, complete with the mole at the base of his jaw.

There were not many things that surprised Fate but this certainly did, and he frowned as he looked from the sitting Luca to the dead Luca lying on the second slab. He noted the same features, the same hair and the same burned hands, but he also noticed that the dead Luca appeared shorter with a somewhat lighter build.

Understanding dawned and Fate arched an eyebrow as he turned to look at the man standing between the two slabs.

'The Butcher of Guile indeed,' he said with a smile.

22

Luca's Tale

The Butcher's cave was surprisingly homely with a table, three chairs and hundreds of books lining crude wooden shelves set into the walls. Light was provided by glass jars filled with brightly glowing fungus. A low cot lay against one wall and it was here that Weasel was sitting beside Madam de Lorni's son. Luca appeared anxious while Weasel looked distinctly pleased with himself.

Sitting in one of the chairs, the Tutor looked up at the 'bogeyman' as the troglodyte handed him a stone cup of water.

'Thank you.'

'His name's Cradlop,' said Weasel.

'Thank you, Cradlop,' said the Tutor.

Weasel laughed at his attempt to imitate the bizarre name, but the troglodyte merely dipped his head with a pebble-plop sound that almost certainly meant, 'You're welcome.'

Across the cave Fate accepted a similar bowl from the Butcher. The large man walked with a stiffness that spoke of sore joints and the sorcerer watched him closely as he lowered himself into the remaining chair.

'You're a replicantis,' said Fate and the Butcher gave a soft laugh.

'I haven't heard that term since my mother died more than twenty years ago.' His voice was deep and mellow, a voice well suited to the echoing acoustics of a cave.

'A replicantis?' asked the Tutor.

'Someone who can transfer the physical properties of one living thing to another,' said Fate.

'*Similar* living things,' clarified the Butcher. 'And the changes I can make are largely superficial.'

'You were able to modify the skin of a troglodyte,' said Fate as his gaze moved to Cradlop. 'There's nothing superficial about that.'

The appearance of the troglodyte's pale skin fell somewhere between human skin and mottled stone.

'That took some time,' said the Butcher.

'But without it, Cradlop would have died,' said Fate. 'A troglodyte cannot survive for long without the mineral waters of its home.'

'He was getting weaker when I found him,' said the Butcher as the two friends looked at each other. 'We saved each other.'

'Your eyes,' said Fate and the Butcher nodded.

The Butcher had the pale skin and pink eyes of an albino, but his eyes also glowed like Cradlop's, and the glowing eyes of a troglodyte can see in the dark.

'I was born with a condition that made me susceptible to sunlight,' the Butcher explained. 'Even a brief exposure would lead to blisters and burns.'

'I have heard of such a condition,' said Fate.

'Well, the people in my neighbourhood thought I was cursed,' the Butcher went on. 'My mother was a healer and, while she lived, she protected me from the cruelty of ignorant folk. When she died I lost that protection and the people drove me out of my home. One boy slashed me with a knife.'

Here, the Butcher paused.

'I think it was the fear that awakened my power... When the boy tried to stab me again, I grabbed his leg and the cut in my shoulder appeared in his thigh. There was so much blood that I knew he wouldn't survive, and so I fled into the sewers.'

Another pause.

'For months I lived in a twilight world; lost to the day and scared of the night. And I would have died if I hadn't found Cradlop.'

The Butcher smiled as he looked at Cradlop.

'Cave dweller, like me,' said the troglodyte.

'We both would have died,' the Butcher went on. 'And Cradlop was suffering from some infection of the skin.'

'Bleed skin, no breathe,' said Cradlop.

'So you transferred some human qualities to Cradlop,' said Fate and the Butcher nodded once more.

'I shared my skin and he shared his eyes,' said the Butcher. 'And that allowed us to carve out a life in the tunnels beneath the city.'

'And now you use your skills to save those who fall between the cracks.'

The Butcher smiled and inclined his head at Fate's choice of words.

'So, let me get this straight…' said the Tutor. 'You find someone who's wanted by one of the gangs, and then you copy their body to fake their death.'

'They only copy innocent people,' said Weasel.

'We choose people who seem decent,' corrected the Butcher. 'People who have fallen prey to misfortune.'

'Like Luca,' said Fate, and all eyes turned to Madam de Lorni's son.

'But how do you know he's innocent?' asked the Tutor.

'You learn to tell,' said the Butcher. 'There are many reasons why people end up hiding in the sewers of Guile. You'd be amazed at how well their voices carry down the pipes and drains.'

He looked across at Luca, but the young man simply bowed his head.

'Some boast of their crimes, some plead for their lives, and some speak of regret and how foolish they have been. They speak to the darkness as they would to the confessional grille of a chapel.'

'And you listen,' said Fate.

'What else is there to do?' said the Butcher. 'For an exiled troglodyte and a man whose skin dissolves in sunlight... It's the only way we can share in the life of the surface world.'

'And what about the people you save?' asked the Tutor. 'What happens to them?'

'We send them far away,' said the Butcher.

'But where can they go?' the demon hunter persisted. 'The people who want them will be watching the gates. And many of the gangs have contacts in other cities.'

'We don't leave through the gates,' said the Butcher. 'The river that carved these tunnels doesn't stop at the city walls. It flows all the way to the sea.'

'What!' said the Tutor. 'You can follow these tunnels all the way to the coast?'

'Mostly,' said the Butcher. 'Some sections are too narrow so we need to travel overland during the night.'

'And what happens when you get to the coast?' asked Fate.

'We have an arrangement with the captain of a trading fleet.'

'An arrangement?' queried the sorcerer.

'Cradlop has a gift for finding gems and precious metals,' said the Butcher. 'We pay for discretion and two years' passage as a hand on a trading ship.'

'Two years?'

'That's how long we deem it safe for most problems to blow over. But many of the people we save choose never to return.'

'So Luca might need to leave the city for *two years*?' asked Weasel.

'And for all that time his mother will think he's dead?' added the Tutor.

'Better that, than for him to be *actually* killed.'

'But Luca's innocent,' said Weasel, and Fate finally turned to look at the young man.

'Why don't you tell us exactly what happened?'

Still a little wary, Luca looked to the Butcher before answering.

'It started about six months ago when Alonso told me to collect a silver flask from a potion-maker.'

'Inganno,' said Fate.

'That's him,' replied Luca. 'A slimy toad of a man. I gave him a purse of money and he gave me a potion.'

'And what did the potion do?' asked the Tutor.

'It made people obey,' said Luca and Fate shook his head in disgust.

'A potion of compliance,' he said. 'A slave potion, if you will. Their use has been outlawed for almost a century.'

'Like Inganno's love potions,' said the Tutor.

'Worse,' said Fate. 'A love potion changes the way a person feels so an affected person could actually be happy, whereas a potion of compliance can compel a person even if they despise what they are doing.'

'He used it on women,' said Luca, 'serving girls mostly.'

'There were other victims?' asked Fate in a dangerous tone and Luca nodded.

'Most were just abused, but I heard rumours about others that went missing.'

The blue ice in the Tutor's gaze matched the golden fire in Fate's.

'But then he used the potion on his cousin, Eliza.'

'Lord Medici's niece,' clarified the Tutor.

'He'd been tormenting her for weeks,' Luca went on. 'But he was running out of the potion... he didn't have enough for a full dose and so he lost the ability to control her. He kept her in the house while he waited for a new batch to arrive, and that was when she wrote the note.'

At this, the Butcher placed a crumpled letter on the table in front of Fate.

'She gave the note to me...' said Luca, his eyes glazing over as he remembered the fear in Eliza Medici's eyes as she pressed the hastily written letter into his hand...

*

'Please,' said the pretty young woman. 'Just deliver it to my father, that's all I'm asking.'

'I can't,' said Luca. 'Alonso'll kill me if I betray him.'

'Please,' she begged. 'You're not like the others. I know you're not. Please help me.'

Eliza's blue eyes were swimming with tears as she held onto his hands.

'All right,' he said at last. 'I'll try.'

'Thank you,' gasped Eliza as Luca slipped the letter into his trouser pocket.

Overcome with relief, she pulled Luca into an awkward embrace before pushing him behind the door as she stepped through into the adjacent room from where Alonso's voice now rose up.

'And where have you been hiding?' he demanded.

'Nowhere,' said Eliza as she moved away from the door. 'I was just...'

Smack!

'You're lying!' said Alonso, and Eliza stumbled into a table as Alonso delivered another backhanded slap to her face. 'You were trying to escape, weren't you? Trying to flee back to dear old daddy.'

Still hiding behind the door, Luca hardly dared breathe. He peered through the narrow gap and froze as he caught a glimpse of crimson robes. It was Alonso's Don'Sha'Vir and Luca was terrified that the mystic warrior might sense his presence.

'Don't you realise that you belong to me,' Alonso continued. 'You're my favourite toy and I will never let you go.'

Luca heard a lighter slap.

'Why, you!' came Alonso's angry reply, and this was followed by the sound of a heavier blow.

Eliza screamed.

'It's no good,' said Alonso with sadistic glee. 'The house is empty. My father won't be back till morning so we have the whole night to enjoy ourselves. And you know what...' he added as if the thought had just occurred to him, 'I think it's even more fun without the potion.'

Risking another glimpse, Luca saw Eliza running towards the door behind which he stood. She was almost at the door when she fell forward and Luca saw a slender dagger protruding from her shoulder.

'Oops!' said Alonso, lowering his hand after throwing the dagger.

The next few minutes were too awful for Luca to recall, but finally the scuffles and the stifled cries gave way to silence and Luca risked a final peek through the crack in the door.

A dishevelled Alonso was rising to his feet, while Eliza's body lay on the bloodstained floor.

Stabbed… strangled… dead.

In a state of shock, Luca backed away from the horrific scene as the voices resumed in the adjacent room. He heard Alonso say something about family, but it was the next sentence that prompted him to act.

'Oh, don't worry,' Alonso continued. 'We'll blame it on the new footman. Now *he* can hang for the death of my dear cousin.'

Sheer terror gripped Luca.

Stripping off his footman's jacket, he moved to the patio doors, his hands trembling as he tried to turn the key. He was just about to leave when a thought occurred to him. He had the letter that Eliza had given him, but without the potion he would have no physical proof.

Turning back into the room he dashed over to a drinks cabinet where Alonso kept the potion. Through a cloud of cold vapour he caught a quick glimpse of a small silver flask and reached out to grab it. Then, before anyone even knew he was there, he slipped out of the patio doors, sprinted across the lawn and scrambled over the boundary wall before disappearing into the night-time streets of Guile.

Knowing it would be too dangerous to return home, Luca ran until he reached the river. He needed somewhere to hide so he scrambled down the bank and forced his way through a thicket of blackthorn bushes where he found a large storm drain that opened into a cave.

Reaching the shelter of the storm drain, Luca sat down on a mound of sandy earth. He was still holding the silver flask in his hand and now he removed Eliza's letter from his pocket. Together, these things should be enough to save him from the hangman's noose. But then he removed the cap of the silver flask and all hope turned to despair as he caught the unmistakable smell of brandy.

It was the wrong flask.

In his haste to escape from the Medici mansion, he had taken the wrong flask.

*

'That's where the sergeant found me,' said Luca as he completed his tale.

'Your mother's friend?' said the Tutor and Luca nodded.

'He went to get the potion flask but he never returned,' said Luca. 'I was waiting for him to come back when I saw Medici's men coming along the riverbank...'

'And that's when Cradlop took Luca,' said Weasel who had been waiting impatiently for them to get to the part of the story that included him.

'Took him to make safe,' said Cradlop.

'Scared me half to death,' added Luca. 'I thought I was going to drown when he dragged me into the water, and then those nightmare fish started biting.'

'They're horrible,' said Weasel, and the young wayfinder grew uncharacteristically serious as he relived his own encounter with the subterranean lamprey.

'We cut them off quickly,' said the Butcher. 'They didn't have time to do too much damage.'

'So what are you planning to do now?' asked Fate.

'We are going to copy Luca's features onto a nameless corpse,' said the Butcher. 'In fact we've almost completed the replicating process. We do it a bit at a time because the process is painful.'

'And you chop the body up to obscure other differences like height and weight.'

'Correct,' replied the Butcher with a nod. 'And the river helps. Even a few hours in the water will change the appearance of a corpse, so people just look for identifying marks.'

'But what about the bodies you use?' asked the Tutor.

'Unclaimed bodies from various morgues,' replied the Butcher. 'It might take a few days, but it doesn't take long for someone to die without anyone to notice they've gone.'

He exchanged a sober look with Cradlop.

'We treat them with respect, and the fact that they are saving another person's life gives meaning to their deaths.'

'So what about Luca?' asked Fate, and the Butcher shrugged.

'There was nothing we could do to prove his innocence so we planned to go ahead with sending him to the coast.'

'And Weasel?' asked the Tutor.

'Young Weasel poses a different problem,' said the Butcher. 'If we let him go then we run the risk of our actions being unmasked. We were trying to decide if we could trust him to keep a secret.'

Fate turned to look at the young wayfinder.

'You can trust him,' he said, and Weasel bowed his head in embarrassment. No one had ever shown that kind of faith in him before.

'But what if we could prove that Luca is innocent?' asked the Tutor. 'What if we could retrieve the potion?'

'Then Luca could prove his innocence and return to his mother,' said the Butcher. 'Do you think you can retrieve it?'

In the pale light of the Butcher's lair the demon hunter and the sorcerer exchanged a glance.

'I would think so,' said Fate. 'But first we need to take care of a dog.'

'A dog!' said Weasel excitedly. 'Are we getting a dog?'

23

Ensnared

It was an hour before dawn when Fate and the Tutor made their way back to Blackfell House. Cradlop had led them to a different exit from the tunnels so there was no need for them to go back through the sump, something for which they were both extremely grateful. Veils of mist lingered in the air so they moved with caution, checking every side street and alleyway for any sign of a dark wolf-like creature that had attacked them earlier in the night.

'Do you think it's healed by now?' asked the Tutor.

'Difficult to say,' replied Fate. 'Your sword cut pretty deep, but effigies like that are not easily destroyed.'

Nodding in agreement, the Tutor drew his sword and Fate noticed that there appeared to be no stiffness or pain from the deep gashes that the manitu had inflicted.

'How's the shoulder?'

'It feels good,' replied the Tutor. 'How's yours?'

'Sore.' said Fate.

'At least it still looks like you,' said the Tutor. 'The skin of my shoulder is now so pale it makes me look ill.' He flexed his recently injured shoulder and Fate smiled.

Before leaving the caves, the Butcher had used his gift to heal the gashes inflicted by Vulpyrac's hound. However, to do so he needed the 'template' of a healthy shoulder and, purely out of professional curiosity, Fate had volunteered his own.

Getting them to lie down on the stone slabs, the Butcher had reached out his hands, one to the Tutor's injured shoulder and one to Fate's. He closed his eyes and the two men winced as their shoulders were suffused by a fierce tingling warmth. When the Butcher removed his hands the gashes in the Tutor's shoulder were gone and the demon hunter's dark skin displayed the vague outline of a pale hand.

'That's because Fate's skin tone is lighter than yours,' said the Butcher. 'It will fade in time,' he added, but the Tutor seemed indignant.

'You mean to tell me I've got part of *him* in my skin?'

'Not really,' said the Butcher. 'It's still your skin. It's just that an echo of Fate's pigment was replicated along with the healing.'

'I would be interested to learn more about the process,' said Fate as he sat up and rubbed his own shoulder.

'And I would be happy to show you,' replied the Butcher.

A short while later, they were ready to leave and Fate explained to Weasel that it would be unwise for him to leave right now.

'It's all right,' said the young wayfinder. 'I like it here. So long as you don't send me off to sea,' he added with a suspicious frown.

'Just lie low till we sort things out,' said the Tutor, giving Luca a reassuring smile.

They were just getting ready to follow Cradlop into the tunnels when the Tutor stopped.

'It's just struck me,' he said, turning back to the Butcher. 'We don't even know your name.'

'Culpepper,' said the Butcher with a smile. 'Samuel Culpepper.'

The three men had shaken hands and with that, they left the tunnels leaving Weasel and Luca in Samuel's care until they were able to prove Luca's innocence, or not.

Now they were back on familiar roads and Blackfell House had just come into view when Fate noticed a change in the Tutor's demeanour.

'What is it?' he asked.

'I'm not entirely sure,' said the Tutor. 'A twinge of sensation from my tattoo.'

The tattoo on the demon hunter's chest offered protection from magical harm, and in some cases it acted as a warning system, alerting the bearer to threats of a magical nature.

'Do you think it's the hound?' asked Fate and the Tutor nodded as his blue eyes stared off into the distance.

'It's close.'

'Quickly then,' said Fate, and the two men began to jog towards the sanctuary of the sorcerer's home.

The Tutor's tattoo was pulsing with alarm as they hurried into the kitchen of Blackfell House where Motina was dozing in a chair by the fire. The housekeeper had spent the early part of the night trying to persuade Daisy to stay at the house. However, the young wayfinder had insisted that she would be safer with her friends and, after everything that had happened, it was hard to disagree. After sending the girl home with a large bundle of food, Motina had started working on Fate's net before falling asleep in her chair.

'What's happened?' she yawned, rising stiffly from her chair as Fate reached up to a large net that was hanging from a clothes pulley attached to the ceiling.

'Excellent,' said Fate. 'You finished it. Did you have time to soak it in rosemary?'

'Never mind the net,' said Motina. 'Tell me what happened... did you find Weasel and Luca?'

'We did,' said the Tutor.

'So, where are they? Are they all right?'

'They're fine,' said Fate, clearly distracted as he pulled the net off the drying pulley.

'Oh, don't mind me,' said the frustrated housekeeper. 'I've only been worrying myself sick... I've only spent the entire night making you a blasted net.'

'I'm sorry,' said Fate as he gathered the still-damp net onto his arm. 'Weasel's alive and well, and we'll explain about Luca when we have the time but for now, the Tutor and I need to try and snare the creature that's trying to kill us.'

'What, *now*?' asked Motina. 'But you've only just got back.'

'The sooner the better,' said Fate as he looked to see if the Tutor was ready. 'People mustn't know that Luca is alive until we can prove his innocence, and we can't do that with a murderous hound snapping at our heels.'

'What!' cried Motina in alarm. 'Weasel was taken by the Butcher?'

'No,' said Fate. 'Well, yes he was, but it's not as you might imagine.' He shook his head to bring his thoughts back into focus. 'Now,' he said. 'Did you soak the net in rosemary or not?'

'No,' said Motina in a sarcastic tone. 'That's why the whole kitchen smells of rosemary.'

Fate gave an embarrassed smile. 'What I meant to say...'

'I know what you *meant* to say,' interrupted Motina. 'And the answer is yes.'

Walking around the table, Fate placed his hand on the small woman's arm.

'Thank you,' he said, and Motina gave a distinctly unimpressed humph!

'So how are we going to do this?' asked the Tutor as they left the house and followed the driveway to the gate in the perimeter fence.

Fate paused as he put his hand on the gate.

'Manitus like this have a base level of cunning, but not so much in the way of actual intelligence. It might be wary of the fence, but if we go into the open, it should attack us.'

'So, we're the bait?' asked the Tutor.

'Well, you're probably better with the net, so I'll play the role of bait.'

The Tutor raised an eyebrow as Fate handed him the net.

'But why trap it at all?' he asked. 'Why not just kill it?'

'We might only succeed in injuring it and then it would just retreat like it did last time. And besides...' said Fate as his dark eyes glittered with flecks of gold, 'I have other plans for this accursed hound.'

With that, Fate opened the gate and stepped beyond the protection of his home. With a sigh, the Tutor straightened the net on his arm and moved to follow as Fate headed off up the street.

'Can you see it?' asked Fate.

'No,' said the Tutor, 'but it's definitely close.'

Fate nodded. There was no direct sign of it, but every now and then they caught the distinctive whiff of tar.

'There!' said the Tutor as a dark shape crossed the gap between two buildings.

'Are you sure?'

'Unless someone's been breeding glossy black boar hounds.'

Fate pursed his lips. 'Over there then,' he said, pointing across the street. 'In that corner beyond the well.'

The Tutor nodded and the two men scanned the misty streets as they backed into the corner that would prevent the hound from getting behind them.

'Are you sure this net will hold it?' asked the Tutor as he adjusted the net for throwing. 'Won't the hound just flow through it like it flowed around your dagger?'

'No,' said Fate. 'The rosemary has a constraining effect and, judging by the faint metallic sheen, I suspect Motina has also imbued it with some kind of spell or enchantment.'

'I thought I could feel something,' replied the Tutor, then Fate hissed as the distinctive shape of the hound came into view.

Emerging from the mist, the manitu looked like something from the urban legend known as *The Hound of the Border Vales*. It advanced cautiously as if it remembered the pain of their last encounter, but still it came on, its glowing eyes switching from Fate to the Tutor and back.

The Tutor was wondering how close the hound would come before it decided to attack. He felt a strong urge to draw his sword, and he stepped a half pace ahead of Fate in a gesture that betrayed his instinct to protect.

'No,' said Fate. 'Move to one side and let it come for me.'

The Tutor frowned at what seemed like an unwise strategy, but then he realised they would have a better chance of catching it if they could predict who it was going to attack. He took several steps to the left as the black hound skirted the well. He was about to take another step when the hound suddenly attacked.

The manitu leapt at Fate, but the Tutor had been waiting for it. Sweeping his arm forward, he cast the net over the creature even as it was flying through the air. However, the net did not stop the manitu and Fate staggered back, throwing up his left arm as the creature went for his throat.

The sorcerer gave a hiss of pain as the hound's teeth clamped down on his forearm, and the only thing that prevented serious damage was the enchanted net that was now pulled tight over the creature's ravening maw.

Letting go of Fate's arm, the manitu whipped round to attack the Tutor and the net slid off its head. Once again, the Tutor felt the urge to draw his sword, but he resisted it as he kicked the hound in the jaw, stepping back quickly as the manitu slashed at him with its talons. Three of the claws got snagged in the net almost pulling it from the Tutor's grasp, but then he clenched his fists and threw himself over the hound, drawing the net with him as he went. As the Tutor hit the ground the net was pulled tight and the hound stumbled as its tangled leg was pulled up under its body.

Falling to the ground, the enraged manitu now snapped at the Tutor who was lying on the ground beside it using his own body weight to pull the net tight over the hound's thrashing form. The demon hunter turned his head as the hound's jaws snapped and gnashed just inches from his face. He was caught in a bind...

If he released his hold the manitu would break free, but if he remained where he was, the writhing beast would soon be chomping on his face. The smell of sulphur and tar was overwhelming and he could feel the heat of the creature's body. The manitu's snapping jaws bit into the leather armour on his right shoulder and the Tutor knew the next bite would find his flesh.

However, at that moment the manitu gave a piercing shriek as Fate stabbed it in the rump with his dagger. At the same time, the sorcerer grabbed a flapping edge of the net and wrapped it around one of the hound's scrabbling legs. Using his knife for purchase, Fate pulled the net tighter restricting the creature's movement even further. Now the Tutor was able to adjust his position. Shifting to one side, he grabbed two loose corners and pulled the two edges of the net together.

Feeling itself constrained, the manitu began to thrash about in a frenzy and Fate bit back another cry of pain as the creature's claws raked his right hand as he grabbed the final loose edge and pulled it tight. And then it was done.

Vulpyrac's Hound was caught in a homemade net, the magical ferocity of its enchantment constrained by the mysterious properties of a simple herb and the spells of a Karuthian witch. Trussed up like a butcher's ham, the shining black creature continued to struggle and snarl as Fate and the Tutor sewed up the net with additional pieces of cord.

As the first glow of dawn appeared on the horizon, Fate and the Tutor dragged the snared beast back to Blackfell House.

'What a foul creation!' exclaimed Motina as they dragged it up the steps and into the house.

In the confined space of the hall, the smell of sulphur and hot tar was almost overpowering.

'We'll take it down to the basement,' said Fate, and together they wrestled the snarling beast through a doorway and down a flight of stone steps.

The steps led down to an impressive room filled with objects collected from every corner of the world. Weapons, shields and exotic masks hung on the walls beside pictures and tapestries, while various tables boasted numerous sculptures and obscure instruments that were clearly of a magical or scientific nature.

One wall of the room was dominated by an enormous circular door, forged from metal and embossed with images of fire, dragons and armoured warriors wearing eyeless helms. It was the door of Fate's vault; the place where his most valuable items were kept. The vault was protected by powerful wards and magical spells. It required magic to open it, and Fate no longer used magic so the vault, and all its secret contents, would remain locked away forever.

As they dragged the manitu to the centre of the room the Tutor was reminded of the last time he had been in this room. It had been the night of the 'penance moon', a night when Fate allowed a certain type of Faerie to share in the memories of all the terrible deeds he had committed while under the thrall of magic. It was a painful and difficult night, but it was just one part of the debt that Fate now paid to make up for the misdeeds of his past.

'Move that chair,' said Fate, and the Tutor's thoughts were broken as they cleared a large space in the centre of the room.

Even though it was now constrained, the manitu continued to struggle and snarl as they looked down at the netted bundle of fury.

'What do you need?' asked Motina.

'I need a bowl of cooking oil, a few rags, and a bottle from the desk in my study.

'Any bottle in particular?' asked Motina.

'Yes, said Fate. 'It's the small potion bottle I took from Inganno.'

'I thought that bottle was empty,' said Motina.

'It is,' said Fate and Motina shook her head in exasperation as she turned to leave the room.

'What exactly are you going to do?' asked the demon hunter.

'You'll see,' said Fate and the Tutor found himself sympathising with Motina.

'*Yes*,' he thought… '*very annoying.*'

*

Going quickly to the kitchen, Motina collected a copper basin, a large bottle of cooking oil and a bundle of rags. She placed them on a sideboard in the hall before heading upstairs to Fate's study. The sorcerer's desk was in one corner near a leaded window that looked over the garden. Sure enough, the small potion bottle was sitting in the middle of the desk. Still curious about what it had contained, Motina picked up the bottle and was about to head back downstairs when something at the window caught her eye.

Shining with a faint silvery light, it was a dandelion seed.

Moving over to the window, Motina looked down into the garden. The tree-lined driveway was still shrouded in darkness, but now there was a patch of light shining between the trees. The pale silvery light had the vague shape of a reclining figure and Motina immediately recognised it as a being from the realm of Faerie.

The housekeeper felt a shiver of disquiet prickle her skin. She was not afraid of the Fair Folk and yet somehow they made her feel nervous. As a witch, Motina was keenly attuned to the laws of nature, but the realm of Faerie conformed to different laws, laws that no mere human could hope to understand.

With another shake of her head, she collected the potion bottle and made her way downstairs. When she returned to the basement room Fate and the Tutor were still holding down the net to restrict the manitu's movements.

'Good,' said Fate. 'If you could pass me the rags and put the bottles on the table.'

Motina put the copper basin, the oil and the potion bottle on the table then...

'You have a visitor,' she said as she handed Fate the rags.

'This is no time for visitors,' said Fate with some annoyance.

'I think you'll make time for this one,' said Motina. 'He's outside on the driveway, and currently reclining in a bower of dandelion seeds.'

Fate looked up with a sudden intensity in his eyes.

'He was here earlier,' Motina went on, 'although he didn't show himself.'

Allowing Motina to take his edge of the net, Fate straightened up and strode from the room.

'Must be some visitor,' said the Tutor, and Motina arched an eyebrow.

'His name's Carduus Thistleblade, a Faerie Lord.'

'Fate didn't seem best pleased.'

'Carduus is a deoraíocht... an outcast,' explained Motina. 'He lives in the wilderlands of Faerie, forbidden to leave them by royal decree.'

'So what's he doing here?'

'I've no idea,' said Motina as she looked down at the writhing manitu. 'But if Carduus has defied the will of his queen, then it can't be anything good.'

144

24

Lord of the Thistleblade Sword

Fate was distinctly wary as he made his way out of the front door and down the shallow steps onto the driveway of Blackfell House. And there, sure enough, was the tall figure of a man, or rather a faerie lord that looked like a man. Dressed in dark green robes that swirled like smoke, the man was no longer reclining on a cloud of dandelion seeds. The silvery motes now floated around him while he looked up at the leafless trees that lined the gravel driveway.

The faerie's gaze finally came to rest on the hole in the lawn where one of the trees was missing. And when he spoke it was as if the essence of a wolf had suddenly found its voice.

'You've lost one,' said the faerie in a growling voice that spoke of humour, and cunning.

'It died well and served its purpose,' said Fate as the rest of the dark trees quivered in the cold still air.

'Would you like me to replace it?' asked the faerie.

'No,' said Fate. 'The original number was payment enough.'

'You know that I don't agree,' said the faerie and he suddenly looked at Fate with eyes of liquid silver. 'Do you know how long it would have taken me to die in the wilderlands of the Blessed Realm?'

Fate did not answer, but only met that silver gaze with ebony darkness and gold.

'Centuries,' said the faerie. 'I might have suffered for centuries if you had not given me a way to survive.'

'I merely offered a suggestion,' said Fate and the faerie smiled.

'Oh, it was far more than that,' he said and, raising his arms, he closed his eyes and tilted his head as if in communion with something that Fate could not see. When he opened his eyes the air around him was filled with a dozen orbs of pale blue light.

Small enough to hold in two open hands, the orbs moved with a purpose. Some went to hover at the faerie's shoulder while others flew up before coming to rest among the bare branches of the trees. Then one of the orbs flew directly towards Fate and, as it did so, the blue light gave way to reveal a tiny female faerie; a warrior sprite with black armour, silver skin and gossamer wings that shone like sapphires. It was a Lannari.

As the tiny warrior streaked towards Fate, it drew a silver grass-blade of a sword and lunged straight for the sorcerer's face. The needle-sharp point came to a halt just a finger's width from his left eye, but Fate did not even flinch. Instead, he frowned slightly as the warrior sprite sheathed her sword and gave a tiny smile as she spun in the air and flitted away to hover at the male faerie's back.

'You introduced me to my daughters,' said the faerie as the rest of the blue orbs condensed into their true faerie form. 'You gave me a family.'

'What do you want, Carduus?' asked Fate with a degree of impatience. The faerie lord belonged to his past and he had no wish to revisit it, especially if it meant incurring the ire of a faerie queen.

'I came to warn you,' said Carduus.

'Warn me about what?'

'Bohr's power is growing.'

Carduus was referring to Oruthian Bohr, the emperor's personal sorcerer.

'Bohr's power was always going to grow,' said Fate.

'But he is getting bolder too,' replied the faerie and now Fate's eyes narrowed in interest. 'He set a trap for one of the border sentinels,' Carduus went on. 'Lured her with what appeared to be a demonic breach within the emperor's grounds.'

'It wasn't?' queried Fate and Carduus shook his head.

'It was a ruse... but the sentinel was fooled and she pushed through the veil.'

'Into the grounds of the palace?'

Carduus inclined his head.

'If she broke through without invitation then the sentinel's life would be forfeit.'

'And there it is.' Carduus's tone conveyed a sense of finality.

'Has she been executed?'

'Worse,' said Carduus, but then he paused. 'Bohr has constructed a chamber,' he explained. 'A magical chamber lined with blue tiles.'

'I've heard of it,' said Fate.

'The chamber is designed to absorb the magical power of anything placed within it, and to transfer that energy to the person operating the device.'

Fate's gaze darkened.

'Has the queen responded?' he asked.

'There's nothing she can do,' said Carduus. 'The law is clear. The sentinel was killed, her power was absorbed by Bohr, and Lonrúil Croí could only rage in her garden and scorch the air with her fury.'

'And what has any of this got to do with me?'

'Why nothing, as yet. But I don't think Bohr will be satisfied with the power of one unfortunate sentinel.' Carduus walked in a small circle until he stood with his back to Fate. 'There are tremors in the wilderlands that suggest he is trying to break The Bond.'

The gold in Fate's eyes flickered with a dangerous light.

'And I've even heard whispers from the human world... rumours suggesting that the Sacred Trees should no longer be given protection.'

'Even Bohr wouldn't be so foolish,' said Fate.

'Not yet, perhaps,' said Carduus. 'For now, I think he has his sights set on Confluence.'

Fate shook his head. 'It'll be years before Bohr is strong enough to challenge the council at Confluence.'

'Not if he keeps using his blue-tile chamber to drain the power of sentinels.' Carduus was still standing with his back to Fate, but now he turned slightly, speaking over his left shoulder. 'And not if he keeps arresting members of the Arcanium.'

For the first time, Fate seemed genuinely alarmed.

'Who?' he asked.

'Oh, I don't know any names,' said the faerie. 'Humans live so short a time, it's barely worth remembering their names.'

'Is that the only reason you're here?' asked Fate. 'To warn me about a threat to Confluence.'

'I thought it was important,' said the faerie. 'But I'm also here to offer my help.' Turning back to face Fate, he placed a hand on the crystal hilt of his sword and a green light spilled from the scabbard as the blade began to glow. 'You know that Bohr had a hand in my downfall, and if Bohr is to be opposed then I would like to help.'

'I don't need your help?' said Fate, but Carduus just laughed.

'You might,' he said as the cloud of dandelion seeds began to swirl around him. 'Now that you have unmanned yourself... you might.' The blur of silvery motes grew faster until the dark-robed figure was obscured.

Up in the trees, the blue-winged Lannari dissolved back into glowing blue orbs before flying into the swirling maelstrom of seeds.

'Just remember,' said the voice of Carduus as Fate raised a hand against a sudden gust of wind. 'If ever you need him... the Lord of the Thistleblade Sword is at your command.'

And with that, the cloud of swirling dandelion seeds vanished and Fate was left alone on the driveway of his home. He was about to turn away when he noticed a single dandelion seed floating towards him. He tried to swat it away, but it swirled around his hand and came to rest on the left breast of his robes. With a snort of irritation he removed it and flicked it away into the air, but the stubborn seed floated on hidden currents and returned to rest against his chest.

'Just plant the seed,' said a disembodied voice and with that the presence of the faerie lord was gone.

Shaking his head in irritation, Fate turned back to the house.

25

The Taming of the Hound

'Is there a problem?' asked the Tutor as Fate returned to the basement.

'No,' said Fate. 'Just an acquaintance from my past.'

'Carduus Thistleblade,' said the Tutor, and Motina just shrugged as Fate gave his housekeeper an accusing glance.

'What did he want?' she asked as Fate crouched down to take the edge of the net from Motina.

'He came to give me some news,' said Fate, tightening his grip as the manitu continued to struggle.

'News?' pressed Motina, and Fate gave a sigh. It was clear that he did not want to talk about it, but their curiosity had been aroused.

'Bohr has made a move against Confluence.'

'So soon?' Motina's voice held a note of concern, and even the Tutor's expression darkened at the mention of Bohr's name. 'What's he done?'

'He's arrested a member of the Arcanium.'

'The mage council of Confluence,' said the Tutor.

'That was a bold move,' said Motina. 'Do you want me to find out who it was?'

'Yes,' said Fate. 'But first, I want you to help us redirect the murderous thoughts of a magically conjured entity.'

'Should we be worried?' asked Motina.

'Perhaps,' said Fate. 'It sounds like Bohr's getting more confident. He's testing the limits of resistance.'

'And what if that resistance is weak?' asked the housekeeper.

Fate did not answer, but his face was grim as his thoughts turned inwards. He was clearly troubled, but the

Tutor could see that this was not the time for such a discussion so he drew their attention back to the matter in hand.

'So, how are we going to do this?' he asked, and Fate seemed relieved by the change of subject.

'We're going to discover what the hound was using to find us. And then we're going to purge it from the creature's mind.'

'And how exactly do we do that?' asked Motina.

'We'll start by making sure it can't break free.'

'We could tie it, if you have some rope,' said the Tutor, but Fate shook his head.

'The net is strong enough. We just have to secure it to the floor.' Still holding his edge of the net, he gestured towards a squat cabinet of dark exotic wood. 'Have a look in there,' he told Motina. 'On the bottom shelf you'll find a series of stone disks.'

Moving to that cabinet, Motina opened the doors and, sure enough, the bottom shelf held eight silvery stone disks each about two fingers deep and a hand's width in diameter. And lying on the top of each disk was a thin finger of darker stone, the ends of which had been shaped into points.

'How many do you want?'

'All of them,' replied Fate.

'How will these help?' asked the Tutor as Motina began to place the stone disks beside them.

'They're stone magnets,' said Fate. 'We can use them to anchor the net to the floor.'

Still holding down his edge of the net, the Tutor reached out for one of the stones. He noticed how the slender piece of stone on top of the disk remained in place like some kind of lodestone. He watched as Fate grabbed a loose edge of the net and tucked it under one of the stones. The sorcerer then rotated the dark finger of stone a full half turn and there was a faint grating sound as the disk was pulled tight against the stone flags of the floor. Fate dipped his head in satisfaction and gave the net a tug to make sure it was securely clamped.

'Work your way around the net,' he told the Tutor. 'Just rotate the dipole until you feel the magnetic force engage.'

The Tutor did as instructed and the net was soon stretched tight over the manitu's writhing form.

'That should do it,' said the demon hunter as Motina turned to Fate.

'But *how* do you purge the mind of a creature like this?' asked Motina.

'By enduring a great deal of pain,' said Fate and with that, he removed his long-coat and rolled up the sleeve of his robes. He then crouched down beside the hound which was lying on its side with its head held firmly against the floor. With his left arm braced against the floor, Fate then narrowed the fingers of his right hand and took a deep breath.

'Wait,' said Motina as Fate met the manitu's furnace gaze. 'You're not going to...'

The rest of the sentence stuck in her throat as Fate reached through one of the squares in the net and plunged his entire hand into the manitu's gleaming black chest. The hound gave a shrieking howl and tried to break free, but the magnets along with Motina's spell of confinement held it fast. Even so, it thrashed and snarled as Fate gritted his teeth against the searing heat that engulfed his hand.

Even though the net seemed secure the Tutor dropped down to hold it tight. Doing his best to keep the struggling creature still, he glanced across at Fate who

152

was rummaging in the manitu's chest as if he were feeling for a lost penny in a murky pond.

'I can feel... something,' hissed Fate, adjusting his hand and turning his face away from the heat that was radiating from the manitu's shining black skin. 'Got it!' said Fate and, withdrawing his hand, he held up a few strands of matted black hair.

Reaching over to the table, Motina passed him one of the rags and Fate's hand trembled with pain as he wiped away some of the glutinous black tar before laying the hairs on the cloth.

'I think these are yours,' he told the Tutor. 'I think this is what Inganno used to mark you as a target.'

'And what about you?' asked the Tutor.

'He probably used my blood,' said Fate. 'If you recall, my hand was bleeding after Inganno threw the glass beaker. He must have used some of the dried blood.'

'But that would just be fragments,' said Motina. 'You can't fish around in that thing for tiny specks of blood.'

'No I can't,' said Fate. 'But I might be able to override my scent with another.' Reaching over to the table he retrieved the small potion bottle that Motina had brought from his study.

'That was the potion Inganno used to make himself stronger,' said the Tutor and Fate nodded.

'It was still wet with his saliva when I took it.'

'So you're going to replace the scent of your blood with his saliva?'

'If I can keep my hand inside for long enough.'

'Rather you than me,' said the Tutor.

Even just holding the net his hands felt raw from the heat of the infernal hound. He glanced at Motina and the housekeeper's face was tight with concern as Fate gripped the potion bottle in his hand. He took a few deep breaths then pushed his fist back into the manitu's body. Once again, the hound howled and thrashed, its claws scraping on the stone floor as Fate challenged the focus of its summoning.

The creature's struggles became so intense that the Tutor began to fear that it might break free, and even Motina got down on her hands and knees to try and hold the net in place. Meanwhile, Fate's face was contorted with pain as he fought to purge all traces of his blood from the manitu's mind. Sweat beaded on his face and he bared his teeth as the tar around his wrist began to glow.

Even constrained as it was, the hound tried to reach Fate with its wicked silvery teeth, and the sorcerer gave a low moan as he struggled to keep his hand in place. The Tutor was just on the verge of reaching for his sword when the wild thrashing suddenly ceased and the fearsome light went out of the manitu's eyes.

The creature did not pant with exertion, but its body relaxed and its snarls and growls became less intense as Fate slowly withdrew his hand. He screwed his eyes shut and gritted his teeth against the pain as Motina retrieved the rags and oil from the nearby table.

Kneeling down in front of him, she gently wiped the hot tar from Fate's partially broiled skin. The pain was written on his face, but then he gave a sigh of relief as Motina poured over some of the cold, cooling oil. The oil diluted the viscous tar making it easier to wipe off and Motina had positioned the copper bowl to catch the noxious mixture before it hit the floor.

'Is it done?' asked the Tutor who was still reluctant to relax his hold on the net.

'I'm not sure,' said Fate. 'I certainly succeeded in neutralising the substances linked to us, but I'm not sure if the sample on the potion bottle was strong enough to focus the manitu's mind.'

'So what do we do now?'

'Well, it looks pretty calm,' said Fate as Motina helped him clean the last of the tar from his arm. 'So I suggest you remove the stone magnets and set it free.'

It was clear from his expression that the Tutor doubted the wisdom of this move. However, the hound was no longer struggling to break free and the ferocious light had faded from its eyes.

'I guess there's only one way to find out,' he said. 'But if I hear so much as a snarl, I'm going to kill it!' He hesitated a moment longer then, shaking his head, he knelt beside the first of the stone magnets.

Fate and Motina watched as the Tutor began to remove the magnets. One by one, he deactivated the stone disks and slid them aside. The tension on the net was now gone, but still the manitu made no attempt to escape. Still not completely convinced, the Tutor took a loose edge of the net and began to lift it clear of the hound's black body.

Sitting in the nearby chair, Fate's dark eyes glittered with interest. Slowly, the Tutor pulled the net back, but then he tensed and reached for his sword as the manitu suddenly straightened up from its prone position.

'It's all right!' said Fate and sure enough, the hound merely righted itself before slowly coming to its feet.

The net was now bundled up on the floor and for a moment the summoned creature looked at it as if the knotted cord stirred some memory in its primaeval mind. It raised its head to look at the Tutor who stood with his hand on the hilt of his Hadean blade. The heart-stone in the sword's pommel glowed with a clear light and, if the manitu made one threatening move, then the demon hunter would cleave the creature in two. But the hound just stood there, turning its head and raising its muzzle as if it were scenting the air. For a moment it turned to look at Fate and the light in its eyes gave the smallest of flares, but then the brightness faded and the manitu turned towards the steps leading up from the basement room.

'Don't try to stop it,' said Fate, and the Tutor moved aside as the hound started forward.

With liquid grace it ascended the steps.

'Open the front door,' said Fate as they followed the creature into the dark hallway of the house.

Moving ahead of the manitu, the Tutor opened the front door almost as if he were letting a pet dog out into the garden. The light in the hound's eyes remained intimidating, but there was no recognition in its gaze. It merely looked at the demon hunter with indifference before turning away and heading out through the main door of the house. It descended the steps, walked down the gravel driveway and slipped through the bars in the perimeter fence.

For a moment it stood, turning its head in the darkness, then it loped away into the night.

'Do you think it will find him?' asked the Tutor.

'I don't know,' said Fate.

'And what if it doesn't?'

'It won't harm anyone,' said Fate. 'It will simply wander aimlessly until the magic of its conjuring is no longer strong enough to hold its form, at which point it will collapse into its constituent parts.'

'It'll become a puddle of tar.'

'Indeed.'

'So what now?' asked the Tutor and Fate looked up at the sky.

'Well, it's too late to call on Medici now,' replied Fate. 'We should get some sleep and visit Medici first thing in the morning.'

'Sleep,' said Motina from the steps of the house. 'That's the first sensible thing you've said in days. Now come inside and let me treat your scalded arm and the cuts on the Tutor's shoulder.'

'Those cuts are healed,' said the Tutor.

'Are they indeed?' said Motina. 'And how exactly did you manage that?'

Fate smiled at the indignation in her voice.

'Come inside,' he said as he climbed the shallow steps and put a hand on his housekeeper's shoulder. 'We'll tell you the story of a man called Samuel Culpepper, and how he came to be known as the Butcher of Guile.'

'But what about Weasel?' exclaimed Motina. 'You still haven't told me what's happened to Weasel!'

'Ah, but it was Weasel who found the Butcher,' said Fate.

'Found him *where*?' asked Motina.

'In the sewers and tunnels beneath our very feet,' said Fate and then their voices faded as the front door of Blackfell House was closed.

26
Stay Strong

In the port city of Dymhaven, Sienna Blade opened the doors of a disused coach house as a bell chimed midnight. The coach house lay just across the street from the keep in which Isaac was being held.

'Be careful,' said Amos as Sienna emerged from the double doors.

Sienna gave Amos a nod and checked that the coast was clear before she approached the dark wall of the keep. Along the base of the wall were a series of barred windows leading to the cells that sat just below street level. Keeping an eye out for the guards, Sienna bent down to the first window and whispered through the bars.

'Isaac! Are you there?'

There was no answer from the first cell and only a confused groan from the second, but as Sienna moved to the next she saw two hands grasping at the bars.

'Sienna,' said a desperate voice. 'Is that you?'

Rushing to the cell, Sienna crouched down.

'It's me,' she said as she caught a glimpse of Isaac's pale and dirty face.

'You have to get me out,' said Isaac, his green eyes glinting with gold. 'I can't take much more of this.'

'Have they hurt you?' asked Sienna.

'Not physically,' said Isaac. 'But Divine Servant Arden keeps testing my power with this foul white light. It looks pure but it burns into your mind like acid.'

'Can't you stop him?'

'I've tried,' said Isaac. 'But even a hint of magic and these bracelets burn like hell.'

From back at the coach house Sienna heard a whistle, a warning that a patrol was returning to this side of the keep.

'We're going to get you out,' Sienna told Isaac. 'Two days from now at midnight. Be ready to climb out.'

Isaac's sigh of relief was almost like a sob.

'Psst!'

Sienna heard the urgent hiss from Amos and she knew it was time to go.

'Two days, Isaac,' she said in a fierce whisper. 'Stay strong.'

27

An Unlikely Assassin

Alonso Medici smiled as he left Inganno's house. The potion-maker had appeared unusually nervous, jumping at every noise from the street and insisting that they talk behind the steel door in his basement workshop.

'What's the matter with you?' asked Alonso. 'I paid for your release from the sheriff's office. Don't tell me you have other people who wish you harm.'

'I need to stay hidden for a few days,' said Inganno, glancing at a cauldron that smelled of tar. 'I'm sure it will only take a few days.'

The young man's chubby face was beaded with sweat, and Alonso's lip curled in distaste. He did not enquire as to the nature of Inganno's problem. Indeed, he would have nothing to do with the odious young man if it were not for his skill with potions.

'You succeeded, then?' he asked as Inganno held out a potion.

'Yes,' said Inganno distractedly. 'But I must warn you,' he added, his hands reaching out as if he considered taking the potion back. 'This mixture is far more potent than the previous concoctions.'

'That is what I paid you for, is it not?' said Inganno with irritation.

'Indeed,' said Inganno with a simpering smile. 'But taking this potion without diluting it will be fatal.'

'Fatal?' said Alonso. 'How can the affected person carry out instructions if the potion is fatal?'

'Not immediately,' cried Inganno. 'The victim won't die immediately. But after a few hours, if the potion's more toxic components aren't neutralised, they will die.'

'Perfect,' said Alonso, and with that he left Inganno's house and returned to the street where two of his men were waiting for him.

'Well?' he said. 'Have you found a suitable person to carry out the task?'

The two men glanced at each other before one of them spoke.

'Seems he doesn't have many servants,' said the man. 'Just a groundsman and a housekeeper.'

'A housekeeper?' said Alonso.

'Cleans his house… prepares his meals.'

'And the mercenary is also living at the house,' added the second man. 'So he's probably eating the same food.'

'The housekeeper it is then,' said Alonso with satisfaction. 'What?' he asked when he saw the men exchange a glance.

'People say she has magic,' said one of the men.

'She's a witch,' said the other.

'No matter,' said Alonso. 'Torvik will be with us. I'm sure he can handle the magical powers of a domestic help.' The two men appeared somewhat reassured. 'Can it be done tonight?' asked Alonso, but one of the men shook his head.

'Apparently, the sorcerer's home is protected by magic,' he explained. 'We need to wait until she leaves the house.'

'Tomorrow then,' said Alonso holding up the small potion bottle. 'We'll wait for this 'witch' to leave the house, and then we'll turn the housekeeper into an assassin.'

28

Monsters

The following morning found the Tutor, Fate and Motina gathered around the table in the kitchen of Blackfell House. It was raining outside and Motina pulled on a waxed cotton cloak as she prepared to visit Madam de Lorni.

'What should I tell her?' she asked as Fate took a sip of his tea.

'You can't tell her anything,' replied Fate. 'Not until we know how Lord Medici reacts to the news that his son is a murderer.'

'Tell her we're still looking,' said the Tutor.

'This is so unfair,' said Motina. 'That a rich killer wanders free while an innocent young man is forced to hide in the sewers.'

'But the world isn't fair,' said Fate. 'You, of all people, know that.'

'True,' said the small hunchbacked woman. 'But that's not going to stop me complaining about it!' Fastening the cloak across her chest, she gathered up a basket of food that was sitting on the table. 'Well, I hope you manage to convince Lord Medici that his son is a raging psychopath. Then maybe I can return to Madam de Lorni with the news that her son is alive.'

'We'll try,' said the Tutor.

With a final sigh Motina left the kitchen and moved into the main body of the house before heading towards the front door. Passing through the hall, she stopped at a sideboard on which lay a slender box made of finely grained laburnum wood. Opening the box, she took out a wand; her wand.

A twisting spindle of polished wood, the wand had lived in that box for years, only being taken out occasionally when she needed it for a particular spell. However, following the recent attack by the Kane twins, Motina had started taking the wand with her when she left the house. After a few days the sense of danger had faded and the habit had lapsed, but now that sense of danger had returned... dismembered bodies, enchanted hell-hounds, and sadistic fops who enslaved girls with illegal potions.

Motina slipped the wand into the sleeve of her blouse and headed out of the house. The rain had now stopped, but still she gathered in her cloak as she opened the gate and left the grounds of Blackfell House. It was a thirty-minute walk to Madam de Lorni's house and Motina was not looking forward to the visit. It was one thing to tell the anxious woman that there was no news about her missing son. It was quite another thing to lie about the fact.

Hunched against the wind, Motina set off up the road. She was so distracted that she did not notice the two figures following her as she moved into the narrower streets of Guile.

*

A few minutes later, Fate and the Tutor were also in the streets. They were halfway to the Medici mansion when they caught sight of Alonso Medici crossing the road to speak with a man whose teeth glinted with a touch of gold. The young Medici was accompanied by two armed guards and his Don'Sha'Vir bodyguard.

Staying hidden behind the corner of a building, Fate and the Tutor watched as Alonso had a brief exchange with the gold-toothed man.

163

'He's up to something,' said the Tutor and Fate gave a slow nod of agreement.

They watched as Alonso gave the man a 'lead on' gesture before following him into the side street with the rest of his men in tow.

'Should we go after him?' asked the Tutor.

'No, said Fate. 'This will give us the chance to speak with Lord Medici alone.'

And with a final glance at the disappearing Don'Sha'Vir, they continued on their way until they reached the main gate of the Medici residence where two armed men were guarding the driveway.

'How are we going to do this?' said the Tutor. 'After what happened at the storm drain, they're unlikely to just let us in.'

'You'd be surprised,' said Fate. 'Men like Medici believe they're untouchable, but they are wary of anything that might threaten their hold on power, especially if it is something that could harm the family.'

'Well, I'm sure we can handle a few house guards if things turn nasty,' said the Tutor as he and the sorcerer began to approach the gate.

'It's not the guards that worry me,' said Fate. 'It's the shimmering patches of air that shadow Lord Medici's movements. I'm not sure what they are, but he definitely has some form of magical protection.'

'Then let's hope he listens to reason,' said the Tutor, laying his hand on the hilt of his sword as the two guards moved to bar their way.

'We're here to see Lord Medici,' said Fate in that tone of unwavering authority.

'Wait!' said one of the guards. 'You're the ones who nearly killed Nayler.' The two guards took a step back and drew their swords.

'We stopped the sadistic brute from killing a girl if that's what you mean,' said Fate. 'Now kindly tell Lord Medici that Decimus Fate has information that could be very damaging to his household.'

'He won't see you,' said one of the men.

Unperturbed, Fate reached into a pocket and pulled out the black and gold medallion that he had used on their last visit, and handed it to the guard.

'Tell his Lordship that I relinquish my membership and claim the Ward of Final Parting.'

It was clear that the guard had no idea what he was talking about, but he disappeared with the medallion, and five minutes later they were standing in the parlour of the Medici mansion with no less than five armed guards watching them from the side of the room. All the men were clearly on edge, but the Tutor was not overly concerned. He knew they would not do anything unless ordered to by the lord of the house. Another minute passed before they heard the sound of footsteps and Lord Medici swept into the room.

'Out!' he commanded. 'All of you, out!'

The men hesitated, only moving when Lord Medici's valet chivvied them along with a curt gesture of the hand.

'You too, Niles,' said Medici, and with a somewhat disgruntled bow, the valet also left the room closing the door behind him as he went. It appeared that Lord Medici was now alone with two dangerous individuals, but both Fate and the Tutor could still make out the faint areas of shimmering air that moved forward as if they were adopting a position from which they could block any attack on Medici's person.

'Now,' Lord Medici went on with Fate's medallion clearly visible in his hand. 'What's this all about? And it had better be important. You almost killed one of my guards and this coin is the only reason you are still alive.'

'No,' said Fate. 'We're alive because you wish to know what we have learned.'

A dark smile tugged at Lord Medici's eyes.

'Well?' he demanded. 'Have you found the villain who killed my niece?'

'No,' said Fate. 'Not yet,' and even the Tutor could detect no trace of deception in the sorcerer's tone. 'But we have learned something important about the murder itself.'

'Oh? And what might that be?'

Fate smiled and the Tutor could not believe how calm he appeared.

'If we could go back to the drawing-room in your son's apartment, I will explain everything,' said Fate.

The hint of a frown tightened Lord Medici's brow, but then he rolled his eyes.

'Oh, if we must,' he said as if he found the whole matter tedious.

As they moved through the mansion, the Tutor watched the shimmering patches of air and wondered what they might be...

Some demons projected a field of magical force that made it difficult for an attacker to get close, while other 'invisible' forces could burn or freeze anyone who moved into the enchanted area. Whatever they were, they remained close to Lord Medici as they entered the drawing-room of his son. Fate was about to speak when Lord Medici gestured towards the sorcerer's chest.

'You've something on your... robes,' he said, waving a disapproving finger at the dandelion seed that was still attached to the fabric of Fate's clothes.

Glancing down, Fate plucked off the seed and flicked it away but the feathery little parasol merely drifted for a moment before settling back against his chest.

'Static attraction,' said Fate, and Medici grunted as if he could hardly be less interested.

'So, what is it you have to tell me?' he asked, his tone communicating the fact that his patience was wearing thin.

'Before we go on,' said Fate, moving to the magically chilled cabinet where Alonso stored his potions. 'I would like your permission to take something from this cabinet.'

'As you wish,' said Medici and Fate smiled at his annoyance.

He opened the door and a cloud of condensed vapour plumed about his head as he bent down to remove a small silver flask, a flask that was almost identical to the one that Luca had given them.

'Here is the answer to this mystery.'

The frown on Lord Medici's brow grew deeper as Fate held up the potion.

'A drinks flask,' he said. 'How can a chilled liqueur tell us anything about the death of my niece?'

'This might help,' said the Tutor and, reaching into his doublet, he removed the letter that Eliza had given to Luca.

'I can't read that scrawl,' said Medici, giving the muddy letter a cursory glance.

'Then allow me,' said Fate.

Taking the letter from the Tutor, Fate angled it towards the window and began to read.

To my dearest father

It is with a heavy heart (and no small measure of fear) that I must tell you about the horrors I have

167

endured in your brother's house and the terrible darkness that resides in your nephew's heart.

Alonso and I have known each other since childhood, and he has always had a propensity for cruelty. However, what seemed like playful dominance has now become something far more sinister. After years of abusing servants and street girls, he has started using potions to ensure their absolute obedience to his perverse desires.

But now, dear father, he has turned his attentions to me. I have not yet mentioned this to your brother; for I fear the damage this might do to the family.

Thus far, Alonso has only used the potion to embarrass and humiliate me, but last night I overheard him boasting of what he intends to do when his stock of the potion is replenished.

Please help me, father. Alonso's appetites are growing ever more extreme. There is even talk of girls going 'missing' from the town, and I am beginning to fear for my life.

I need your help, dear father, or at least your permission to return home to our estate near Confluence. Please act quickly. Alonso is a danger, not only to me but to the reputation of the Medici family itself.

Your loving and devoted daughter
Eliza

As Fate read the letter, Lord Medici's expression had grown more severe until his face was set like the marble from which his home was built.

'So you see,' said Fate. 'This is not just a flask of some expensive spirit. It is an illegal potion that can rob a person of their own volition.'

'And just what are you implying?' asked Lord Medici.

'I am not implying anything,' said Fate. 'I am offering you evidence that your niece was not killed by a hired servant who has now gone into hiding. Rather she was killed by a young man who has become intoxicated by the power he can exert over others.'

'You are suggesting my son is a killer?'

The Tutor's hand strayed towards the hilt of his sword as the expression in Lord Medici's eyes took on a murderous edge.

'I'm afraid so,' said Fate and for several tense seconds the two men just looked at each other.

'And you would be right,' said Medici with a sigh. Walking over to a drinks table, he poured himself a glass of brandy. 'Alonso has always been a troubled soul,' he went on. 'How does the saying go? What's cunning in the kitten…'

'Is cruel in the cat,' finished Fate.

'That's it,' said Medici extending a finger from the glass as he took a sip of his drink. 'I have always taught Alonso the importance of being able to control people,' he went on as if he were imparting some wisdom about the raising of children. 'But I think he took the lessons too literally,' he added with a laugh and a wistful shake of the head.

'You *knew* that Alonso killed your niece?' said the Tutor.

'Of course,' said Medici. 'I know everything that goes on in this house. And do you really think my niece was the first?'

'So the accused servant is in the clear…'

'Goodness, no!' exclaimed Medici. 'I can't let my brother know that Alonso has killed his only daughter. The old stick would insist on justice and then I'd have to kill *him* too.' He rolled his eyes as if this would be a terrible inconvenience. 'And just think of the shockwaves it would send through the family… Our enemies would like nothing better than for the Medicis to be weakened by a domestic squabble.'

'The murder of a young woman is not a 'domestic squabble',' said the Tutor, and the two shimmering patches of air closed in as he took a step forward.

'You would do well to calm yourself, demon hunter?' Medici made a small movement with his head as if he were directing the shimmering patches of air to stand down.

'What if *we* were to tell your brother?' asked Fate, and the murderous glint returned to Lord Medici's eyes.

'That would not be wise,' he said.

'And what if we were to tell the authorities?'

Lord Medici gave a contemptuous sniff. 'The authorities know better than to challenge me, and neither approach will help the young man who is currently hiding somewhere in the city.' Lord Medici drained the last of his drink. 'He will die for the murder of my niece,' he went on. 'The young man's life is already forfeit.'

'What have you done?' asked Fate, and Lord Medici smiled.

'I have issued an open contract.'

'In the city?' asked Fate.

'In all the Seven Vales,' said Medici with relish. 'Paid in full with the Concilio Condemnabitur.'

'The Council of the Damned,' said Fate.

'The very same,' said Medici.

'Then there is nothing we can do to change your mind?'

'Changing my mind would not change the young man's fate,' said Medici. 'Even if I were to die on the spot, the young man would still be killed by someone wishing to claim the bounty from the council.'

'That is unfortunate,' said Fate.

'That is life,' said Medici. 'Now, I really must be getting along. I think this medallion has bought you more than enough time. But let me warn you...'

'You are warning me?' said Fate, and the Tutor recognised the dangerous tone in the sorcerer's voice.

'Indeed I am,' said Medici. 'I have heard the rumours about you giving up magic. Indeed, I would never have believed them if I hadn't heard it from Master Veleno himself. He tells me that you refused to use magic even when your life depended on it... Ha!' he exclaimed as he saw the confirmation in Fate's dark eyes. 'So, it's true! The great Decimus Fate is now nothing more than a washed-up do-gooder, the Sage of Blackfell House... champion of the poor.'

The Tutor did not need to see Fate's eyes to know that the gold streaks would be glowing like fire. Lord Medici seemed supremely confident, revelling in the denigration of someone who was once considered powerful. But then Fate smiled, Lord Medici's poise faltered, and the shimmering patches of air moved forward to flank him as the Tutor's hand returned to the hilt of his sword.

'Thank you for your time, my Lord,' said Fate with a gracious bow.

'Enough of these niceties!' snapped Lord Medici. 'You come into my home and threaten my family with talk of division and scandal... Get out of my house before

I ignore this medallion and break the Ward of Final Parting. And if you ever harm one of my employees again...'

'Yes?' said Fate with an eagerness that was distinctly unnerving.

'I will place a bounty on *your* head and kill one random citizen every twelve hours until your lifeless body is left at my gate.'

'Hmm...' Fate gave a nod and pursed his lips. 'A most impressive threat.'

'Not a threat,' said Medici. 'But a promise.'

'And do the Medicis keep their promises?'

'Always,' said Medici and with a word, the audience was over and Fate and the Tutor were escorted from the house.

'How can people like that live with themselves?' said the Tutor as they left the grounds of the Medici mansion.

'Because they are damaged,' said Fate. 'And because they think they are beyond the reach of consequence.' He glanced back at the enormous building. 'That's what power does to you. It makes you believe you can do anything you please,' he continued. 'And if you never learned empathy or honour as a child...'

'Then you become a monster,' said the Tutor, and the look in Fate's eyes made it clear that he had faced such a monster in himself. He took a deep breath before placing a hand on the Tutor's arm.

'Come now,' he said. 'We have to tell Samuel Culpepper that the Butcher needs to dump another doppelganger in the river. And then I need to tell Motina that we failed to help Madam de Lorni's son.'

Fate knew Motina would be terribly disappointed. What he did *not* know was that, even as they headed back to Blackfell House, Motina was fleeing from Medici's men.

She had noticed them following her as she left Madam de Lorni's home. Three men dressed like mercenaries, one with a gold tooth that glinted in the light. For almost a mile they had followed her and now Motina was breathless, her hunched back aching as she hurried towards the safety of Fate's magically protected home.

Turning into an alley, she headed for the main street where the presence of bystanders might offer some protection. She was barely halfway to the busier street when two figures appeared in the alley ahead of her. Motina stopped and turned, only to see Medici's men closing in on her from behind. The two figures ahead of her now also began to approach. One was tall and wearing the fine-cut clothes of a gentleman. The other was dressed in the crimson robes of one who lived in the desert.

Motina's heart beat rapidly in her narrow chest. There was something unsettling about the robed figure and she could sense that he was a creature of magic.

Reaching into her sleeve she pulled out her wand, her eyes flitting from the men behind her to the two figures approaching from the front. At the sight of the wand the Medici guards began to back away, but the powerful figure in the desert robes came on. His eyes were covered by a silk scarf tied around his head and, even though he could not 'see', the figure looked down at her wand. His mouth twisted into a mocking sneer and Motina's heart almost quailed.

Those grey lips were stitched together.

29

Motina's Pantry

Motina was trapped; three men behind her, two men ahead. The only option left was to fight. Glancing to front and rear, she quickly assessed her opponents. The three men behind her looked like soldiers or mercenaries. Any one of them was strong enough to subdue a small woman like her. Ahead of her, the well-dressed gentleman seemed the least dangerous, strange considering he was probably the instigator of this attack. But the well-dressed fop was not alone. He was accompanied by the nomad figure in the crimson robes, and *he* was clearly the most dangerous of them all.

Even as she watched, the terrifying figure came forward, moving with the confidence of one who knows he cannot be harmed.

Gripping her wand, Motina took a breath and drew in the forces of nature which were frustratingly meagre in the dim alleyway of a city. As the nomad closed on her, she bound this energy to her own spirit and channelled it into her wand. The enchanted wood focussed the energy, magnifying it until the wand began to glow.

'Dedzinoša bultiņa!' cried Motina, and her wand suddenly flared as a burning arrow of light shot forward to strike the nomad in the shoulder.

The magical attack burnt a hole in the nomad's crimson robes and the tall figure reeled back with a snarl of pain, but the mystical brands in his dark skin glowed as they absorbed the worst of the damage. Motina knew she could not stop him, but that had not been her intention. The pause in his advance gave her just enough time to reach into a pouch at her waist and grab a handful of fennel seeds.

Like many common-or-garden plants, fennel was rich in magical properties, the myths of which went back to the time when humans stole fire from the Gods. Today, Motina would make use of that latent power.

'Užsidegti siršė!'

Calling out the spell in her native tongue, Motina flung the fennel seeds at the three men blocking the alley behind her. Instantly, the seeds burst into flame and began flying towards the men like a swarm of wasps. The men cried out and swatted the air as the enchanted seeds stung their flesh with searing barbs. While they were distracted, Motina tried to slip between them. She might well have got past them had an invisible force not reached out and grabbed the back of her cloak.

Motina's feet left the ground as she was yanked backwards, sailing through the air before landing heavily on the rain-soaked flagstones. Shaken and winded, she shifted round as the crimson-robed figure loomed over her. Looking up into that blindfolded face, she raised her wand for one last burst of magical force. The polished wood began to glow and Motina was just about to unleash the fire when the nomad's large hand closed around it. The flesh of his hand began to smoke and the nomad released a growl of pain before clenching his fist and snapping the wand in two.

Even now Motina tried to crawl away, but the nomad took hold of her, lifting her off the ground as if she weighed nothing at all.

'Hold her!' said a voice and Motina felt herself being constrained as a muscular arm folded across her chest while a strong hand clenched tight in her hair.

'Open her mouth.'

Panic surged through Motina as the man with the gold tooth stepped forward, leering unpleasantly as he grabbed her chin and forced her mouth open.

Eyes wide and staring, Motina now saw the well-dressed man coming towards her with something in his hand. It was a small bottle, the kind of bottle that was often used for medicine or potions. Once again Motina began to struggle, but the arm tightened across her chest and her thoughts grew fuzzy as some foul hypnotic magic forced its way into her brain. The dim alleyway seemed to close in around her and noises echoed strangely as she lost the will to resist.

Almost as if it were happening to someone else, Motina felt the cold neck of a bottle clack against her teeth. A sweet liquid trickled into her mouth and she was too dazed to resist the instinct to swallow. The liquid burned slightly, but it was not unpleasant and the heady fumes rose up into her nose relaxing her mind and reducing the urge to struggle.

'It's working,' said the well-spoken voice. 'You can let her go.'

The arm around Motina's chest relaxed its grip as she was set back on her feet, those same strong hands now steadying her as she fought a wave of dizziness. A plume of fear rose up in her mind as she opened her eyes. She was being held upright while several strange men stared at her.

'You're safe,' said a voice that she *knew* was dangerous and yet somehow she believed and trusted.

'Safe,' she repeated in a dreamy voice.

'Yes,' said the voice. 'Now listen to me... only to me...'

Motina's gaze came into focus on the face of a good looking man in expensive clothes. He reminded her of someone who had trapped her in an alley, but Motina's mind now wallowed in a haze between fear and a strong desire to hear what he had to say.

'I want you to drink the rest of this,' he told her and Motina glanced down at the half-empty potion bottle.

'What is it?' she asked.

'Something that will make you feel better,' said the man. 'Now drink.'

With only the slightest hesitation, Motina took the bottle and put it to her lips.

'*Salvia divinorum*,' she thought as she recognised one of the components. '*Betel and peyote sap.*' These rare and mind-altering extracts could be toxic and a dim note of alarm sounded in her mind, but it was completely overridden by the man's instruction for her to drink. She thought she detected several inorganic compounds, but then a less suspicious thought entered her mind... '*I wonder what they used to sweeten it.*'

Motina was mildly embarrassed by the banality of the thought, but her critical thinking was slowly being subsumed by an overwhelming sense of compliance.

'Good,' said the man as he noticed the faint sheen of silver appear in Motina's raven-black eyes.

For her part, Motina felt a strange combination of pleasure and repugnance at his praise. Almost absently, she tucked the empty bottle into a pocket as she tried to think what she should do next.

'You might be feeling a little confused,' said Alonso Medici and Motina nodded. 'You might have forgotten where you were going or what you intended to do next.'

Another nod and a slight smile from Motina.

'Well, you visited an actress called Madam de Lorni and now you are going to continue on your way as if nothing out of the ordinary happened.'

177

'As you wish,' said Motina, but Alonso held up a finger.

'No,' he said. 'It must be as *you* wish.'

'Of course,' said Motina with something of her customary fire. 'I don't need a young upstart like you to tell me what to do.'

'No you don't,' said Alonso. 'But there are a couple of things that I would like you to do for me.'

'Certainly,' said Motina as if such a thing were entirely normal.

'Excellent,' said Alonso. With a nod, he directed his men to retreat down the alley before putting his arm around Motina's shoulders and leading her towards the mainstreet. 'First, you will forget about being followed and you will forget that this encounter ever took place.'

'All right,' said Motina obligingly.

'And then, at the earliest time of your convenience, you will kill the man called Decimus Fate and the demon hunter known as the Tutor.'

Somewhere deep in her mind, Motina railed against the very thought of harming Fate. However, as the powerful potion was slowly absorbed, that fierce resistance began to sink away as if Motina herself were drowning in a dark body of water. Finally, all resistance vanished and only obedience remained.

'Killing them won't be easy,' said Motina in a voice devoid of emotion.

'You're a witch,' said Alonso with a cynical laugh. 'I'm sure you will find a way.' He seemed entirely satisfied with the way things had gone, but his men seemed nervous.

'We should get out of here before someone sees us,' said one of the men.

'No,' said Alonso remembering what his father had said about subtlety. 'Someone might have seen us *enter* the alley. It will be better if they see the housekeeper emerge unharmed.' He turned to Motina. 'You will join us as we go up onto mainstreet,' he told her. 'I will drop a handkerchief and you will pick it up for me.'

'With pleasure,' said Motina, although the smile on her face did not appear completely natural.

With a very different kind of smile, Alonso walked away with his Don'Sha'Vir just a step or two behind. Emerging onto the mainstreet, he reached into a pocket allowing a silk handkerchief to fall onto the cobbles.

'Excuse me, sir,' said a voice behind him, and he turned round to see Motina bending down to retrieve the handkerchief from the ground. 'You dropped this.'

'Why thank you,' said Alonso, noting how one or two people looked across to witness the exchange.

'Good day, sir,' said Motina and with that she continued on her way.

Alonso smiled again as he watched her go. His father had been right... employing a bit of subtlety was very satisfying. Feeling entirely pleased with himself, he turned in the direction of the Medici mansion.

Motina had the strangest sensation as she continued along mainstreet. It almost felt as if she were waking from a dream. Pausing on the road, she glanced back the way she had come. She remembered leaving Madam de Lorni's house, and she remembered a sense of anxiety as she turned into a narrow alleyway. And yet she had no memory of being in the alleyway itself.

'I must have been daydreaming,' she muttered to herself. 'Now, what else do I need to do today?' Her words trailed off as she went through the list of jobs in her mind.

'*I need to get some diced lamb for a stew... And, now that it's stopped raining, I need to mangle the washed bedding and hang it out to dry... Cut back the rosemary and plant the garlic bulbs... And what was the other thing?*'

'Ah, yes,' Motina murmured to herself. 'I need to kill Fate and the Tutor.'

So powerful was the potion that she did not experience even the slightest concern about the prospect of committing murder.

'Tricky,' she mused as she turned into the road on which Blackfell House was situated. 'I could stab them in their sleep, but they both sleep lightly, except for Fate on the night of the Penance Moon.'

'A sleeping draught might work, but Fate would notice the effects long before he fell asleep.' She paused in thought. 'Poison would do it,' she murmured with a nod.

'*But not just a straightforward poison,*' she thought to herself.

Fate had enchanted tattoos that would alert him to the presence of toxins, so a straightforward poison would not work.

'*But if I used two substances that weren't poisonous on their own... two substances that only became deadly when they came together in the victim's stomach...*'

Yes,' said Motina as she reached the boundary fence of Blackfell House. 'That would do the trick.'

Feeling a bizarre sense of satisfaction, she reached out to open the gate then recoiled with a cry of pain as the metal flared with fire that burned her hand. The wrought iron fence was enchanted with magic to keep out anyone who intended harm towards Fate, a magical protection that now included Motina herself.

The hunchbacked witch was now in a quandary. Her most pressing imperative was to kill Fate and the Tutor and yet she could not accomplish this if she was unable to get past the fence. For several minutes she struggled with this problem, and so intense was her determination that she even tried the fence a second time before withdrawing her hand in pain. Even standing close to the fence she could feel the 'hum' of its resistance.

And then the strangest thing happened...

She began to wonder what might happen if she thought about 'not' killing Fate, and even as she entertained the thought, so the hum of blocking energy seemed to recede.

'That's it,' she said to herself. 'All I need to do is decide *not* to kill him and the fence will let me through.' And sure enough, as this thought grew stronger, so the hum of magical force grew less.

So effective was this approach that Motina actually began to question killing Fate at all.

'What was I thinking?' she asked herself. 'Why in the world would I want to harm the man who saved my life?'

The troubling thought was so distracting that Motina was barely conscious of reaching for the gate. There was only the slightest tingle of magical energy as her hand closed on the handle.

'Something happened on the way back from Madam de Lorni's,' Motina frowned as she opened the gate and passed through the perimeter fence. 'I was being followed,' she murmured.

Strange memories began to creep into her mind; shadowy memories that were almost like a dream... a dark alleyway, men blocking her way, and a tall figure in red desert robes. Feeling fearful and confused, Motina proceeded down the gravel driveway but, even as she tried to make sense of them, the disturbing images began to fade away.

The desert figure's eyes were covered by a headscarf, Motina remembered and his lips…

You will forget that this encounter ever took place.

His grey lips were…

You will forget that this encounter ever took place.

'Lips,' said Motina as her thoughts returned to murder. 'I must make sure they taste nothing on their lips.'

Climbing the shallow steps, Motina paused at the front door of Blackfell House. Her mind was now clear, but she had the strangest feeling that she was being followed. Turning around, she scanned the driveway before raising her gaze to the streets beyond the fence. And there, partially concealed behind the corner of the adjacent property, were two armed men that looked like mercenaries.

Even as she looked at them, the men hid behind the corner and Motina shifted her gaze in the opposite direction where another man was watching Blackfell House. Like the others, he was also armed, but unlike the others, this individual was smiling and Motina caught the faint glint of a gold tooth. Then the man ducked back from view and the housekeeper shook her head and gave a little snort at her silliness.

'You're imagining things,' she told herself as she opened the front door.

Moving into the hallway she stopped as a wave of dizziness washed over her. A twinge of discomfort clutched her stomach and she wondered if she had eaten something that disagreed with her. She had no memory of swallowing a potion that was concentrated enough to kill a fully grown man. But Motina was much smaller than your average man, and the potion's dangerous strength was already showing its effects.

As the moment of discomfort passed, Motina found herself looking at the slender box lying on the sideboard, then she reached into her sleeve and frowned.

Where on earth was her wand?

She remembered taking it out of the box, and she *thought* she had taken it to Madam de Lorni's. However, the concern about her wand began to interfere with the list of jobs she had to do, and slowly it too faded from her mind.

With another shake of her head, she hung up her cloak and made her way through to the kitchen and opened the pantry, one wall of which was lined with shelves containing a huge range of herbs, spices and ingredients for use in spells. Motina's collection would have put many an apothecary to shame and she tapped a thin finger against her lips as she considered her options.

'Now,' she thought. 'What can I use to kill two strong and healthy men?'

30

Swallow or Die

Fate and the Tutor were in a sombre mood as they headed back to Blackfell House. Before returning home they had taken a detour to the storm drain where Weasel and Cradlop were waiting for them. The troglodyte had swum through the sump, Weasel had wriggled his way through the hole in the wall of the cave, while Luca and Samuel remained in the tunnel. They listened as Fate told them what Medici had done.

'And there's no chance he could call off the contract?' asked Luca.

'It wouldn't matter if he did,' said Fate. 'He's already lodged it with the Concilio Condemnabitur.'

'The Council of the Damned,' said Samuel and Fate gave a dour nod.

'It's not fair,' said Weasel as Luca hung his head in despair. 'Rich people always get to ruin other people's lives, and they never pay the price.'

'Sometimes they do,' said Fate meeting the Tutor's gaze as they remembered a once wealthy man who had recently been turned into gold.

'What now?' asked Weasel.

'Now I must complete my work on replicating Luca,' said Samuel.

'So that's it?' said Weasel. 'We dump a stranger's body in the river and Luca spends the rest of his life at sea.'

'It's better than death,' said Fate.

'And we still have another person to find,' said the Tutor for they had not forgotten Jane's missing love, Fidanza.

'Well I'm staying here till it's done,' said Weasel. 'Luca could do with the company and Samuel's teaching me to play chess.'

With nothing else to be done they had taken their leave and headed for home. It was after midday and both men were hungry so it was with a pleasant sense of anticipation that they caught the smells of cooking coming from the kitchen of Blackfell House.

'Well?' said Motina wiping her hands on a towel as they entered the kitchen. 'How did you get on?'

'Not well, I'm afraid,' said Fate as he and the Tutor sat down at the table. Their coats were wet and their boots were muddy, and Fate was surprised that Motina made no comment.

'Was Lord Medici not in?' she asked.

'Oh, he was in,' said Fate.

'So you showed him the evidence.'

'Of course.'

'And?'

'And he doesn't care,' said the Tutor.

'Doesn't care that his son's a murderer,' exclaimed Motina as she set out two bowls and brought over a pot of stew from the stove.

'He already knew,' said the Tutor.

'And he doesn't care so long as it doesn't hurt the family,' added Fate.

'But his own niece was killed!' said Motina.

The housekeeper was clearly appalled, and perhaps that was why her hand shook as she ladled out the stew. Leaning over the table she removed a muslin cloth from a freshly baked loaf of bread, but as she straightened up she winced from a sudden pain in her stomach.

Fate's eyes narrowed in concern as he watched Motina put a hand to her stomach.

185

'The death of his niece doesn't concern him,' he said. 'Not now they have a scapegoat that they can blame for the murder.'

'Could you not tell the girl's father?' asked Motina.

'It wouldn't help,' said Fate. 'Medici has already paid in full to have Luca killed.'

'The swine,' said Motina, and Fate frowned in confusion as she leaned over the table and pushed the bowl of stew away from him.

Sitting across the table, the Tutor also noticed the bizarre action and they exchanged a puzzled look as Fate retrieved the bowl and began to eat.

'So, how did things go with Madam de Lorni?' Fate took a mouthful of stew and offered the bread to the Tutor before tearing off a piece for himself.

'What?' said Motina, her hands clenching and unclenching as she watched the two men eat their stew.

'Madam de Lorni,' said Fate. 'How was she when you visited?'

'Not well,' said Motina. 'And she's going to be a whole lot worse when she thinks her son is dead.' Her hand suddenly flicked out as she knocked the spoon from Fate's hand.

Fate's eyebrows shot up in surprise while Motina's face twitched with anxiety.

'I'm sorry,' she said. 'I thought I saw a spider on your hand.'

Once again Fate frowned as he turned his hand over, looking for any sign of an arachnid. Looking more closely at his housekeeper he retrieved his spoon and continued with his meal.

'Are you all right, Motina?' he asked, trying to sound casual as he dunked a piece of bread into the heavily seasoned stew.

'I'm fine,' said the housekeeper, but once again she winced as with a spasm of pain. 'I'm just upset by the whole affair, and angry that people like the Medicis can get away with whatever they want.'

'That's just what Weasel said,' said the Tutor.

'You saw Weasel?' said the housekeeper, her tone lightening despite her obvious discomfort.

'He's fine,' said Fate. He exchanged another look with the Tutor and it was clear that even the demon hunter had noticed that Motina was not herself.

'Are you sure you're all right?' Fate asked her again. 'Did something happen while we were away? Has Master Veleno been bothering you again?'

'No,' said Motina. 'It's nothing like that.' Picking up a tea towel, she opened the warming drawer beside the oven and took out a baking tray of small pies. 'I'm just worn down by all this worry.'

A serving plate was already sitting on the table, but instead of filling it with the pies Motina turned towards a bucket that was used for collecting kitchen scraps.

'Motina,' said Fate as he saw that the housekeeper was about to tip the pies into the bucket.

'Hm?' said Motina then, 'Oh, my!' she exclaimed. 'Whatever was I thinking?'

'I don't know,' said Fate, 'but they smell like pork.'

'Indeed they are,' said Motina. 'And they're always better when they're still warm.' She transferred the pies to the plate on the table. 'They might taste a little different,' she added. 'I was trying out some new herbs.'

'I'm sure they'll be delicious,' said Fate. Taking a pie he began to study his housekeeper more closely. She seemed unusually anxious and there were beads of sweat on her forehead as if from a fever. Her wrinkled face creased with pain and Fate put down his pie.

'You're not well,' he said, but Motina raised a hand to forestall any concern.

'Just a stomach cramp,' she said, leaning on the table as another spasm gripped her belly. 'I'll go for a lie down just as soon as you're finished. Go on,' she said, gesturing for them to continue eating. 'You know how I pride myself on my pork pies.'

'They're delicious,' said the Tutor licking crumbs from his fingers as he swallowed the last of his pie.

Fate took a bite, and he was so distracted by his concern for Motina that he did not notice the faint tingle of alarm coming from a tattoo on his right forearm. He swallowed and then raised an eyebrow as Motina sat down on a chair.

'Thank goodness!' she said. 'I thought you were never going to eat the second component, although I did add a third component to the bread, just to be sure.'

'What do you mean, a third component?' said Fate, his tone suspicious as an unthinkable possibility began to dawn in his mind.

'A third component of poison,' said Motina and now her face crumpled as she began to cry. 'I didn't want to do it,' she croaked, her voice cracking with emotion. 'But somehow, I couldn't stop myself.'

Even as she spoke, the Tutor felt the first twitch of pain grip his own stomach. His face started to tingle and his tongue felt swollen as his vision began to blur. Fate had only taken a bite of his pie, but he too could feel the effects of poison seeping into his veins. His gaze quickened as he looked at the food on the table... the stew... the bread... the pies.

Laying them out in a line, he began to wave his right hand over the various foods.

'That won't help,' said Motina, her small body hunching and twitching as Inganno's potion polluted her flesh. 'I knew you'd sense it if I tried to poison you directly.'

In a flash of comprehension, Fate realised what Motina had done. Gathering the food, he mixed it together in the half-empty dish of stew. Immediately, the tattoo on his right forearm began to glow and throb.

'What have you done?' he asked as his diaphragm convulsed and the muscles in his throat began to tighten.

'I did what I had to do,' Motina sobbed even as she slumped forward over the table, her eyes fluttering and her breathing shallow.

The Tutor was in no better shape, he looked distinctly alarmed as he felt the poison's grip on his body tighten.

Knowing he had no time to lose, Fate stood up from the table and hurried over to the water tank beside the sink. He grabbed two glass tumblers and filled them with water before adding large handfuls of salt from a ceramic pot beside the stove. Stirring the mixture quickly, he winced as a bout of cramp pulled tight across his stomach. His head swam and his ears rang as he carried the glasses back to the table.

'Drink this!' he told the Tutor, almost dropping the glass as the muscles in his arm tightened with a jerk.

Groaning in pain, the Tutor fumbled for the glass and managed to get it to his mouth. His teeth clenched involuntarily, but somehow he was able to get most of the heavily salted water down his throat. Beside him, Fate did the same while Motina was now slumped forward across the table, her cheek resting in a puddle of drool.

'You need to vomit,' Fate told the Tutor, the words blurring together as his tongue began to swell.

The Tutor's chair scraped across the floor as he got to his feet and moved to the sink as he felt bile and saltwater rising in his gorge. Black blotches had begun to darken his vision and he could not seem to get enough air into his lungs. Glancing up, he saw Fate stumble from the kitchen, his shoulder striking the door frame as he struggled to make his way. For a moment he thought the sorcerer was abandoning him and then his stomach lurched.

As the Tutor brought up the contents of his stomach, Fate careened off the walls until he reached the hall where a doorway gave onto a set of stone steps leading down to his basement room. Feeling increasingly dizzy, Fate stumbled down the steps and into the large room that was filled with all manner of antiques and curiosities. His eyes struggled to focus as he lunged towards a glass cabinet lying against the left-hand wall of the room. Leaning against the cabinet, he felt his stomach heave as he vomited saltwater and the remains of Motina's poisoned lunch onto the floor.

Fate's vision was growing blurry, but in a moment of clarity, he saw what he was looking for... a small silver box with a hinged lid. He reached out to grab it, but he had forgotten to open the cabinet and his hand was cut as it smashed through the glass.

Ignoring the cuts, Fate clutched the small box to his chest and opened the lid to reveal a handful of what looked like small silver pebbles. Trying to stop his hand from shaking, he took one of the pebbles, slipped it into his mouth and swallowed. Then, closing the lid, he gripped the box tightly as he headed back towards the kitchen. However, he was barely halfway up the flight of stone steps when a burning pain surged in his stomach and he collapsed to his hands and knees.

Fate's mouth stretched wide and wisps of white energy emerged from his throat as the stone released its magic and his body was suffused by a fierce light. For several seconds the silvery light coursed through his body until even his veins glowed white. As the incandescence faded Fate collapsed onto his face.

For a moment it appeared that he was unconscious, then his head came up and he managed to get one hand under his chest. With a great effort, he pushed himself up from the floor and reached for the box that had slipped from his grasp.

The sorcerer crawled up the steps and blinked away the brightness before stumbling back to the kitchen where he found the Tutor in a heap on the floor beside the sink. The demon hunter looked barely conscious and this filled Fate with dread. The silver pebble he had swallowed was a theriac stone, a magic panacea that could purge the body of almost any toxic substance or poison.

The purging was painful and quick. However, having done its work, a theriac stone would also induce a brief period of somnolence, or sleep. Even now, Fate could feel his limbs getting heavier and his eyelids drooping as he slipped towards a deep, if short-lived, slumber. But it was now clear that Motina had also been poisoned and he could see that she was even closer to death than himself or the Tutor. If he could not get a stone into her stomach in the next few minutes then he was sure the housekeeper would die.

'Motina,' Fate told the Tutor as the drowsiness took hold of his body. 'You must give one of these to Motina.'

Twitching with the spasms that wracked his body, the Tutor managed to open his eyes.

191

'Take one of these,' said Fate, his words trailing off as sleep rose up to claim him. 'And give one... to... Motina.'

The sorcerer's eyes closed and the silver box fell from his hand as he fell sideways into a brief, but irresistible sleep.

The silver theriac stones spilled across the kitchen floor and the Tutor merely stared at them through a haze of pain and confusion.

'*Silver pebbles,*' he thought. '*What the hell am I supposed to do with silver pebbles?*'

The Tutor was on the verge of passing out when Fate's last words echoed through his mind.

'*Take one of these... give one to Motina...*'

Fighting against the convulsions, the Tutor reached down and groped for the pebbles. Like a child trying to feed itself, he managed to get one of the pebbles into his mouth. He swallowed and the small stone felt huge as he forced it down his constricted throat. With a great effort, he managed to haul himself up, almost falling again as he doubled over from the cramps in his stomach. Through his failing vision, he saw Motina sprawled forward over the table.

'*Give one to Motina.*'

The Tutor was just reaching for the woman when he felt a burning sensation flare in his stomach. The surge of magical energy seemed to engulf his entire being and he gave a cry of effort as he grabbed Motina and hauled her small body onto the table. A clear white light suffused his vision and veils of silvery energy swirled in his breath as he parted Motina's lips and pushed a pebble into her mouth. The housekeeper was in a fugue of delirium, but the pebble worked its way to the back of her throat and she began to gag.

With the last of his strength, the Tutor leaned over the table and put his mouth to Motina's ear.

'Swallow,' he mumbled. 'Swallow or you will die.'

Then, not knowing if the housekeeper had heard him or not, he collapsed to the floor as white light flooded his veins and he sank into the engulfing arms of sleep.

31
Trust

Fate woke to the harsh cries of ravens, a dozen ravens
flapping and pecking at the kitchen window of Blackfell
House. The birds were frantic; desperately worried about
the small hunchbacked woman lying unconscious on the
kitchen table. The birds were black, but the light
emanating from Motina's body was white, and Fate
struggled to think why this was important.

He remembered pain, discomfort and fear, and then
he heard a groan. Looking around, he saw the Tutor lying
on the floor beside the table. The demon hunter looked
like he had been drugged.

'*Drugged...*' thought Fate. '*Or poisoned.*'

They had been poisoned.

In a flood of recollection, it all came back to him.
Crawling across the floor, he put a hand on the Tutor's
shoulder.

'Tutor,' he said, but the demon hunter was still half
asleep. 'Alexander!' said Fate in a louder and more
insistent tone. 'You have to help me... Motina is too
small to survive a theriac stone. She'll die if we don't
help her.'

Something in Fate's voice managed to break through
the Tutor's torpor and he began to stir.

'Is she alive?' he murmured. 'I tried to give her a
stone.'

'She's alive,' said Fate. 'The light is still purging her
body, but the magic will kill her if I can't draw off some
of its power.'

Getting to his feet, Fate swayed as he leaned against
the table, his eyes squinting against the brightness that
shone through Motina's pale and fragile skin. Whatever

194

was poisoning her had clearly spread through her entire body. Her back was arched and her mouth was open in a silent scream.

'Take off her dress,' said Fate, and the Tutor looked at him askance. 'Her dress!' Fate repeated as he began to remove his own tunic and undershirt. 'I might be able to help her, but it will need skin to skin contact.'

The urgency of the situation left no room for propriety so the Tutor merely snapped the laces on the front of Motina's dress and pulled it up over her head. Beneath the dress, Motina was wearing a white shift that left her arms and legs bare.

'That'll do,' said Fate. 'Now, pass her to me.'

The sorcerer was still wearing his charcoal grey trousers, but his chest was bare and for a moment the Tutor stared at the scars and arcane symbols that covered his skin.

'Quickly!' said Fate as he sat in a chair and held out his arms.

Still not really understanding, the Tutor lifted Motina from the table and passed her into Fate's arms. Her body felt light and fragile, such a contrast to the strong and sharp-witted housekeeper he had come to know.

'Stand back,' said Fate as the white light from Motina's body seemed to ignite a series of magical symbols that extended across Fate's shoulders and down his arms. The glowing symbols obviously caused Fate discomfort and the sorcerer gritted his teeth as he wrapped his arms around Motina's small frame.

'Will your magic save her?' asked the Tutor.

'Not my magic,' hissed Fate. 'The symbols will simply absorb the stone's power before it kills her.'

'I can feel heat,' said the Tutor as the light of the arcane symbols grew even fiercer. 'Does it hurt?'

195

'Like the very devil,' groaned Fate, then he closed his eyes and held Motina tight as the power of the theriac stone burned his flesh.

Outside the window there was a cacophony of squawks and dark flapping wings, while inside the kitchen the light was so bright that the Tutor squinted against it and, when it finally faded, the air in the kitchen was filled with the metallic tang that follows a lightning strike.

Hunched over Motina's body, Fate gave a heavy sigh as the symbols on his body stopped glowing. Slowly, he relaxed his arms and looked down at Motina who sat on his lap with her head nestled against his chest. For several seconds he thought she might be dead, but then her shoulders shifted as she drew a breath.

Outside the window, the flapping had ceased and a single bird let out a deep-throated caw as it peered into the kitchen.

'Motina,' said Fate. 'Can you hear me?' Motina's narrow chest continued to rise and fall. 'Raven Mother…' urged Fate and still there was nothing until Motina opened her eyes.

'You smell terrible,' said the witch and Fate smiled.

'That's what happens when your housekeeper tries to poison you.'

*

Fate and the Tutor recovered surprisingly quickly from their brush with death. After washing, the Tutor put on a clean shirt and scrubbed down his black leather doublet while Fate donned a fresh set of robes. Standing in his bedroom, the sorcerer frowned at his reflection in the mirror as he watched Carduus's dandelion seed settle back on his chest.

Within an hour they felt almost normal, if a little shaky and sore. By contrast, Motina was completely wiped out by the potion that had overwhelmed her body, and by the theriac stone that had finally cleansed it from her system. After waking in Fate's arms they had carried her up to her room where she slept soundly for five straight hours. It was well into the evening when she finally woke. Even though she was weak and disorientated she insisted on coming downstairs to talk about what had happened. Fate and the Tutor had cleaned up the mess, but there remained a lingering smell of upset stomachs and magical force. The two men sat quietly as Motina leaned on the table, fighting against her weariness as she struggled to recall the events of the day.

'I remember leaving Madam de Lorni's house,' she said, her hands restless as she stared into space. 'I was being followed,' she added. 'Three men... armed and ugly. One of them had a gold tooth.' She glanced up as if the clarity of this memory surprised her.

'I tried to get to the mainstreet, but two other men blocked the way.' Motina frowned as the fear of that moment returned. 'One was about your height, dark hair, fine clothes,' she added, glancing up at Fate. 'The other man was taller and darker... He was dressed in crimson robes like the nomads who live in the desert.'

Fate and the Tutor looked at each other. It was clear that she was describing Alonso Medici and his Don'Sha'Vir.

'I tried to fight,' said Motina, her breath quickening. 'Tried to burn them and escape, but the nomad had magic, and he was strong... very strong.'

Motina was trembling and Fate put a hand on her arm.

'It's all right,' he told her. 'We can do this tomorrow when you're feeling stronger.'

'No,' said Motina. 'We do it now.'

Fate removed his hand and sat back as she continued.

'They made me drink something, and then everything changed,' Motina's voice took on an air of wonder. 'I stopped struggling and all I wanted to do was obey.'

'Inganno,' said the Tutor and Fate nodded.

'I would have done anything,' Motina went on. 'Anything he told me to do, I would have done it.'

'And what did he tell you to do?' asked Fate and Motina hung her head.

'He told me to kill you,' she murmured. 'You and the Tutor.'

'How did you get past the gate?'

'I had to stop thinking about killing you,' said Motina, 'which wasn't easy because I knew they were watching.'

'Who was watching?'

'The three armed men... I think they were making sure that I carried out my task.'

The Tutor glanced at Fate. Those three men were probably still watching the house.

'And what about you?' asked Fate. 'Did you take the same poison you gave to us?'

'No,' said Motina. 'I think it was the potion they gave me. Even as I drank it, I could tell it was too strong... concentrated to the point of being dangerous.'

Fate's eyes glittered with sparks of gold.

'He told me to kill you,' Motina repeated to herself. 'And I tried,' she added, shaking her head in disbelief. 'I actually tried to kill you.' Motina could not bring herself to look at Fate.

'Yes, you tried,' said the sorcerer. 'And you would have succeeded if it weren't for the box of theriac stones I had tucked away in the basement.'

'Is *that* what you gave me?' said Motina, her eyes widening in surprise. 'It felt like I'd swallowed a star.'

'They do burn some,' said the Tutor and the three survivors smiled.

'And now,' said Fate. 'I think I'd like a cup of tea.'

The Tutor began to get up, but Fate waved him back down as Motina got slowly to her feet. Making her way over to the stove, she opened a lidded jar and put several spoonfuls of crushed mint leaves into a teapot before adding hot water from the kettle.

'I can't believe you're asking me to make the tea when I tried to kill you with poison.' Her voice contained a note of disbelief as she made her way back to the table where the Tutor had now laid out three ceramic cups.

'It wasn't poison that was used to try and kill me,' said Fate. 'It was trust.'

Motina bowed her head in shame, but then Fate put a finger under her chin to raise her face.

'Before today, I trusted you with my life, Varna Motina.' The sorcerer looked deep into the housekeeper's small black eyes. 'And on my oath, I trust you still.'

Fate's normally stern face was softened with a smile as a tear ran down Motina's cheek.

They sat in silence as they finished their tea, and Motina's eyes drooped with tiredness, but there was one more thing Fate had to ask of her before she could go back to her bed.

'You said there were three men watching the house?'

Motina nodded.

'Can you show us?' he asked and some of the weariness faded from Motina's eyes as she pushed herself up from the table and led them to a room where the window looked out onto the street.

'They're definitely watching the house,' said the demon hunter as he studied the hiding places that Motina had pointed out.

Fate gave a slow nod and his face was set like stone as he turned to Motina.

'We need to leave you for a while,' he told her. 'Will you be all right?'

'I'll be fine,' said Motina. 'But maybe it would be better if we just forgot about...' Her voice trailed off as Fate shook his head.

'What was it you told me about cruel people with power?'

'They need to be opposed,' said Motina with a sigh. 'Cruel people grow crueller if they are allowed to go unchallenged.'

The witch and sorcerer exchanged a meaningful look before Fate turned to the Tutor.

'You know what I have to do,' he said.

'Yes,' said the Tutor. 'You're going to kill Alonso Medici. I also know that Lord Medici will murder half the city to find you if you kill his son.'

'You don't have to join me,' said Fate, but the Tutor just shrugged.

'They tried to kill me too,' he said. 'Besides,' he added, 'my diary happens to be clear for the next few days.'

Fate's dark eyes shone with streaks of gold.

'So, how do we get out of the house without them seeing us?' asked the demon hunter.

'*We* don't,' said Fate. 'I'll go out the front door and make it look like I've been poisoned. If Medici's men are there, they'll move in to finish the job and then you can attack them from behind.'

'And just how am I supposed to do that?'

'Follow me,' said the sorcerer and with that, he led them down to the basement where the sorcerer opened a large cabinet to reveal an array of weapons and armour.

'Take whatever you want,' said Fate, but the Tutor shook his head.

'I have everything I need for Medici's men.'

'And for the Don'Sha'Vir?'

'Crossbows and throwing knives won't help against an opponent like that.'

'And what will?'

'The skills of a demon hunter,' said the Tutor and the two men exchanged a smile.

For his part, Fate took a pair of steel bracers that fitted snugly beneath the sleeves of his robes. In addition to his dragon-handled daggers, he now buckled on a three-quarter length rapier before selecting a small hand crossbow with five black bolts in a small belt quiver. Closing the cabinet, he began to cross the room then stopped as he passed the massive circular steel door of his vault.

'Is there anything in there that would help?' asked the Tutor.

'Oh, yes,' said Fate. 'But wielding such power always comes at a cost.'

The Tutor could almost feel the power of Fate's temptation, and he wondered again at the sorcerer's reasons for giving up magic.

With a sigh, Fate squared his shoulders and turned away from the vault before glancing down at a table where three small white spheres sat in a black onyx bowl.

'Although, one of these might help,' he told the Tutor as he slipped one of the small spheres into a pocket.

With a final glance at Motina, he walked towards the far corner of the room. There was no door in that direction and the Tutor simply assumed he was going to collect something else until the sorcerer touched a particular block in the wall and the corner of the room hinged open to reveal a spiral stairway leading down into the ground.

'A secret passage,' said the Tutor. 'Why am I not surprised?'

Standing beside the secret opening, Fate smiled as he reached up to take one of his elongated crystals from a stone sconce set into the wall. He gave it a shake, and the crystal began to shine with a pale blue light as he held it out to the Tutor.

'Follow the passage for about fifty yards and then take the right-hand fork.'

'Where does it come out?'

'The right-hand fork leads to a cemetery about two hundred yards from the house. The exit is canter-levered so it should slide away without any trouble. Then make your way back to the house. I'll give you about ten minutes to get into position.'

The demon hunter dipped his head in agreement then raised the glowing blue crystal as he started down the narrow spiral stairs. 'This place is just full of secrets.'

'You have no idea,' said Fate.

32

Wounded and Bleeding

Two hundred yards from Blackfell House lay the Glan Ogwen graveyard, the resting place of wealthy families in the First Quarter of Guile. With over a hundred tombs and mausoleums, the graveyard was a quiet and solemn place, and so there was no one around to hear the dull scrape of stone as the lid of one particular grave slid back to reveal a flight of stone steps leading down into darkness.

The Tutor emerged cautiously. A few oil lamps burned in the nearby streets, but apart from that, the night was dark and quiet. Checking that the coast was clear, he slid the tomb's capstone back into place and there was just enough light for him to read the inscription.

'In memory of Kristyn Fermi,' he whispered as he read the name of the grave.

For just a second he wondered who Kristyn Fermi was then he made his way out of the graveyard and took a moment to get his bearings before heading back towards Blackfell House. As he drew closer he moved slowly, searching for any sign of Medici's men. Skirting the grounds of one property, he hugged the wall, edging forward until he caught sight of the man he had seen from the window. Armed and wary, the man was keeping to the shadows as he kept watch on Fate's house.

There was still no sign of the other two men, and the Tutor was beginning to wonder if they were out there when the man leaned out from his hiding place and looked across to a thick stand of laurel bushes on the far side of the sorcerer's property; perfect cover for someone who was trying to remain hidden. It was late now and the streets were quiet, so the Tutor moved with care as he made his way round to a point between the two hiding places.

Like a leather-clad shadow, he crouched behind the protruding edge of a large stone gatepost. He had just got into position when the front door of Blackfell House opened and Fate staggered out, stumbling down the steps and onto the gravel driveway as he headed towards the gate. The sorcerer looked unsteady on his feet, hunched over and gripping his stomach as if he was in pain.

The demon hunter saw movement to his left as two men emerged from the dense leaves of the laurel bushes. And then, over to his right, he saw the first man edging his way forward as Fate fumbled with the gate before staggering away from his home and into the open street.

The Tutor tensed. He did not want to give away his presence by striking too soon.

Fate had reached the open space of the crossroads when Medici's men finally broke from cover. Moving in from both sides, they converged on the 'poisoned' sorcerer; two knives and a sword glinting in the darkness as they went in for the kill.

And now the Tutor moved. He knew Fate had the element of surprise, but that would not save him from three dangerous opponents. The man they had seen from the window was the first to reach Fate, gripping his knife as the sorcerer sank to one knee as if from a spasm of pain. The man's knife drew back and he was just about to strike when Fate twisted round and shot him in the stomach with a small crossbow bolt.

The attack clearly took the man by surprise and he froze, glancing down at the black bolt protruding from his leather jerkin then he sucked in a grunting breath as Fate's rapier stabbed up into his chest.

The Tutor saw the man's legs give way as Fate got to his feet, withdrawing his rapier as the man pitched forward onto his face. The first of Medici's men was dead and Fate turned just as the remaining two men closed on him.

They came in fast, each drawing an additional weapon so that both were armed with dagger and sword. There was no time for Fate to re-cock his crossbow so he simply raised his rapier to meet his attackers. The two men diverged to split Fate's defence, and it would have ended badly for the sorcerer until one of them cried out as the sharp points of a throwing star stabbed into his back. The startled man turned just in time to see the black-clad figure of the Tutor bearing down on him.

The man was clearly a veteran and his instinct to survive eclipsed the pain from the throwing star. Raising his weapons, he managed to deflect the Tutor's first blow, turning his parry into a counter-attack with surprising skill. He slashed out with his sword and blocked a second attack with his dagger before the Tutor's superior skill brought the confrontation to an end.

With blistering speed, the demon hunter unleashed a rapid series of attacks until his blade slipped past the man's guard to deliver a fatal thrust. The man barely had time to gasp before the Tutor withdrew his sword and strode past him to engage the man now fighting with Fate.

Even against a trained soldier Fate was holding his own, his robes flaring out as he parried attacks with his rapier.

'You're... supposed... to be dead!' hissed the man as he tried to close the sorcerer down.

Fate's face was tight with concentration as he focussed on his opponent, but his eyes widened as he saw the Tutor moving in for the kill.

'No!' he cried. 'I want him alive.'

With a twist of the wrist, the Tutor changed the angle of his attack to strike with the flat of his blade. The man's legs went wobbly and he collapsed to the floor.

Silence returned to the street while in the distance a dog barked into the night, but no one appeared to have noticed the fight that had taken place in this more sparsely populated part of the city. Two men lay dead with a third groaning as he hovered on the edge of consciousness.

'What should we do about these two?' asked the Tutor, but Fate just shrugged.

'Nothing,' he said. 'It's not uncommon for mercenaries to die fighting in the street.'

'And what about this one?' he asked as the dazed man started to come round.

'He's dead,' said Fate. 'He just doesn't know it yet.'

'Are you just going to slit his throat?' asked the demon hunter, and Fate's gaze did not flinch as he jerked his chin towards the man.

'Don't you recognise him?' he asked, and now the Tutor could see that one of the man's teeth was glinting in the lamplight. It was Gold Tooth.

'This man took pleasure in beating an innocent girl,' said Fate. 'He also forced Motina's mouth open so they could give her the potion that would have killed both her and us. He's going to die, but he's going to help us get to Alonso before he does.'

Hauling Gold Tooth to his feet, they bound his hands, put a dagger to his side, and marched him off into the night. By the time they reached the river, the man had recovered sufficiently to try and wheedle his way out of his predicament.

'It wasn't my fault,' he cried as they stumbled down the grassy bank towards the river. 'I was only doing what Master Alonso told me to.'

'Did he tell you to beat a defenceless girl?' asked the Tutor as he pushed the man through the thorn bushes surrounding the storm drain.

'That was just a bit of fun,' said the man as if this light-hearted reply might help his situation. He was wrong.

'And did he tell you to kill us?' asked Fate.

'Only if the hunchback failed,' said the man. 'And only if we could do it without anyone seeing. But I wouldn't do it again,' he added as if he suddenly realised that he might have spoken out of turn.

'Of course you wouldn't,' said Fate, and the man gave a hiss of pain as Fate made a small cut on the man's arm with the blade of his black dragon-handled dagger.

The man recoiled, struggling against his bonds, but the Tutor held him fast as Fate reached into his robes and took out a small vial of liquid. 'Do you know what this is?' The man shook his head. 'It's an antidote,' said Fate.

'An antidote to what?' asked the man.

'To the poison on the blade of this dagger.' The sorcerer held up his black dragon-handled dagger. 'The smallest cut from this weapon is enough to kill a man.' The man's eyes grew wide as he stared down at the cut on his arm. 'A stab wound will kill you in seconds,' Fate went on. 'But a small cut is different. A big man like you might survive for an hour or more if the cut isn't too large. But even a small cut will lead to death unless you can drink this antidote before you pass out.'

'What do you want me to do?' asked the man, his face beading with sweat as if he could already feel the effects of the poison. 'I'll do anything... just name it.'

Fate remembered the fear in Motina's face as she recalled how she had been forced to swallow the potion. He remembered the shame in her eyes when she told them what she had done. And he remembered her small frame contorted with agony as the power of the theriac stone purged the harmful potion from her body.

'I want you to return to Alonso,' said Fate with no trace of mercy in his dark eyes. 'I want you to tell him that we are wounded and bleeding and waiting for a boat to carry us out of the city. Tell him we're hiding out in the storm drain where his men were looking for Luca.'

The man was nodding frantically.

'And who knows,' Fate went on. 'If you get back quickly enough, there might still be time for the antidote to work.' He held up the small bottle and the man nodded some more. 'Cut him free.'

With a slice of his dagger, the Tutor cut the man's bonds and he stumbled away from the two intimidating men that had just let him go.

'Don't dally,' said Fate. 'You wouldn't want to collapse and die before you can get back for the cure.'

Fear, hatred and desperation flashed in the man's eyes.

'Alonso'll kill me if I betray him,' he said as his gold tooth glinted in the darkness.

'Not if he dies tonight,' said Fate.

'You'll never kill Alonso,' the man snorted. 'You'll never get past Torvik.'

'Alonso's bodyguard,' said Fate.

'He's a freak,' said the man. 'A father once came looking for his daughter... one of Alonso's girls,' he added with disturbing ambiguity. 'He drew a sword on Alonso, but Torvik merely grabbed the blade and put a hand to the man's chest.' He paused, staring into space as

208

he remembered the scene. 'He set the man's heart on fire... right there in his chest. We could see it glowing through his ribs.' The man raised his eyes to look back at Fate. 'I'm dead if I betray Alonso.'

'And you're dead if you don't,'

'Some choice,' said the man bitterly.

'It's more of a choice than you gave my housekeeper.'

'This is crazy!' said the man. 'All this for a few dead girls and a crippled old crone.'

Clenching his jaw, the Tutor started forward, but Fate put out a hand to stop him.

'How are you feeling?' he asked the man who still seemed reluctant to leave.

'Dizzy,' said the man.

'Then I'd hurry if I were you,' said Fate as he held up the small vial of liquid.

Finally, the man realised that he had no choice. Maybe it was his imagination, but he could almost feel his chest getting tight and his heart beating faster from the effects of poison.

'Fine!' he snapped. 'I'll do it,' and with a last baleful glance he turned away from the storm drain and disappeared into the night.

'Do you think Alonso will come?' asked the Tutor.

'Yes,' said Fate. 'It's nighttime, in a secluded location, and we're both "wounded and bleeding". He'll be cautious, but yes, he will come.'

'And what about Lord Medici?' asked the Tutor. 'I wasn't joking when I said he would kill half the city to find you.'

'I know,' said Fate.

'And he'll have extra security at the mansion once he marks you for dead.'

'No he won't,' said Fate. 'Mere guards won't protect him from a notorious sorcerer like me, so he will call on the protection of the Juoda Pakta.'

'The dark sisters?'

'Precisely,' said Fate. 'By midday tomorrow Lord Medici will have the protection of thirteen dark witches.'

'So, how the hell will we get to him?' asked the Tutor, but Fate just smiled.

'One depraved nobleman at a time, my friend' said Fate. 'You just focus on how you're going to defeat a man who can set fire to your heart while it's still alive and beating in your chest.'

'I'd rather tackle an entitled brat like Alonso,' said the demon hunter.

'No,' said Fate. 'Alonso is mine.'

The Hunt Resumes

As Fate and the Tutor waited for Alonso and his mystic bodyguard, a deadly shadow was prowling the streets of Guile. The dog-like form of the manitu was still wandering the streets of the city, keeping to the shadows as it tried to discern its purpose. The human sample inside of it was not strong enough to allow it to home in on its prey and so it drifted aimlessly.

Only when it reached the walls of the city did it have the sense that it was going too far; that its target lay somewhere behind in the twisting warren of streets. From the tall tenements in the Second Quarter to the crowded slums of the Third it wandered. But eventually, it began to move towards the more affluent areas of the Fourth Quarter; a part of the city where a wealthy widow had once died in her sleep, leaving the house and all her estate to her only son, a troubled young man with a fleshy cherubic face.

Standing on a bridge over the Norward Canal, the Manitu hunched its shoulders and lowered its head. Somewhere in its chest, the trace of its target matched the scent of something on the air. The trace was weak and hidden away, but finally it was strong enough to hunt.

Hobson's Choice

The night was dark and the black expanse of the river shimmered with the light from distant street lamps. Fate and the Tutor were waiting on the patch of open ground in front of the storm drain. The two men were looking down at the object Fate had taken from the black bowl in the basement room of Blackfell House. It was a sphere of milky white glass about the size of a hen's egg. The object was illuminated by the faint glow of Fate's firefly charm which hovered about six inches above the sorcerer's hands.

'Are you sure that'll work?' asked the Tutor.

'No,' said Fate. 'But it might give us a chance if Alonso brings more guards.'

'Just how bright is it?' asked the Tutor.

'It'll blind you for a day if you look directly at it.'

'Where the hell do you get this stuff?'

'The Sutākirā assassins use them as diversions,' said Fate. 'I found four in the belt pouches of an assassin who failed in his mission.'

The Tutor arched an eyebrow. He did not need to ask who the assassin's target might have been. Glancing back towards the storm drain, he changed the subject. 'I'm still not sure about including the others.'

'They want to help,' said Fate, but the Tutor was not convinced.

After sending Alonso's man on his way, Fate and the Tutor had met Samuel and the others in the storm drain, telling them how Alonso had tried to kill them and what they planned to do about it. Samuel had agreed to help, but Weasel and Cradlop were also keen to do something.

'But this is dangerous,' insisted the Tutor.

'They'll only come out if we have things under control,' said Fate. 'And the darkness gives us the advantage. Now hush… Someone's coming.'

He tucked the firefly charm in a pocket as the sound of someone approaching along the riverbank grew louder. The area in front of the storm drain was surrounded by a fringe of blackthorn and, peering through the bushes, they could see a figure with a dim lantern hurrying along the bank towards them.

'It's him,' said the Tutor, 'the one with the gold tooth, and he looks a little shaky on his feet.'

Fate said nothing, only pursing his lips as the man pushed through the thorn bushes to speak with them.

'I did it!' he gasped. 'I told Alonso.'

'Is he coming?' asked the Tutor.

'He is,' said Gold Tooth. 'With two of his men and the Don'Sha'Vir.'

'Which way?' asked Fate.

'That way,' said the man, pointing back the way he had come. 'They'll be here soon. Please, I need the antidote now.'

Fate retrieved the small bottle from his robes. 'How long do we have?' he asked.

'About ten minutes,' said the man. 'I ran on ahead while they were getting ready.' He held his hand out to Fate. 'Please,' he begged. 'I did what you asked; now I need to get away before they see me.'

The Tutor's brow was furrowed with suspicion. He did not trust the man and he was surprised when Fate held out the antidote.

'Very well,' said the sorcerer. 'Drink that and be gone with you.'

Edging forward, Gold Tooth took the bottle from Fate. Backing away into the thorn bushes, he broke the

213

wax seal and there was a quiet pop as he removed the tiny cork. Putting the bottle to his lips, he drank it down before tossing the empty bottle aside. He retreated further, and there was just enough light to see that his lips were parted in a gold-toothed smile.

'You're dead!' he sneered. 'No one defies the Medicis... the both of you are dead.'

Hardly had he finished speaking when two more lanterns blossomed in the darkness revealing the presence of *six* armed guards, while behind them stood two more figures. It was Alonso and his bodyguard bathed in the faint light of magical energy that was centred around the Don'Sha'Vir's hand.

'I think Gold Tooth has double-crossed us,' said the Tutor.

'Of course he has,' said Fate as the treacherous man emerged onto the grassy riverbank beyond the thorn bushes.

'Now!' he cried. 'Take them now!' He pointed towards the storm drain then his face creased with pain as he clutched his stomach and collapsed to his knees.

'I guess the antidote came too late,' said the demon hunter.

'No,' said Fate as he cocked his crossbow and drew his sword. 'The dagger that cut him is only toxic to things of demonic origin, whereas the poison he just drank will kill a man in seconds.'

The Tutor stared at him in the darkness. 'Has anyone ever told you that you're a frightening man?'

'It has been said,' replied Fate and the two men readied themselves as Medici's guards moved in. The six guards came on slowly, fanning out as they pushed their way through the bushes. Their lanterns lit up the immediate area but failed to penetrate the cave-like mouth of the storm drain. As they came closer, Fate raised his crossbow while the Tutor gripped one of his steel pointed throwing stars.

'Say the word,' said the Tutor as the guards moved into the clearing.

'Now!' said Fate.

The crossbow bolt and the throwing star flew out, but neither was aimed to kill. Instead, the projectiles targeted the two lanterns. Fate's crossbow bolt punched through the glass bulb of one lantern, extinguishing the flame and causing the guard holding it to jerk back his arm in alarm. The second lantern swung wildly as the Tutor's throwing star bit into the bearer's arm. The unexpected attack made the guards pause and then they watched as Fate lofted the milky white sphere into the air. The ball of white glass did not appear threatening and yet the guards tensed as it fell towards the hard-packed earth.

'Eyes!' cried Fate as the sphere hit the ground and shattered to release a blinding white light.

Even though he had turned away and covered his eyes, the Tutor could still see the bright flare of light. It lasted only a second, but that was enough to blind the Medici guards. That was when Fate and the Tutor attacked, and they were not alone.

Stunned and dazed by the exploding sphere, the Medici guards stumbled blindly as Fate and the Tutor moved in. The plan was to get them into the storm drain before Alonso realised what was happening. Rushing up to one guard, Fate put a dagger to the man's throat.

'Walk!' he hissed, pressing his dagger harder as the man started to resist.

Beside him, the Tutor arched back to avoid the sword of another guard who had managed to close his eyes in time to avoid the worst of the blinding effects. Still a little stunned, the guard swung his weapon in wild arcs until the Tutor disarmed him and punched him in the stomach before grabbing his collar and dragging him into the cave.

At the same time, another figure emerged from the storm drain, a figure with broad shoulders, short legs and long powerful arms. It was Cradlop, and the powerful troglodyte quickly grabbed two guards and dragged them bodily into the cave where Weasel was waiting with a handful of leather cords to tie up the befuddled guards.

In no time at all, the six Medici guards were bound and gagged, squinting and groaning as they tried to expunge the flaring blob of darkness that was now seared onto the retina of their eyes. One of them gave a muffled cry of warning, but then quickly stopped as Weasel cuffed him around the side of the head.

'Keep quiet, you oaf!' he hissed.

Cradlop was also crouched nearby, his arms outstretched as he restrained two of the guards with his powerful hands. Fate turned to the Tutor.

'Allow one of them to speak,' said the sorcerer as he prepared to leave the storm drain. 'Try to draw Alonso in, but give me time to get into position.'

'Be careful of the Don'Sha'Vir,' said the Tutor.

'Don't worry,' said Fate with a smile. 'I'm leaving the lethal bodyguard to you. We just need to make sure that Alonso doesn't escape,'

'Then be quick,' said the Tutor.

Reaching into a pocket, he drew out one of the blue light-crystals that Fate had given him earlier. Then, without another word, Fate dimmed the firefly charm as he snuck out of the storm drain and curved round to the right. His aim was to climb up the bank, circle around and come at Alonso from behind.

Barely a minute passed before they heard Alonso's voice.

'Dorsan,' he called out. 'Have you got them? Dorsan, are you there?'

One of the guards reacted to his name being called and the Tutor put his dagger to the man's throat before removing his gag.

'Tell him to wait,' whispered the Tutor putting a dangerous amount of pressure on the sharp edge of his dagger.

'Just a minute, my Lord,' cried the man. 'We just need to make sure they're dead.'

The Tutor gave the man a nod and relaxed his dagger as Weasel replaced the man's gag.

The Tutor checked to make sure the guards were securely tied then tensed as he heard footsteps as someone approached the fringe of thorn bushes. He turned to Weasel.

'Get ready to run,' he told the boy. 'If things go badly then you and Cradlop flee back into the caves.'

Weasel's shoulders slumped but he dipped his head in a reluctant gesture of assent.

The Tutor rose to his feet, drew his sword and walked out of the cave, the soft light of the crystal casting a blue highlight on his black clothes and armour. Even his dark Southern Isles skin took on an ethereal glow that matched the blue of his eyes.

'You!' said Alonso backing away as he caught sight of the demon hunter. 'I thought you were…'

'Dead?' interrupted the Tutor as he pushed his way through the thorn bushes. 'Wounded and bleeding?' he suggested. The Don'Sha'Vir bodyguard drew a sleek one-handed scimitar and moved to block his advance as the Tutor stepped free of the trees.

'Dorsan!' cried Alonso, his voice shrill with anxiety. 'Marcus... Cooper...'

'I'm afraid your men are a little tied up,' said the Tutor, his eyes moving from Alonso to the Don'Sha'Vir as the two warriors measured each other up.

'Where's the sorcerer?' said Alonso, his eyes darting behind the Tutor as he looked for some sign of Fate.

'He had to leave on an errand,' said the Tutor. 'But I'm sure he'll be back soon.'

'Not before you die,' said Alonso. 'And then there'll just be one of you to kill.'

'I wouldn't be too sure of that,' said the Tutor trying not to look over Alonso's shoulder as Fate's dim silhouette appeared in the darkness some twenty paces behind him.

'Enough of this!' snapped Alonso. 'Kill this fool!' With a wave of his hand he directed the Don'Sha'Vir to attack.

The arcane brands in the nomad's skin suddenly flared as he closed on the Tutor who stepped to the right in an effort to draw the bodyguard away from Alonso. Even though he could not see, the mystic's 'gaze' followed the Tutor's movement, then he lunged forward with such speed that the demon hunter was almost taken off guard.

The Tutor reacted instinctively, blocking the Don'Sha'Vir's sword with his own before attempting a counter-strike that sliced the air as the robed figure leaned away from the Hadean blade. Even in this first exchange, the Tutor got a sense of his opponent's skill and he sharpened his focus as he realised just how dangerous this desert nomad was.

Stepping back, he raised his sword to block a blistering series of blows before launching an assault of his own. The energy of his attack now rose to a new pitch and for a moment the Don'Sha'Vir appeared vulnerable, but then the blindfolded figure flung out his free hand and the Tutor reeled back as a gout of orange flame engulfed his head.

The magical flames burned hot, and it was only the protective energy of the Tutor's demon hunter tattoo that prevented him from suffering burns. As it was, his face was scorched and the air was filled with the smell of singed hair. The Don'Sha'Vir used this distraction to launch a new attack which the Tutor was unable to completely avoid. He escaped a lethal thrust to his chest then gasped as the nomad's curved blade sliced through the black leather of his breeches.

Stepping backwards, the Tutor blocked another series of attacks. Then, parrying a thrust to his chest, he maintained contact with the mystic's blade and pushed forward to inflict a cut to the Don'Sha'Vir's shoulder. The blindfolded man hissed through his stitched lips then thrust his free hand forward, unleashing a pulse of energy that struck the Tutor like a kick from a carthorse. The Tutor staggered backwards as the Don'Sha'Vir started towards him, but then the nomad stopped as he 'sensed' a fleeting shift in the Tutor's attention.

For just an instant, the Tutor's focus had shifted to the shadowy figure of Fate who was now closing in behind Alonso. Following his gaze, the mystic turned just in time to see Fate raising his crossbow to shoot Alonso. The small weapon issued a muted 'twang' but the black bolt shot wide of its mark as the Don'Sha'Vir used some invisible force to grab Fate's arm as he made the shot.

Alerted by the sound of the crossbow, Alonso spun round and recoiled in surprise. The sorcerer in the charcoal grey robes was right there behind him and

Alonso fumbled for his own sword as he backed away from his attacker who was struggling to break free of the Don'Sha'Vir's mental grip.

The nomad's magical grip was strong, but Fate's willpower was stronger. Focussing his mind he began to pry himself free, but this required effort and he was slow to notice Alonso rushing in for a surprise attack.

Fate was forced to twist to one side as Alonso's blade stabbed a hole in his outer robes. The sorcerer's movement was still hampered by the grip of the Don'Sha'Vir until the Tutor attacked the mystic and the restraining force vanished. Fate's rapier whipped up to challenge Alonso and the cowardly lordling turned to flee. Fate knew the younger man could outrun him, so he simply loaded another crossbow bolt and shot Alonso in the back of the leg before he got too far away.

Alonso gave a cry and stumbled forward as he felt the stabbing pain in the back of his thigh. Glancing back, he saw the dark outline of Fate walking towards him. Distant street lights glinted off his slender blade, and Alonso thought he saw the faint glint of gold in the sorcerer's shadowed eyes.

'Torvik!' he cried. 'Torvik, where are you?' The desperation in Alonso's voice was palpable as Fate came closer and closer, but Torvik was otherwise engaged.

The Don'Sha'Vir turned his head as he heard Alonso calling, but the spoilt young noble was finally beyond his help. A demon hunter stood between them and the mystic warrior gripped his curved sword as he turned to face his blue-eyed opponent.

In the darkness the pommel of the Tutor's Hadean blade had begun to glow and the graceful blade seemed to ring with a high melodic note. Once again, the brands in the Don'Sha'Vir's skin glowed red as he attacked; a vicious attack followed up with arcs of fire and mental assaults that struck like punches from an invisible fist.

And the Tutor absorbed it all.

He parried the blade, resisted the fire and shrugged off the blows that were intended to hurt him. Each time one of his mental blows was repulsed, the Don'Sha'Vir recoiled and the Tutor pressed his advantage.

The Don'Sha'Vir's scimitar remained dangerous and the quiet of the night echoed with the ringing clash of steel. The exchange was brief and brutal and it ended with the Tutor stabbing the Don'Sha'Vir in the pit of his right arm. The mystic's sword fell from his grasp and he stumbled back as the Tutor struck down with a killing blow. However, the blow never landed as the Don'Sha'Vir grabbed the blade with his hand.

Once again they locked wills, Don'Sha'Vir magic versus demon hunter will, as the mystic held the blade with his enchanted flesh. Putting all his strength behind the sword, the Tutor stared into the Don'Sha'Vir's veiled 'eyes'. Through his stitched lips, the mystic snarled, but he was not dead yet. Still holding the sword, he raised his free arm and placed his hand on the demon hunter's chest.

Almost immediately, the Tutor felt the magical force engulf his heart. He felt his heart beat faster and his vision darkened as the mystic's fire burned in his chest. A weakness began to creep through the Tutor's body and he thought his legs might give way. But then, with a final effort, he wrenched his sword free of the Don'Sha'Vir's grasp and spun around with a horizontal sword-stroke aimed at the Don'Sha'Vir's head.

The scything blow removed the top of the mystic's skull, taking with it the headscarf that covered half his face. In a fleeting moment, the Tutor caught of glimpse of poisoned veins and hollow eyes, the sockets burned black and empty. It was a vision of nightmares, but then it was gone as the Don'Sha'Vir collapsed to the ground.

For a moment the Tutor looked down at his fallen enemy and then he looked up as he heard Alonso's voice coming from further up the river bank.

'That's no choice at all,' whined Alonso as the Tutor ran over to where Fate had the young Medici cornered.

'It's the only choice you have,' said Fate, the tone of his voice cold and final. 'Either you admit to your crimes and accept your punishment, or you die where you stand.'

'Pah!' said Alonso. 'They'll hang me for what I've done.'

'Yes, they will,' said Fate. 'But you might stay alive for another few weeks.'

Fate had Alonso trapped against a small rock face that overlooked the river. It was too steep to climb and the only other way out was past the sorcerer who stood with his rapier poised.

'Curse and damn those blasted girls!' hissed Alonso, turning round with his sword in his hand as the finality of his situation dawned. He put his free hand to his head and grabbed a fistful of his own hair then... 'My father will pay you,' he said desperately. 'My father will pay you a fortune if you just let me go.'

'There's no amount of money that will make up for what you've done,' said Fate and, even in the darkness, he could feel the hatred in Alonso's eyes.

Silence followed as Alonso weighed his options until finally...

'All right,' he said at last. 'I'll turn myself in.' Relaxing his sword he shambled towards Fate with his head bowed. 'My father owns some of the best lawyers in the city. He'll be able to...

The sentence went unfinished as Alonso suddenly snatched up his sword and lunged at Fate. His blade was aimed straight for the sorcerer's heart, but Fate was ready. With a mere flick of the wrist, he caught Alonso's blade with his rapier, forcing the thrust to go wide as his own sword slid down the length of Alonso's blade and into the depraved man's chest.

Alonso's body went stiff and he coughed up blood. His eyes stared up at Fate and then his legs gave way and he collapsed to the ground. He ended up kneeling, slumped back on his heels with barely the strength to raise his own head. A final spasm of pain twitched through his body and he died.

'The Don'Sha'Vir?' said Fate without taking his eyes off Alonso.

'Dead,' said the Tutor.

'Are you all right?'

'Cuts and bruises,' said the Tutor. 'Nothing serious.'

'Good,' said Fate, and the Tutor was surprised by the matter of fact tone of his voice.

'Medici will see you dead for this.'

'Yes, he will,' said Fate with something approaching a smile. 'Now, help me get him back to the storm drain. It's time to introduce Alonso Medici to the Butcher of Guile.'

The Plan Unfolds

Only one of the Medici guards had managed to close his eyes in time to avoid being blinded by Fate's exploding sphere. With his hands tied behind his back, the man now stood in the mouth of the storm drain looking down at Alonso's dead body.

'You don't understand,' said the guard. 'Lord Medici might kill me just for delivering the news that his son is dead.'

'Not if you tell him who did it,' said the Tutor.

The man looked up at the demon hunter, but the Tutor nodded towards Fate.

'Decimus Fate,' said the sorcerer. 'Tell Lord Medici that Decimus Fate killed his son and dumped his body in the river.'

'You're mad!' said the man in a disbelieving tone. 'Lord Medici will tear the city apart to find you. And he won't stop until he sees you dead.'

'I know,' said Fate. 'Now, are you going to lead these men back to the mansion or shall we just kill you here?'

The guard glanced around at his companions who were all still blinking their eyes in vain attempts to clear their vision.

'I'll do it,' said the man and with that, they were all hauled to their feet.

The Tutor cut their hands free and then arranged them in a line with each one resting a hand on the shoulder of the man in front.

'Don't go too quickly,' Fate told the guard who would lead them. 'I'd hate for one of your friends to lose his way and go stumbling into the river.'

The man tilted his head in a gesture of resignation then, walking somewhat haltingly, he led the line of men out of the storm drain and into the darkness of the night.

'Hey! Wait! Ow!' came various cries as the flash-blinded guards picked their way through the prickly thicket of blackthorn bushes.

Fate waited until they were out of earshot then, heading back into the storm drain, he leaned in close to the hole in the wall of the cave.

'Are you there?' he asked.

'We're here,' said the voice of Samuel Culpepper who was standing on the other side of the hole with Luca. 'It sounds like you've had an exciting night.'

'It's not over yet,' said Fate as the Tutor, Cradlop and Weasel came to stand beside him. 'Are you still willing to do this?'

'Of course,' said Samuel. 'The question is, are you still willing to go through with it? Luca here, can tell you that it's not an easy process. '

'It hurts like hell,' Luca confirmed, but Fate was determined.

'I have no choice,' said the sorcerer. 'It's the only way to make Medici drop his guard, and to stop him from hurting people in an attempt to find me.'

'Very well,' said Samuel. 'Bring the young man's body round to the Ludgate entrance. And I'd be quick about it, if I were you. From the look of the sky, we only have about an hour or two until sunrise.'

'See you in a few minutes,' said Fate before turning away from the hole to address the Tutor. 'Shall we take him together?'

'It's probably easier on my own,' said the Tutor.

Crouching down, the demon hunter began to haul Alonso's body up from the ground. However, the difficult task was suddenly made easier as Cradlop stepped in to help. The troglodyte was incredibly strong and displayed little effort as he helped the Tutor get the limp body onto his shoulder.

'Are you all right?' asked Fate.

'I'm fine,' grunted the Tutor as he adjusted the weight across his shoulders. 'Nothing I like better than carrying the corpse of a sadistic killer through the night-time streets of Guile.'

Fate gave a wry smile then stopped as Weasel started to follow them.

'What?' said the young wayfinder. 'I'm coming too.'

'No you're not,' said Fate. 'I need you to do something else.'

'What is it?' asked Weasel suspiciously. He had been looking forward to seeing Samuel perform his 'magic'.

'I need you to call on Master Veleno.'

'What!?' exclaimed Weasel. 'You've just declared war on one murderous noble, now you want me to go and call on another.'

'I take it you know where Veleno lives?' asked Fate.

'I'm a wayfinder,' said Weasel with an affronted air. 'Of course I know where he lives.'

'Then get him out of bed and show him this.' Fate handed the boy his white dragon-handled dagger. 'Tell him Lord Fate has a proposition for him.'

'What proposition?'

'Tell him, I want him to dump my dead body at the gates of Lord Medici's mansion.'

Weasel's face broke into a smile as he realised he was not being kept out of the action. Instead, he was being given a key role in the deception that Fate had devised. The sorcerer went on to give Weasel some details including the time and place where Veleno would find Fate's "body".

'Tell him there will probably be a reward,' he added as a final note. 'That should brighten Veleno's mood after being dragged from his bed.'

With that, Weasel said a quick goodbye to Cradlop and Luca.

'And one more thing,' said Fate as Weasel headed out of the storm drain. 'After Veleno, go to Blackfell House and ask Motina for a set of my robes.'

'Any particular colour?' asked Weasel, and the Tutor snorted back a laugh at the boy's subtle wit. With a final grin, the young wayfinder disappeared into the night.

'Come on then,' said the Tutor. 'Let's get this done before I give myself a hernia.'

Turning away from the storm drain, the two men set off towards the alternative entrance to the tunnels, an entrance that lay hidden in the glazed brick walls of the Ludgate Sluice.

36

Lord Medici's Wrath

The sky was beginning to brighten as the Medici guard led his five 'blind' companions through the main gate of his employer's mansion. They were met by more house-guards who woke Medici's valet, who then went through to the Lord himself. Dressed in a silk dressing gown, Lord Medici made his way down the grand staircase into the main reception hall of the house flanked, as ever, by two shimmering patches of air that hovered at his shoulders like barely visible ghosts. Lord Medici moved to stand in front of the guard from the storm drain and his face darkened as the guard delivered the news about his son.

'What do you mean, dead!?' he demanded, his rage not diminished by the casual nature of his attire.

'He was killed, my Lord, by the sorcerer known as Fate.'

Medici's face was tight with fury as he cast a disgusted glance over the incapacitated guards who stood, heads bowed and still blinded by the brightness of the Sutākirā sphere.

'And what about my son's Don'Sha'Vir?'

'He's dead too,' said the guard. 'Killed by the demon hunter.'

Medici's shoulders sagged in shock, but then his lip curled in a sneer.

'But you all survived,' he said in a dangerous tone.

'We were blinded,' said one of the men. 'The sorcerer used some kind of magic to blind us.'

'Magic?' snapped Medici. 'I was told he had stopped using magic.'

The man chose not to contradict his master as the two shimmering patches of air drew in a little closer to Medici who was now looking around as if Fate could be hiding in some corner of the room. He turned to his valet.

'Sound the alarm,' he told the man. 'Have the guards patrol the grounds and fetch my Black Pact medallion.'

'You're going to use it, my Lord?' asked the man.

'Of course!' snapped Medici. 'This is Decimus Fate we're talking about; the man who slew the demon of the vale. Do you really think this shower of useless bastards can protect me from a man like that?'

'But people say he has given up magic.'

'And these men say he used magic tonight,' said Medici. 'No... I'll be far happier once we have a coven of dark witches patrolling the grounds.'

'Of course, my Lord,' said the valet.

'And put out the word,' Medici continued, his tone darkening with resolve. 'I want Fate found.'

'The Council of the Damned, my Lord? Like we did for the servant?'

'That could take too long,' said Medici. 'I want this over quickly.'

'A reward for anyone in the city then?' suggested the valet.

'That'll do for the carrot,' said Medici.

'And for the stick, my Lord?'

'Let it be known that I will kill one random citizen each day at sunset until the sorcerer is delivered to me. I won't feel safe until I know that Fate is dead.'

37

In the House of Master Veleno

As the leader of a large criminal organisation, Master Veleno was not easily unsettled. His influence in Guile meant that there were few threats to a person like him, but even he was wary of upsetting a powerful family like the Medicis. The normally suave man yawned as he sat in the throne-like chair of a grand reception room. Wearing an expression of suspicion, he looked down at the young street urchin who had got him out of bed. The boy had spoken clearly, but Veleno shook his head as if he had misheard the request.

'He wants me to do *what*?' he asked, staring at Weasel as he turned Fate's dagger over in his hands.

'He wants you to dump his corpse at the gates of Lord Medici's mansion,' said Weasel.

The young wayfinder had never been in such a grand house before and his mind was overwhelmed by the sheer opulence of the place. Like everyone else, Weasel knew of Veleno's love of gold. Indeed, much of that gold was on display in the room, including one impressive piece that made Weasel feel distinctly uncomfortable.

It was a life-sized statue made entirely from gold. It was by far the most realistic statue that Weasel had ever seen and he kept glancing at it as if he expected it to suddenly come to life.

'And why would Fate want me to dump his corpse?' asked Veleno.

Weasel was about to answer, but then he stopped himself and looked at the guards and Veleno's personal magic-user who was standing nearby. The magic-user, in particular, seemed especially interested, but Weasel did not trust him. The man's expression suggested anger and bitterness, and the left side of his face appeared to be formed from some kind of smoky black glass.

Veleno noticed Weasel's hesitation and waved his men out of the room.

'Out!' he commanded. 'All of you, out! You too, Xanda,' he added when the magic-user did not move.

The man called Xanda was clearly frustrated by the order to leave, but finally he left the room and closed the doors.

'Now,' said Veleno. 'Tell me why my old friend would want me to carry out such a bizarre and unexpected task.'

'Because he killed Lord Medici's son,' said Weasel, and the Lord of the City was suddenly wide awake.

'Alonso?' he said and Weasel nodded. 'Fate has killed Alonso Medici?'

'Yes,' said Weasel.

'Good!' said Veleno with conviction. 'That young whelp always was a sadistic little shit.' He leaned forward and his eyes glinted with mischief as he beckoned Weasel to come closer. 'Now,' he whispered as a conspiratorial smile spread across his face. 'What's the plan?'

38
The Juoda Pakta

As Weasel explained what Fate had in mind, so dawn was breaking over the grounds of the Medici mansion. It was a bitter morning and the manicured lawns were white with frost as Lord Medici stood on the grass with his personal valet.

'It's very cold, my Lord,' said the valet. 'Wouldn't you rather summon the dark sisters in the drawing-room?'

'No,' said Medici shaking his head. 'This needs to be done outside.'

'And will they arrive on broomsticks?' asked the valet without any trace of sarcasm.

'I've no idea,' said Medici as he stared down at the Black Pact medallion with its disturbing design of the three-fingered hand. 'Do you have the payment?' he asked and the valet's lip curled in distaste.

'I do, my Lord,' said the valet, holding up three leather pouches of differing size.

The smallest pouch contained five carats of the purest rubies crushed into a fine powder. The second held twenty ounces of pure gold. While the third was damp with the blood of thirteen severed fingers that Medici's guards had somehow acquired from the poorer quarters of Guile.

'What next?' asked the valet as he held the bloody pouch away from his body.

'Just a drop of my blood on the medallion,' said Medici. With that, he took a fine silver lancet and made a small nick on the side of his hand. Then, holding his hand over the medallion, he squeezed out a single drop. The bead of blood appeared to soak into the medallion and the three-fingered hand suddenly flared as the thirteen symbols began to glow.

'They're coming,' said Medici as the cold morning air grew even colder.

'There!' said the valet as a nearby patch of grass began to steam and smoke as if it were being scorched by some intense heat from below. 'And there,' he repeated as several more patches appeared.

Even as they watched, the grass in each patch burned black and the smoke rose up to form columns of writhing shadow; thirteen columns of smoke that slowly coalesced into the forms of thirteen women. The women were thin and dressed in sackcloth with skin the colour of ash. The tops of their heads were shaved to leave a fringe of dark hair hanging down over their back and shoulders. And each of them wore a belt of rope from which hung various leather pouches plus a number of dark crystal spheres held in crude string nets.

The witches were largely indistinguishable from each other, but one individual stood out. Slightly taller and standing more upright, this woman had the bearing of a leader. Her ash-coloured face was marked by a white cross that extended across her eyes, down through her lips and up over her bald and cindered skull. For a moment the witches took in their surroundings and then the leader turned to look at Lord Medici.

'Who invokes the protection of the Juoda Pakta?' she asked.

'I do,' said Medici holding up the medallion.

'Against which threat?'

'A sorcerer,' said Medici. 'A man by the name of Decimus Fate.'

'The slayer,' said the witch and her sunken eyes seemed to pulse with darkness. 'This man is known to

233

us,' she continued with a sneer that revealed black and rotten teeth. 'It will be a pleasure for the dark sisters to serve.'

She gestured to one of her fellow witches who came forward to take the three pouches from the valet. As she did so, Medici noticed that the first finger from her left hand was missing.

'You will stay until he is dead?' asked Medici trying to hide his fear.

'Or until we take him alive,' said the witch.

39

Two of Him

The Butcher's cave was filled with a cold white light as Fate lay back on the waist-high block of stone. On the slab beside him lay the lifeless body of Alonso Medici.

'There's no need to do the whole body,' said Fate as he rested his head on the stone. 'We're about the same height, and of similar build, so just focus on the face, hands and some of the tattoos. But be careful not to copy them exactly,' he added. 'I wouldn't want you to get hurt.'

Samuel nodded his understanding. 'The process is painful,' he said. 'Normally it would be done over several different sessions.'

'We don't have time for that,' said Fate. 'Just do what you need to do.'

To one side of the cave stood the Tutor with Cradlop and Luca.

'It does hurt,' said Luca. 'I could only stand it for a few minutes at a time.'

'It's his choice,' said the Tutor looking at the concentration on Fate's face. 'People like Fate are no stranger to pain.'

Luca and Cradlop turned to look at the demon hunter. The Tutor was referring to the sorcerer, but somehow they knew that he was also talking about himself.

With everything ready, Samuel moved to stand between the two lying figures. Reaching out, he laid a hand on Fate's chest in the way a doctor might try to calm a nervous patient.

'Try to remain still,' he told the sorcerer. 'And just let me know if you want to stop.'

Fate dipped his head to show that he understood, and Samuel extended his arms until his hands hovered over the two men's faces. Then the big man closed his eyes, and the Tutor sensed a tingle of magical energy as Samuel's brows came together in a frown of concentration. The replicantis slowed his breathing and his pale body began to pulse with a faint white light. The pulse slowed until it matched the rhythm of Samuel's heartbeat and a faint mist began to form over the bare skin of his arms.

As the Tutor watched, he saw the mist flow down Samuel's arms until it was concentrated around his hands and filled the air above the faces of the two men on the slabs.

'This is when it starts to happen,' whispered Luca, and Cradlop made a guttural noise of agreement. 'It feels cold,' Luca went on. 'Like a cold mist that burns your skin with a thousand tiny pinpricks.'

The Tutor glanced at the young man who had gone through this procedure himself. Luca's own doppelganger had been stored away in a lower chamber that always remained cold. This delayed the process of decay, but they would need to dispose of the body soon.

'Look!' said Luca. 'Samuel is starting to copy Lord Fate.'

Looking back up to the slabs, the Tutor could now see a rhythmic pulse of light passing through the mist. The pulse began in the cloud covering Fate's face, travelled up the mist on Samuel's arm, across his shoulders and down to the other arm into the cloud of mist covering Alonso's face. Matched to the slow beating of Samuel's heart, the pulses of light continued in a series of gentle waves.

'It really does hurt,' murmured Luca, and now the Tutor could see Fate's hands clenched tight by his side as he resisted the pain of this magical process.

'By now it feels like your skin is being peeled away,' said Luca. 'It still feels cold, but it burns like hell.'

In the silence of the cave they could just hear the faint sound of Fate's constrained breathing; the only audible sign of the intense pain that he now endured.

'How long does it take?' asked the Tutor.

'A couple of hours for the face,' said Luca; 'a few more to do the hands and tattoos.'

'*Two hours for the face!*' thought the Tutor. He knew from his own experience that pain seemed to slow the passage of time, and he wondered if Fate would tap his hand to indicate that he needed a break.

But no, the stoic sorcerer remained still and uncomplaining. In fact, it was Samuel who needed to take breaks as the strain of the magical process took its toll. However, by early afternoon it was done. The pulsing white light faded, the mist dispersed and Samuel took a step backwards, stumbling with fatigue as he leaned on one of the slabs. Moving away from the wall, the others now came forward to see if he was all right.

'I'm fine,' said the replicantis. 'A little drained, but I'm fine.'

Luca held out a stone tumbler of water and then Cradlop helped Samuel over to the side of the cave where he sat down heavily on a crude stone bench.

Now, the Tutor turned his attention to Fate.

'Can you hear me?' he asked, for the sorcerer was still lying with his eyes closed and his hands clenched tight. 'Decimus?' pressed the Tutor. 'Are you...'

'Just give me a minute,' said Fate and slowly his fists unclenched and he opened his mouth to stretch the muscles of his jaw. 'That… was unpleasant,' he said, and the Tutor could only smile at the understatement.

Fate blinked a few times then he opened his eyes and took the Tutor's arm as he slowly sat up. He swung his legs over the side of the slab and gave a nod of thanks as the Tutor handed him a tumbler of water. The sorcerer took a few sips as the two men looked across to the body of Alonso Medici who was now the spitting image of Fate.

'That's uncanny,' said the Tutor, then he glanced at Fate who was studying 'himself' with a critical eye. 'Don't you find that unsettling?' continued the Tutor, 'to be looking at a perfect copy of yourself.'

The corners of Fate's mouth turned down and he raised his eyebrows as if it was not so unusual.

'I once knew a sorcerer who transfigured his own features to look like me.'

The Tutor just stared at him.

'The man tried to kill me and steal my identity.' Fate eased himself off the slab and went over to study Alonso more closely. 'That sorcerer's imitation was impressive, but it was nothing compared to this.' He leaned down to examine Samuel's work more closely. 'Incredible,' he breathed, then he reached out to open Alonso's eyes. 'And you even managed to replicate the eyes.'

'They caused me some trouble,' said Samuel as he sipped his water and rested his head against the wall of the cave. 'It was as if they resisted the process.'

'The eyes of a feral mage contain their own inherent magic,' said Fate. 'They're like a signature that can't be forged.'

'It looks just like you,' said Luca as he and Cradlop came over to view Samuel's work.

238

'Good,' said Fate. 'Lord Medici won't drop his guard unless he is convinced that I am dead.'

'What next?' asked Samuel.

'We wait for Weasel to return with Fate's clothes,' said the Tutor.

'He's here,' rumbled Cradlop as he turned towards the entrance to the cave. 'And someone else too.'

They turned to follow the line of his gaze and soon they could all hear the echoing sound of someone approaching.

'I got them,' said Weasel, holding up a bundle of Fate's robes as he entered the cave.

'Wait for me, you fleet-footed sewer rat!' said a voice behind him, and Fate recognised that familiar tone of annoyance.

It was Motina.

'She made me bring her,' said Weasel when he noticed the disapproving glint in Fate's dark eyes.

'You're damn right, I did,' said Motina as the small hunchbacked woman hobbled into the cave. 'If you are going up against the dark sisters of the Black Pact, then I am going with you.'

'But we're not going against the dark sisters,' said Fate. 'The whole idea is to get them to leave so we can get to Medici.'

Holding one of Fate's glowing blue crystals, Motina was watching where she put her feet. However, as she entered the brighter space she came to a stop and looked up, her small eyes bright with interest as she took in the various people in the cave.

'You must be Cradlop,' she said as she approached the broad-shouldered troglodyte.

Cradlop dipped his head.

'And Luca,' said Motina taking Madam de Lorni's son into a thin-armed embrace. 'Your mother misses you terribly.' She reached up to touch his face. 'I'm sorry we couldn't make things right for you.'

'I'm alive,' said Luca. 'And I'll see my mother again, someday.'

Motina's eyes glistened as she patted his cheek.

'And you must be Samuel,' she continued.

'I am,' said Samuel with a weary smile.

'I hear you're a replicantis,' said Motina. 'That skill began as a form of healing… did you know?'

Samuel nodded.

'My mother was a healer,' he said and Motina's face beamed with pleasure.

'Then I look forward to hearing all about her,' she said before turning to Fate with an expectant expression.

'And this,' said the sorcerer with a little shake of his head, 'is Varna Motina, my… housekeeper.'

With a small bow, Motina took her leave of Samuel and walked towards the two slabs at the centre of the cave.

'What are you doing here?' murmured Fate as she came closer. 'You should be resting.'

'I'm not as frail as I look.' Motina's tone was indignant.

'But you don't even have a wand,' insisted Fate.

Without looking at him, Motina held up a thin rod of hazel that had clearly just been freshly cut and trimmed from the garden. Fate gave a sigh.

'That won't tolerate any kind of power,' he hissed.

'It'll be enough to take down one of those Black Pact harpies,' said Motina as she moved forward to look at the dead body lying on the slab.

'Oh, may the heavens help us!' she cried as she looked from Fate to the transfigured body of Alonso. 'Now there are two of him!'

40

Deception

As Samuel worked on replicating Fate, so word began to spread about the reward for a sorcerer and the threat of retaliation if the sorcerer in question was not found. Not everyone in Guile heard this news. Such information tended to proliferate among the more unsavoury elements of a city, and there was always some confusion.

Was it *any* sorcerer?

And who *was* this person called Fate?

Most people in the city were unaware of such a man, while others knew him only as the Sage of Blackfell House, or the man in the charcoal grey robes. But one thing was certain... once Medici started killing random citizens then Fate's anonymity would come to an end.

'We need to act before sunset,' said Fate as he looked towards the main gate of Medici's mansion with Motina and the Tutor. 'The whole city will turn against me once people start dying, and I won't allow innocent people to be killed because of me.'

They were standing in the corner of a small park just up the road from the main entrance to Medici's grounds. A thick stand of laurel bushes provided the perfect hiding place. From here, they could not only watch the gate, they could also see through into the grounds themselves.

'We just have to hope that Medici is fooled by Samuel's handiwork,' said the Tutor. 'We can handle a few guards, but there's no way we can reach Medici with all those witches patrolling the grounds.'

They stopped talking as one of the witches came into view through the gate. Even from this distance they could see the dark shadow of the witch's sunken eyes.

'They look almost skeletal,' whispered Motina.

'That's the price you pay for dealing with the Daemonaria,' murmured the Tutor.

'And *that's* what they use as currency,' said Motina pointing towards the witch's belt.

Both Fate and the Tutor knew what she meant. She was referring to the dark crystal spheres hanging from the dark sisters' belts. Each of those spheres contained a Diminutian; the smallest type of faerie. The witches caught the faeries and sealed them into spheres for dealing with entities in the realm of demons.

'Just looking at these traitors makes my blood boil,' said Motina.

'Mine too,' murmured Fate, 'but the Tutor's right. It would be suicide to attack while Medici has their protection. Hopefully, he will dismiss them once he believes that I'm dead.'

'The idea of letting them get away makes me feel sick,' said Motina.

'I know,' said Fate. 'But your revenge will have to wait for another time.'

'Psst!'

They glanced round to see Weasel pushing his way through the bushes.

'Thirteen,' said the young wayfinder. 'We counted thirteen witches in the grounds.'

'A full coven,' said Motina and Fate nodded.

'And Veleno?' he asked.

From inside his shirt, Weasel produced Fate's dragon-handled dagger. 'He's on his way,' he said with a smile.

Fate dipped his head in acknowledgement as Weasel returned his dagger, then scowled as the wayfinder moved to join them. 'What are you doing?' asked the sorcerer.

'I'm staying to watch.'

'No,' said Fate. 'I need you to deliver a letter. And then you should go and say goodbye to Luca. He will be leaving for the coast tonight, as soon as Cradlop delivers his doppelganger to the river.'

Weasel's face fell. He hated missing out on the excitement although he would like to see Madam de Lorni's son one more time before he left the city for good.

'What letter?' he asked in a sulky tone.

'To Lord Medici's brother,' said Fate.

'Didn't Medici warn us against that?' asked the Tutor.

'I think we're beyond the point of warnings, don't you?' said Fate. 'Besides, the brother deserves to know what really happened to his daughter. And if we succeed in killing Medici, then he might just stop the rest of the family from coming after us.'

Reaching into a pocket, Fate pulled out a letter and a small pouch of coins.

'Take this to the East Gate pigeoneer,' he told Weasel. 'Tell him to use a reliable bird.'

Reluctantly, Weasel took the letter then his head came up as he heard a distinctive whistle.

'That's Kirsten,' he announced, referring to one of his fellow wayfinders. 'Master Veleno's here.'

Judging by the reaction of the guards on the gate, Weasel was right. Two of them moved to block the gate while a third called back towards the house. A few moments later, Lord Medici himself appeared in the gateway, flanked by the two shimmering patches of air and three of the Black Pact witches.

'Is it him?' Lord Medici asked the guards as he reached the gate and looked up the street to where Veleno was now approaching on his beautiful black stallion. 'Is he dead?'

The guards did not answer. They had no idea if the sorcerer called Fate was dead. All they knew was that the crime boss, known as Master Veleno, was riding towards them.

'Ah, my good friend Medici,' called out Veleno as he drew up to the gate. 'I am sorry to hear about the death of your son, but I have something here that might ease the pain of his passing.'

Veleno was accompanied by a retinue of six guards plus Xanda, his personal mage. He was also leading a second horse, across the saddle of which was draped the body of a man dressed in charcoal grey robes.

'This is it,' whispered the Tutor. 'Now we'll see if Veleno can be trusted.'

'I know how far I can trust Veleno,' said Fate. 'It's the witches that bother me.'

They then watched as Medici's guards came forward to take the body down from the horse. They laid the body on the driveway and stepped back as Lord Medici came forward with his personal valet just a few steps behind.

'It's him,' he said with a note of disbelief. 'It's really him.' He glanced at his guards as if he were looking to them to confirm Fate's identity. Two of the men nodded their concurrence and Medici looked back to Veleno. 'But how?' he asked. 'I was told this man was cunning and dangerous.'

'Indeed he was,' said Veleno, then he raised his voice as if he knew that Fate would be listening. 'But the fool turned his back on magic, and now… he's dead!'

Hidden by the leaves of the park, Fate smiled at Veleno's dramatics.

For a moment longer Medici stared down at Fate's face. 'You… have my thanks, Veleno,' he said.

'It's the least I could do to avenge your son,' said Veleno.

'Don't overdo it,' muttered Fate.

'Have you found Alonso's body yet?' asked Veleno and Medici's lip curled in anger as he was reminded of his son.

'No,' he snarled.

'You will,' said Veleno. 'I'm sure he isn't far away.'

'He just can't help himself, can he?' whispered the Tutor.

Veleno looked like he was trying to suppress a smile as he scanned the surrounding streets. The gesture seemed to suggest that he was looking for Medici's son, but Fate knew he was scanning the area for any sign of where *he* might be hiding.

'In the meantime,' continued Veleno, 'there was some mention of a reward…'

'Yes, yes,' said Medici, gesturing to his valet as he continued to stare down at the man in the charcoal grey robes.

From inside his doublet, the valet produced a large pouch of gold. He started towards Veleno who frowned as if the act of being paid in the street was somehow vulgar. After a moment's hesitation, the valet passed the reward to one of Veleno's men.

'Well if that's everything,' said the Lord of the City. 'Then I'll leave you to your grief and the continued search for your son.'

Lord Medici barely heard Veleno. Seemingly lost in thought, he continued to stare down at the body in the charcoal grey robes.

'What should we do with him?' asked one of the guards.

''What?' asked Medici distractedly.

'The sorcerer,' said the guard. 'What should we do with his body?'

'Oh,' said Medici, shaking his head as if to clear his thoughts then... 'Burn him!' he spat. 'Burn him to ash, and then burn the pile of drab stones that he calls a home.'

'Wait!'

The commanding voice stopped everyone in their tracks as one of the witches stepped forward.

'Maybe we should examine the slayer's body.'

Gesturing for one of her sisters to join her, the leader of the witches approached the body then stopped as Veleno's magic-user, Xanda, summoned a wall of protective force.

The leader of the witches frowned in suspicion.

'What are you doing?' she demanded.

'I am protecting the lives of myself and my lord,' said Xanda as he extended the wall of force to cover Master Veleno.

'From what?' asked the witch.

'From the tattoos on Lord Fate's skin,' said Xanda as if he were stating the obvious.

A glint of alarm flashed in the witch's eyes as she looked from Xanda to the body of Fate.

'The last time I crossed Fate he did this,' said Xanda, indicating the side of his face that was now formed from smoky black glass. 'Every day I live with agony and I have no wish to die from the tattoos that protect this sorcerer's flesh.'

The witch's face twisted with uncertainty as she glanced down at Fate's body where a number of tattoos

247

were visible on his wrists and neck. With a hiss of frustration, she gestured one of her sisters forward.

'You have knowledge of this protective art,' she began. 'Do you sense any danger in examining the body?'

Looking distinctly wary, the witch leaned forward, keeping her distance as she tried to see more of the tattoos.

'I have not seen these particular designs, but they do resemble inscriptions of power.'

Once more the leader of the witches hesitated.

'Enough of this,' cried Lord Medici. 'We'll burn his body, scatter the ashes and that will be an end to it. Now begone,' he told the witches. 'The sorcerer is dead and your presence is no longer required.'

The lead witch's voice took on a menacing tone.

'In Karuthia this man had a reputation for…'

'I don't care about his reputation,' snapped Medici. 'You have kept your side of the Black Pact bargain, and I have paid the appropriate fee. Now go.'

'As you wish,' said the leader, although the expression in her deep-set eyes was not one of obedience. Nevertheless, she made a sweeping gesture with her heron-skull wand and the coven of thirteen witches began to gather on the lawn.

'Thank you, Veleno,' said Medici as the Lord of the City turned to leave. 'I am in your debt.'

'Not at all,' said Veleno. With a final magnanimous wave he led his men away from the gate and Medici turned to the thirteen witches now gathered on his lawn.

From their hiding place, Fate and the others could only see three of the witches, but still they watched as each conjured smoke from their wands and weaved it around themselves until they were fully concealed. The columns of smoke then shimmered with a faint pulse of light and the smoke sank down into the earth, leaving nothing behind but another patch of scorched grass.

'Wow!' breathed Weasel, clearly impressed by this magical feat. 'Can you do that?' he asked Motina whose eyes were narrowed in thought as she stared at the spot where the leader of the witches had disappeared.

'What?' said Motina coming out of her reverie with an indignant humph. 'Can I sink down into the realm of demons just to save myself a few days of travel on the back of a horse?'

'It's more than a few days ride to Karuthia,' added Fate and Motina fixed him with a steely glare.

'No,' she said in a clipped tone. 'I can't.'

Fate put a hand on her arm to convey that he meant no harm. They then watched as Medici dismissed the additional guards he had posted around the grounds. Clearly relieved not to be facing a notorious sorcerer, the men ambled out of the gate and headed off towards the nearest tavern.

'You should get back to the house,' Fate told Motina as the guards disappeared from view. 'And *you* need to send that letter,' he added to Weasel.

'So you're still going after Medici?' asked Motina.

'I have to,' said Fate. 'Right now his guard is down, but sooner or later he will find out that I'm not dead and he won't make the same mistake twice.'

'Maybe I should...' began Motina, but Fate cut her off.

'No,' he said. 'This task is for me and Alexander. Besides...' he added with a glint in his gold-flecked eyes. 'I have a plan.'

'I'm sure you do,' said Motina with a familiar arched brow. 'Come on,' she said to Weasel. 'You send that letter, say goodbye to Luca, and then meet me back at the house for some supper.'

Even the mention of food was not enough to tempt Weasel away, but he knew he had no choice. Reluctantly he hung his head and followed Motina out of the park before they went their separate ways. As they disappeared from view, Fate turned to the Tutor.

'Are you ready?'

The Tutor nodded. 'What do you have in mind?'

'I think we wait for those additional guards to get out of earshot and then go in over the wall. If you enter through Alonso's quarters you can announce your presence and draw Medici out into the garden.'

'Into the garden?' queried the Tutor.

'More room to fight, and quicker to escape if more guards arrive,' said Fate.

The Tutor frowned. He had the distinct impression there was something that Fate was not telling him.

'And those patches of air that follow Medici around... have you figured out what they are?'

'I have my suspicions,' said Fate.

'And?' said the Tutor, his tone making it clear how frustrating Fate's vagueness could be.

'I think they're Don'Sha'Vir,' said Fate; 'Don'Sha'Vir with their presence masked by an enchantment of concealment.'

'And you think I can handle two of them?' asked the Tutor. 'In addition to Medici's guards?'

'I think we'll be fine,' said Fate with that infuriating smile, 'just so long as we can draw them out into the garden.'

'Whatever you say,' said the Tutor. 'But if things get too hairy then I'm high-tailing it over the wall.' Placing a hand on the hilt of his Hadean blade, he pushed through the laurel bushes and checked to make sure the coast was clear. 'After all,' he added as he stepped out into the street. 'It wasn't me who killed Medici's son.'

Fate's smile broadened as he followed the demon hunter round to a point where some trees made it easier to climb over the boundary wall of Medici's grounds. The wealthy nobleman had tried to kill them and now it was time for Lord Alfredo Medici to pay the price.

*

Motina was only a few hundred yards from the Medici mansion when a worrying thought crept into her mind. They had all seen the Black Pact witches departing from the gardens, but Motina recalled the leader's reluctance to leave and now Motina was wondering if the smoke from the leader's column had fully disappeared into the grass.

No... something felt wrong and Motina came to a stop.

The dark sisters were evil and cunning. In Karuthia they had been dismissed as a small and insignificant cult and yet the damage they had done was horrific. The magic-users of Karuthia had underestimated them and Varna Motina would not make the same mistake twice. She was not sure what assistance she might be able to provide, but if her suspicions were correct, then simply warning Fate and the Tutor might be enough.

Turning around, she hobbled as quickly as she could, following the boundary wall to the point where Fate and the Tutor had decided to enter. The branches of the trees were conveniently placed, but for a woman of Motina's crooked build they were a significant obstacle. Slowly she worked her way up until she could see over the wall. And there she stood, breathing heavily and looking through the autumn leaves to the garden beyond.

'Now we'll see if you've really gone,' she murmured to herself.

Halfway to the house, she could just make out a figure in charcoal grey robes tucked into the folds of some dense conifers. And further on, crouched like a shadow before a pair of glazed patio doors, was the black-clad figure of the Tutor. For a few moments, the demon hunter appeared to be working at the doors and then a gap opened up and he slipped inside, but only a minute passed before there was a shout from inside the house.

Candles flared in the windows of the house and now Motina could see movement inside. A moment later the Tutor appeared back at the open doors where he actually stopped as if he was waiting for someone to catch up.

'It's the hunter!' came Lord Medici's frantic cry from inside the room. 'The demon hunter's in the garden! Where the hell are my guards?'

'What on earth are they playing at,' muttered Motina as the Tutor slowly backed away from the doors.

He was halfway to Fate's position when a guard came charging around the side of the house with his sword drawn. Catching sight of the leather-clad demon hunter, the man charged forward, sword swinging as he came, but the Tutor avoided the attack with ease before slamming his elbow into the man's face. The guard dropped heavily on the grass and lay still.

Another guard now appeared from the opposite direction while a third burst out of the patio doors. The first of these new guards aimed a downward attack, but the Tutor sidestepped quickly, caught his arm and flipped the guard onto his back before delivering a kick to the man's jaw. The man's body slumped, insensible, and the

252

Tutor turned to face the guard who had emerged from the doors. This man was more cautious, attacking the Tutor with controlled thrusts and cuts. Once again the demon hunter evaded the attacks before catching the man's wrist and pulling him off balance. As the man stumbled forward, the Tutor got behind him, taking him in a grappling hold with one arm clamped around the man's neck. Holding the man securely, the Tutor stepped back as Lord Medici emerged from the house.

From her vantage point, Motina could not see the two shimmering patches of air, but she could sense their presence.

'He has protection,' she breathed as she watched the Tutor back away, the man in his grip slowly becoming weaker as the Tutor constricted the blood vessels in his neck. The guard finally went limp and the Tutor dropped the unconscious body at his feet.

As Lord Medici continued to advance the two patches of air became visible as they took on human form, and Motina gasped. They were like the desert robed figure that had caught her in the alley, only the silk robes of these nomads were not red. They were black.

Alonso Medici had employed the protection of a Don'Sha'Vir, which when translated means "the blind that see" but the two figures that guarded the life of *Lord* Medici were even more powerful. These two lethal assassins were known as the Don'Sha'Mort, 'the blind that kill'.

As the two robed figures took on their true form so the Tutor drew his sword and, even from a distance, Motina could see that the crystal in the sword's pommel had begun to glow. Now Fate stepped out from behind the trees and Lord Medici gave an animal snarl of rage.

'You!' he cried. 'But you're dead!'

'Clearly not,' said Fate and Motina wondered why he sounded so calm. 'You and your son tried to kill me and my friends,' Fate went on. 'And that is something I cannot allow to pass.'

Spitting with fury, Medici spoke through clenched teeth.

'Don't threaten me, wizard! You might have fooled me once, but now you really will die,' he added with wicked glee. 'Did you really think my son would have better protection than me?' Here he glanced at the Tutor. 'Your pet demon hunter might have bested my son's Don'Sha'Vir, but even he is no match for *two* of the Don'Sha'Mort.'

Even now, Fate did not seem overly concerned and Motina shifted position as she saw him reach up to the left shoulder of his robes. He took hold of something, although it was too far away for Motina to see what it was.

'Ah, the arrogance of the rich,' said Fate. 'Always so confident in the protection they can buy, but no Alfredo, it is you who will die tonight.'

Reaching out his hand Fate made as if to drop something then stopped as if an invisible force had caught hold of his arm.

And now Motina sensed something else... the shadow of a dark soul over to her left. Quickly her eyes scanned for the source and there it was, a column of dark smoke that coalesced into the form of a woman dressed in sackcloth with a shaved head and a crude white cross drawn across the sunken features of her face. It was the leader of the Black Pact witches and she held her heron-skull wand at arm's length as she slowly advanced on Fate.

Lord Medici was clearly surprised by the sudden appearance of the witch, but he recovered his composure quickly and smiled.

'You were saying?' he asked of Fate. 'Something about one of us going to die?' He glanced at the Tutor as if he knew the man was doomed then, with a wave of his hand, he directed the Don'Sha'Mort to attack.

41

Evening the Odds

The moment he felt the invisible force, Fate knew exactly what it was. The magic that held him had the distinctive signature of a witch; earthy and organic, not the polished energy of someone who had spent years perfecting their art. But the purity of this energy had been corrupted. What originally sprang from the living forces of nature was now poisoned and tainted by the befouling touch of the Daemonaria. And yet that connection to the demon realm made the magic more powerful, so powerful that Fate could not break free.

Craning his neck around, he saw the leader of the Black Pact witches standing on the grass, arm outstretched and pointing at him with the bleached shard of a heron-skull wand. Fate tried to pull away, but his arm felt like it was trapped in a bed of hot sand. Cursing his carelessness, he glanced at the Tutor who adopted a defensive stance as the black-robed Don'Sha'Mort attacked.

The two desert warriors came in fast, one throwing out a mental snare to pull the Tutor off balance, while the other cast forth a screed of magic shale that burned into the demon hunter's armour, clothes and skin alike. And as they came, they drew their swords, two curved blades shining black and wicked sharp.

The Tutor stumbled slightly from the pull of mental force. He squinted against the spray of burning stones, but other than that he remained composed. As soon as the Don'Sha'Mort appeared he realised there would be no time for a slow build-up of tempo, no feeling out an opponent before launching an attack. No, on this occasion he needed to explode into violence and that is precisely what he did.

Fate had now seen the Tutor fight on a number of occasions and he was always impressed by the man's speed and skill, but this was something more. In the fading light, the heart-stone in the pommel of the Tutor's blade flared brightly as he charged forward to meet his opponents who seemed surprised by the fact that he had chosen to attack.

The three combatants became a blur of rapid movement and lethal steel. Meanwhile, Lord Medici was screaming at the witch who still held Fate in her magical grip.

'Kill him!' he cried.

'I can't,' hissed the witch. 'He is trying to do something that has the touch of magic. If I let him go then he might succeed.'

Focussing his mind, Fate tried again to move his hand, tried to let go of the tiny object he was holding. His willpower was far stronger than the witch's, but without using *his* magic he could not break free of hers.

'Sisters!' cried the leader as she attempted to recall the other members of the coven. 'If you have not yet completed the journey home, then return to me... return to me now.'

Her voice was tight with the effort of restraining Fate while the Tutor continued to do battle with the Dan'Sha'Mort.

At first it looked like the demon hunter would be overwhelmed, but the mystic warriors had never faced a Hadean blade before. Normally they would add magical attacks to the physical assault, but now they needed to channel power into their swords to prevent them from being cloven in two by the Tutor's glowing blade. This effectively negated their magical powers, levelling the confrontation and turning it into a competition of martial skill, a quality in which Alexander Teuton excelled.

The exchange between them was fast and brutal. For all his skill, the Tutor struggled to counter the attacks from two deadly opponents. It was only a matter of time before one of those curved blades found its way through his defences so he went on the attack once more. With a series of kicks and vicious sword cuts he closed on one Don'Sha'Mort and slammed the pommel of his sword into the side of the nomad's head. The blindfolded figure stumbled backwards, the arcane symbols branded in his skin flaring with light as their unholy magic resisted the force of the blow.

The second Don'Sha'Mort now took the opportunity to attack, but once again the Tutor was too fast and, with a rapid cut, his sword sliced down across the nomad's face and chest. The glowing blade nicked the Don'Sha'Mort's jaw and cut a gash into his neck and chest. The nomad fell onto his back, his free hand trying to staunch the flow of blood from the mortal wound on his neck.

And then several things happened at once…

The Tutor dropped his sword as the first Don'Sha'Mort struck his arm with a bolt of magical force…

Three more columns of smoke rose up from the ground as three more witches appeared on the lawn…

And the leader of the witches smiled as she realised that victory was now theirs.

'Heal the Don'Sha'Mort,' she commanded one of the witches. Then… 'Lend me your strength,' she told the remaining two who drew their wands as they prepared to give the leader enough magical energy to kill Fate.

And through all this, Fate continued to struggle against the force that held him fast. To one side, he saw one of the witches kneel beside the wounded Don'Sha'Mort. Using her wand, the woman opened a rift into the Daemonaria before untying the dark crystal spheres from her belt. Despite his own predicament, Fate felt sick. He knew that the faeries inside those crystals could be traded for healing powers from the demonic realm.

To the other side, Fate saw that the Tutor had now lost his sword to a bolt of magical force.

Such a blast of magic would have broken the demon hunter's arm were it not for the tattoo on his chest. Beneath his black leather doublet, the enchanted tattoo shone brightly as it absorbed the deadly magic. The Tutor had no time to retrieve his sword as the uninjured Don'Sha'Mort attacked him once more. The assassin aimed a downward blow and, with no sword to block it, the Tutor reached up to catch the mystic's arm. The two figures now grappled for dominance and the Tutor might have prevailed, but then the Don'Sha'Mort's body flared with magical flames as his entire body was engulfed in a burst of immolation. The demon hunter tattoo might allow the Tutor to resist the magical flames for a few seconds, but any longer and his flesh would begin to burn.

Seeing all this, Fate clenched his jaw in frustration. If he could not release the object he was holding they were both going to die. Using every ounce of strength he possessed, he tried to open his fingers as he forced his hand down towards the ground.

The leader of the witches gave a hiss of effort as she began to lose her grip on Fate.

'Sisters, help me!' she cried and Fate's body froze as the two remaining witches added their strength to her own.

'What are you waiting for?' cried Medici. 'Kill him now!'

The leader's withered lips drew back in a snarl as tendrils of black smoke suddenly rose up from the grass at Fate's feet. The dark smoke spread up Fate's body before streaming into his eyes, nose and mouth. His vision darkened and his breath was choked off as the smoke filled his lungs. With just seconds of consciousness remaining, he made a final effort to open his fingers, but now the power of three dark witches was focused on him and there was no way he could break free.

Meanwhile, the dark sister trying to heal the injured Don'Sha'Mort was kneeling between the assassin and the rift that glowed with the angry light of fire. Taking one of the crystal spheres, the witch spoke the words of a spell, trading the life-force of a faerie for the power to heal the Don'Sha'Mort. Putting one hand on the assassin's chest, she crushed the sphere to reveal a small male faerie. Grasping the tiny body, she thrust the faerie into the demonic flames, gasping with pain as she snatched her hand back from the rift from where a high-pitched scream of anguish could now be heard.

And there it was...

The Tutor struggled, Fate began to fade, and a faerie writhed in agony as Varna Motina struck.

It had taken the housekeeper several frustrating minutes to clamber over the wall before scrabbling down on the other side. Her thin arms were not long enough for her to reach the ground and she twisted an ankle as she landed among the bushes inside Medici's grounds.

Cursing her frailty, she pushed her way through the bushes and limped onto the lawn where she could see the Tutor wrestling with the Don'Sha'Mort who was now covered in a skin of dark flames. She saw Fate still frozen in place, his body wreathed in clouds of dark smoke. And finally she saw the witch kneeling beside the wounded Don'Sha'Mort. She saw the foul woman break the crystal sphere before placing a faerie into the furnace heat of the demonic realm. Motina heard the cry of unspeakable pain as the faerie's life-force was converted into healing energy. The cut in the Don'Sha'Mort's neck closed up with unnatural speed and the witch rejoined her sisters as the wounded mystic got back to his feet.

Horrified by all the evil on show, Motina drew the thin piece of hazel she was using as a wand. She knew the green stick could not withstand much power, but it was all she had. Drawing in the natural forces from all the plants and animals in Medici's garden she bound that energy to her own and channelled it through the soft fibres of her wand.

A twisting shaft of light shot out of the wand which split and burst asunder in Motina's hand. It was all the wand could handle, but it was enough. The burst of light struck the leader of the witches in the shoulder, burning her dress and searing the withered flesh of her face. With a scream of pain, the leader staggered to the side, her dress and face smoking from the force of Motina's spell.

Recovering quickly, the leader turned to see where this attack had come from, as did her three dark sisters standing close by. All four witches stared at Motina who stood her ground as she met the fury in their sunken eyes. The four witches immediately recognised Motina as a magic-user from Karuthia, one of the few who had escaped the genocide that they had helped to commit.

Their faces were filled with hatred and arrogance. They were four, all strong and hale, and each with a heron-skull wand, while the housekeeper was small, frail and wandless.

And yet Motina smiled.

She smiled, and a fierce fire burned in her small black eyes.

'Oh, Tu niekšinga ir be krūtų paršavedė,' she said in Karuthian. 'Leisk man supažindinti jus... su Likimu.'

Which, roughly translated meant...

'Oh, you vile breastless sows. Let me introduce you... to Fate.'

At this, the four witches looked round to see that Fate was no longer frozen with his arm stretched out, no longer straining to release the thing he held between his finger and thumb. The sorcerer was now kneeling on the grass. The black smoke still lingered around his body, but his dark eyes glittered with gold as he pushed the tiny parasol of a dandelion seed into the earth of Medici's lawn.

'NO!' screamed the leader of the witches as the air was suddenly filled with the scent of silver celandine.

With the witches now focused on Fate, Motina hobbled past to see if she could save the faerie. Throwing herself to the ground she reached into the rift from where the screams of the tortured soul still pierced the evening air. The intense heat burnt Motina's arm, but she did not pull away as she searched for the tiny form of the Diminutia. Finally, her fingers closed around something more delicate than a fledgling wren and she withdrew her arm, the skin of which was now blistered and burned. Ignoring her own pain, Motina cradled the tiny faerie to her chest and summoned all the healing power she could muster, hoping against hope that this desperate soul had not endured too much.

Even as Motina slumped back from the rift, so the lawn bucked with a pulse of power and the four witches stared at the spot where Fate had planted the seed.

'What?' cried Lord Medici. 'What's happening?' and then he looked on in horror as a whirlwind of dandelion seeds suddenly erupted from the ground writhing and twisting until they dissipated to reveal the tall figure of a man, or rather a faerie that looked like a man. Dressed in dark green robes that swirled like smoke, the figure took a moment to take in his surroundings as a dozen pale blue orbs appeared in the air around him.

It was Carduus, Lord of the Thistleblade Sword. When he first appeared he wore a smile of dark amusement. However, as he absorbed the scene, his expression changed to one of anger. Eyes of liquid silver began to glow like white-hot steel and a low growl rose in his throat as he looked at the dark spheres hanging from the witches' belts. His gaze then shifted to the Don'Sha'Mort, one now standing after being healed, and one covered in flames as he grappled a demon hunter with deep blue eyes. The frown on the faerie lord's brow deepened as he recognised the Don'Sha'Mort as men who had been empowered by the sacrifice of faerie souls.

'And what do we have here?' he asked in a dark and menacing tone.

'This is private property!' cried Medici with the arrogance of a man who had not yet realised that all his wealth and power suddenly meant nothing.

Carduus looked at him with utter contempt before switching his gaze back to the witches and the Don'Sha'Mort.

'I think it's time we evened up the odds, don't you?' he asked of no one in particular, and then he gave a sigh as the twelve blue orbs assumed their faerie form, transforming into the warrior sprites known as Lannari. 'It would appear the demon hunter has lost his sword,' said Carduus and four of the Lannari flew down to lift the Hadean Blade from the ground. 'And maybe we should give him a little space so he can face his opponent man-to-man, or man-to-monstrosity, as appears to be the case.'

The smile in the faerie's eyes was dark and mirthless as *green* vines now snaked up from the grass to pull the burning Don'Sha'Mort away from the Tutor who drew a breath of relief to be free of the flames. Then he opened his hand as the Lannari held out his sword.

'I'm sure the demon hunter would like to conclude this combat himself,' suggested the faerie lord.

'Indeed, I would,' answered the Tutor and a touch of warmth crept into Carduus's eyes.

'Then my daughters shall dispatch the second abomination, while I destroy four murdering whores who despoil the very idea of what it means to be a witch.'

The faerie lord turned back to the witches then staggered as three bolts of shadow-force punched into his body while a fourth attack summoned a swarm of faerbane flies, the bite from which could be deadly to faeries.

Strong as they were, the shadowy bolts of energy seemed to have little effect on Carduus. The faerie's swirling green robes simply absorbed the attacks, only darkening slightly as the harmful energy was dispersed. As for the flies... they formed a dense cloud that flew straight for his face, but Carduus merely lowered his brow and uttered a single word.

'Sruthán,' he said in the language of Faerie... burn.

264

The swarm of faerbane flies instantly ignited, each one glowing brightly for a second before falling to the ground in a shower of black ash.

'Withdraw!' cried the leader of the Black Pact witches as she realised this enemy was beyond their power to defeat. The other three witches needed no further command and the ground at their feet grew black as each of them began to disappear within a rising column of smoke.

'I think not,' said Carduus and reaching out his hands he appeared to take hold of the three escaping witches, his fingers curving into claws as if he could snag their souls in his grasp. Fearing for their lives, the witches increased the power of their inter-planar spells, straining to break free of the faerie's grip.

Seeing that Carduus was occupied with her three sisters, the leader decided she had just enough time to end the life of a magic-user who had escaped the Karuthian purge. As her own column of smoke curled about her body, the leader raised her wand to aim a lethal spell at Motina who was still cradling the injured Diminutia.

The deadly curse was forming in the witch's throat, but it failed to reach her lips as Fate stabbed her with a dragon-handled dagger. The witch's sunken eyes went wide, black and empty as the pits of hell and then the veins beneath her skin shone white as her link to the demonic realm was cauterised.

All the power she had bought with the suffering of others was suddenly expunged. She turned to look at Fate, her face contorted with rage, but the sorcerer was not intimidated. With one swift motion, he whipped the blade of his dagger across the woman's throat. She collapsed in a heap of sackcloth and withered flesh, her blood spilling like fine black sand from the ragged gash on her throat.

To either side, her three sisters were being slowly pulled down to the ground where the grass of Medici's lawn seemed to have melted away to reveal a dense tangle of crimson-stemmed brambles. But these were no ordinary brambles... these were rubus carnivora, a dangerous plant from the Wilderlands of Faerie. Their barbed stems hooked the unwary, digging deeper and tighter as one struggled to break free. And thus the victim would be held; bound by hooked cords, slowly dying until their decaying corpses broke down to feed the soil in which the carnivora grows.

Fate watched the witches struggle to break free as Carduus pulled them down into the Wilderlands of Faerie until they vanished and the grass of Medici's lawn reappeared.

And, even as the witches met their end, so the two Don'Sha'Mort were coming close to their own. The one who had been recently healed now found himself beset by a dozen armour-clad faeries. At only ten inches tall, the Lannari were fast and deadly. Bourne upon blue translucent wings, the silver-skinned faeries darted in; slashing with their swords until the Don'Sha'Mort's clothes were torn and his body was lacerated with a hundred bloody wounds. Despite his fury, and the frantic use of magical fire, the desert warrior was dying.

The black-robed figure slumped to one knee as the tendons at the back of one leg were cut. He swiped at a faerie who flitted away as one of her sisters zipped in to slash a vein in the Don'Sha'Mort's neck. The brands in his skin flared red as he tried to heal himself, but the number of cuts was too many, his demonic power too weak.

Finally, the Lannari withdrew, hovering above their defeated foe like lanterns in some enchanted glade. While a few paces to one side, the other Don'Sha'Mort met a similar fate on the point of a Hadean Blade.

Now facing just one opponent, the Tutor regained his composure and prepared himself for a duel to the death. Likewise, the Don'Sha'Mort levelled his blindfolded gaze as he attacked with fire before sweeping in with his scything blade, but the Tutor was ready for him.

The tattoo on his chest flared with energy as it absorbed the force of the Don'Sha'Mort's flames and there followed an impressive display of martial skill until the Tutor's blade whipped up to sever his opponent's wrist. The Don'Sha'Mort's sword fell to the ground and the Tutor spun round to deliver a deep cut to the nomad's stomach. The desert assassin staggered forward, reaching for the Tutor with his remaining hand, a hand that glowed red hot.

The Tutor did not even try to avoid the searing hand and the shoulder of his leather doublet smoked as he drove the point of his sword into the Don'Sha'Mort's chest. Once again the arcane brands in this nomad's skin glowed red, but slowly the light dimmed and the heat faded from the assassin's hand. The Don'Sha'Mort slumped backwards, the hole in his chest smoking as he slid from the Tutor's blade.

'Stop!' came a desperate cry and all eyes turned to Lord Medici.

Seeing his protectors defeated, Medici had tried to flee until two Lannari flew down to block his path. Now he stood beside the demonic rift with two of the dark spheres in his hands. Each one contained a tiny faerie, both of whom would die if the spheres were thrown into the fiery rift.

'Stop!' he cried again as one of the Lannari edged closer. 'Stop or I throw these into the rift.'

'That would be unwise,' said Fate as gold streaks glittered in his dark brown eyes. He glanced to one side to see if the Tutor was close enough to intervene, but the demon hunter was too far away. He looked at Motina who might have been able to hold him with magic if she only had a wand. In the air above the lawn, the twelve Lannari started to move until Medici bent closer to the rift.

'Don't!' he cried. 'I'll do it, I swear.' The Lannari stopped as Medici turned to look at Carduus. 'Surely we can come to some arrangement,' Medici went on. 'I have many precious gems and gold... so much gold that you wouldn't believe.'

Medici's wealth was without question, but no faerie would sell the life of another for something so base as gold. Fate could feel the fury rising in Carduus's chest and, from that moment, he knew that Medici was doomed.

42

Taxus Eternus

Lord Medici's eyes were wide with desperation as he faced the intimidating faerie. His last hope was that his vast wealth would be enough to save his life. Over the years he had dealt with witches and paid a king's ransom for the protection of beings who gained their power from the demonic realm. His wealth and standing had always saved him, but the fair folk of the Blessed Realm cannot be bought. Their allegiance can only be earned.

Medici waited for an answer then flinched as Carduus suddenly produced a dandelion flower with all the flair of a town-square conjurer. He watched as the faerie lord breathed on the yellow flower causing the petals to wilt, giving way to a seed-head that unfurled to produce what children called a dandelion clock. Medici appeared tense and mesmerised, staring at Carduus as if he had expected a powerful spell instead of mere sleight of hand. But then Carduus held the seed-head to his lips, drew a breath and…

Poof!

The faerie lord exhaled with such force that the dandelion seeds shot forth like a cloud of miniature darts. Medici barely had time to close his eyes as the seeds flew into his body, piercing flesh and clothes with hundreds of tiny pinpricks. Cautiously he opened his eyes and then he smiled as he realised the 'attack' had done no damage at all. In fact it had barely even hurt.

'Now,' he said in a tone of growing confidence. 'Are we going to negotiate or shall I throw your kin into the fires of hell?'

Watching from nearby, Fate's gaze darkened as he watched Medici try to blow one of the seeds from the back of his hand. It was as if the sorcerer knew what was about to take place, and he knew it was not good.

'Why, the damn things won't come off!' cursed Medici as he tried to brush the seeds from his clothes. Still keeping hold of the dark crystal spheres, he tried to pull one of the seeds from the flesh of his hand, but his mouth stretched wide with pain as the seed tugged at his skin. 'It won't come off!' he said again and now his tone was edged with panic as he felt each of the pinpricks swell with pain as the dandelion seeds began to root.

'What's happening?' he cried as the roots spread beneath his skin. 'By the gods, I can feel them...'

Medici collapsed to his knees and a low moan of pain emerged from his mouth as each of the seeds grew into a small dandelion plant. But the faerie magic did not stop there. The plants continued to grow and Medici screamed as they fed on his flesh until the wealthy man was completely covered in leaves. No longer screaming, Medici's body convulsed as the plants began to flower. His limbs twitched, and his chest heaved until the flowers opened and his chest ceased to move.

Lord Medici was dead, his flesh becoming mere compost to feed the enchanted plants. And even as Fate and the others watched, those nutrients were all used up. The green leaves withered as the flowers gave way to seed-heads and then each of these puffed into the air releasing thousands of miniature parasols that flew up to form a cloud, a cloud of dandelion seeds that would now add to the power of a faerie lord.

Carduus let out a breath and rolled his head as if to ease a certain stiffness in his neck. Lord Medici's body was now nothing more than a discarded pile of skin and bones wrapped in the remnants of a rich man's clothes. As the Lannari flew down to free their fellow faeries from the crystal spheres, so Carduus moved to stand beside Fate who was now kneeling beside Motina.

'Are you all right?' asked Fate as he tried to assess the damage to Motina's arm.

'Allow me,' said Carduus.

Kneeling beside the injured witch, he gently took the Diminutia from Motina's hands before handing it to one of the Lannari.

'I think he will live,' said Motina, her voice tight from the pain of her burns.

'He will live because of you, Raven Mother,' said Carduus.

Then the faerie lord produced two more plants from thin air, one a silvery bulb that resembled garlic and the other a spear-shaped succulent leaf with barbs along its edge. Carduus crushed them both between his hands muttering what sounded like the lines of a poem before opening his hands to reveal a cloud of silvery mist which he then spread over the burns on Motina's hand and arm. The mist slowly condensed to leave a sheen of silver on Motina's blistered skin.

'Thank you,' she breathed as she felt the pain recede.

'No,' said Carduus. 'Thank you.' He glanced up as one of the Lannari flew down to place a splintered length of hazel in his hands. 'It was you who broke the witch's grip that allowed Lord Fate to summon me. And you did it with *this*!' he added with a note of disbelief.

Carduus held up the shattered wand, waggling it about as if to accentuate just how flimsy the magical aid had been. Then he turned to Fate with a note of censure in his voice.

'I think such a devoted companion deserves a better weapon than this, don't you?' he asked and for once, Fate appeared flustered.

'She only recently lost her wand,' he said. 'I was going to replace…'

'I'm sure you were,' said Carduus as if the sorcerer was making excuses. Then, reaching into his robes he drew forth another dandelion flower before turning to Motina as if he were asking her permission. 'If it please you?'

'Of course,' said Motina a little shyly, and Carduus smiled as he passed the dandelion flower to one of the Lannari who flitted around the lawn for a moment before stopping at a particular spot.

'You're sure?' asked Carduus and the Lannari cocked her head as if he should know better than to ask.

The Lord of the Thistleblade Sword smiled as he moved to the spot where the Lannari was holding the dandelion flower, then, taking hold of the flower, he split the stem with his thumbnail and opened it up to reveal a narrow slit in the fabric of reality. The split stem now formed the edges of an opening into the realm of Faerie.

For a moment Carduus looked into the opening then he gave a nod and reached through. His lips compressed as he gave a pinch of effort and then he withdrew his hand which was now holding a slender branch from some strange Faerie tree.

Nodding in satisfaction, Carduus passed the thin branch to the Lannari who gathered round before going to work with their small sharp blades. And as they worked, Carduus began to recite…

I went out to the elder woods, a flower to cut my bride

But found instead a wand of yew, in the light of eventide

I cut the stem with a silver blade, to keep the pure sap true

And gave instead to a warrior maid, her enemies to rue

Even as he finished the verse, so the Lannari finished their work and Carduus opened his hand to receive a smooth rod of wood.

'And gave instead to a warrior maid, her enemies to rue,' he repeated and then he bent down to offer the wand to Motina. 'I think this is more fitting for one so brave,' he added with a smile.

Motina appeared stunned while Fate just smiled. Over the years he had often wondered if he had done the right thing by defying a Faerie Queen to save Carduus, but now he was sure. Faerie justice could be a cruel unfathomable thing. It was not to be trifled with, but neither was it perfect. Verdicts were often passed in the heat of passion, which sometimes meant that such verdicts were unjust. He wondered if the Faerie Queen known as Lonrúil Croí would ever see it that way.

'So this was your plan?' said the Tutor as he came to stand beside Fate.

'Yes,' said Fate.

'Well, you might have told me that you had a Faerie Lord at your beck and call.'

'Medici consorted with people who trafficked faeries,' said Fate. 'I knew Carduus would be only too happy to help.'

'Faeries are terrifying,' said the Tutor as he watched Carduus stand up from Motina.

'So why did you marry one?' asked Fate, for the Tutor had been married to a woman of Faerie blood.

'Because they can be wonderful too,' said the Tutor and Fate could hear the sudden thickness in his voice.

'Indeed they can,' said the sorcerer. 'Indeed they can.'

They both grew silent as Carduus came to stand beside them and together they watched as the Lannari transformed back into blue spheres of light, taking with them the Diminutia faeries they had now rescued from the dark crystal spheres.

'What will you do with them?' asked Fate.

'We'll take them to the edge of the Wilderlands and push them through into the domain of Lonrúil Croí.'

'But you're forbidden from entering the queen's domain.'

'That's true,' said Carduus. 'And my presence is sure to bring the border guards running, but instead of finding me, they'll find the diminutia and then the queen will care for them.'

'Are you sure?' asked the Tutor.

'Oh, yes,' said Carduus. 'Lonrúil Croí might be angry with me, but she values the lives of all faeries regardless of their size.'

Fate smiled as the cloud of dandelion seeds began to swirl as Carduus prepared to leave.

'I'm glad we were able to save these souls from torment,' he began. 'But the debt between you and I remains. No, don't object,' he added with a twinkle in his liquid silver eyes. 'I won't pester you every day of the year; simply rest assured that from now on... I will be keeping an eye on Fate.'

With a final smile, the smoke-robed figure disappeared as he was swallowed up in a whirling cloud of seeds.

'And don't forget what I told you about Bohr,' came his voice as Fate and the Tutor raised a hand to shield their eyes. 'The emperor's sorcerer is getting bolder. If he collects enough power from his chamber of blue tiles then what happened in Karuthia could befall the entire world.'

And with that, the Lord of the Thistleblade Sword was gone.

'Well, *he* knows how to make an exit,' said the Tutor as the storm of seeds disappeared in a swirl of glowing sparks. 'But what did he mean about Bohr? Is the emperor's sorcerer planning a new purge?'

'I think Bohr's ambitions go far beyond the idea of another purge,' said Fate. 'But there's no time to talk about that now. We should get back to the house before the rest of Medici's guards return from the tavern.'

Crossing the lawn, he moved to help Motina to her feet.

'Can you walk?' he asked as the witch swayed a little.

'I'm fine,' Motina replied. 'My, but that faerie healing is some powerful stuff.'

Carduus's healing salve had reduced the pain of her burned arm, but her twisted ankle was still painful and she was grateful when the Tutor offered her his arm.

'Are we going?' he asked when Fate hesitated.

'Just a minute,' said the sorcerer as he walked towards the Medici mansion.

The shadowy figures of several servants could be seen at various windows, but Fate walked directly to the patio doors where a particular servant now ducked back from view.

'You have nothing to fear,' said Fate as he looked in through the patio doors where Medici's valet now cowered behind a cabinet. 'Not from me, at least.'

The valet peered out from cover. 'What will you do now?' he asked.

'Me... nothing,' said Fate. 'But Lord Medici's brother now knows the truth about his daughter's death. He is probably on his way here as we speak.'

In the dark room, the valet's face grew pale.

'I had nothing to do with that,' he cried. 'And I never took part in their crimes.'

'But you remained in service and you never took steps to stop them,' said Fate.

The man's fear was almost palpable.

'What should I do?'

'If I were you,' said Fate, 'I would make an appointment with the authorities. Speak to someone you can trust, someone like Captain Monetti of the city guard. I've heard that he is an honourable man. Tell him everything you know about the Medicis' crimes and then leave the city and look for a position where you don't have to sell your soul just to earn your keep.'

'And what should I tell this Monetti about Lord Medici's death?' asked the valet and he tensed as Fate's eyes glittered with gold.

'Tell him Medici meddled with demonic forces and paid the inevitable price.'

The valet's life was now in ruins, but Fate had no pity for someone who would knowingly serve a man like Medici. Without another glance, he turned away from the house and returned to the Tutor and Motina. The hunchbacked witch was staring at the wand the Lannari had made for her.

'It's Taxus Eternus,' she said in a voice filled with awe. 'A Faerie wand, cut from eternal yew.'

The Tutor was not familiar with this tree, but Fate was and the sorcerer pursed his lips, nodding in

276

agreement as he acknowledged the significance of such a gift.

'Come on, my warrior maid,' he said with a smile. 'It's time we got you home.'

43

Breakout

In the darkness of his prison cell, Isaac was waiting for the midnight bell. He was tired and traumatised from his continued testing at the hands of Divine Servant Arden. Shaking with cold and nervous anxiety, he looked up at the barred window of his cell wondering if he had got the day wrong or missed the midnight bell. Then Isaac froze as he heard the creak of a door opening from somewhere across the street. He heard the clop and scuffle of hooves on cobblestones and then the soft sound of approaching footsteps until…

'Isaac!'

It was Amos.

'I'm here,' said Isaac as the stable master's face appeared at the window of his cell.

'Quickly,' said Amos, looping a piece of rope around one of the bars. 'We need to get these tied on tight.'

'Where's Sienna?' asked Isaac.

'She's with the horses.'

'What!?'

'You'll see.' Reaching down, Amos removed a lump hammer from a sack along with several steel spikes.

'What are you doing?' asked Isaac as he grabbed the bars and hauled himself up to the window.

'We're getting you out of there,' said Amos and with that, he proceeded to tap the steel spikes into the mortar between the stones holding the bars in place.

Across the road, Isaac could just make out the cloaked figure of Sienna. She was standing between the dark shapes of two enormous horses.

'You're going to…' began Isaac, but Amos cut him off.

'Quiet now,' said the stable master. 'We have to time this just right while the guards are on the other side of the keep.'

They waited in silence for a few seconds until a loud bell rang the first chime of midnight.

'Drop down,' said Amos as he picked up the hammer and waited for the next chime to sound.

The bell sounded and Amos gave one of the spikes a tap. That first blow was a little tentative because he needed to get his timing right. However, as the third chime sounded, Amos struck a hefty blow that drove the steel spikes deep into the mortar between the stones. A fourth chime sounded, and a fifth, but Amos could not use all twelve. They needed to break open the cell before the guards returned to this side of the keep.

As the tenth chime sounded, Amos gave one of the spikes a final hit before giving a low whistle. Almost immediately, the ropes attached to the bars were pulled taut. There was the creak of straining fibres, a faint grinding of stone and then a crash and clang as the bars of the cell were torn free.

'Now!' said Amos, reaching a hand down into the gaping hole. 'Isaac, give me your hand.'

Jumping up, Isaac grabbed the hand and the stable master hauled him out of the cell.

'Run to Sienna!' said Amos as he cut the ropes and began gathering them up as he followed Isaac back towards the disused coach house. He had just reached the corner of the adjoining street when four guards emerged around the side of the keep, quickly followed by a man in the black cassock of a priest.

'Stop!' cried the priest, but Amos ducked into the street where Sienna was now holding the reins of two sleek horses.

'Mount up!' she told Isaac as Amos bundled the coiled ropes into the disused coach house and reached for the double doors. There was just enough light for Isaac to glimpse the rumps of the two much larger horses standing quietly in the darkness.

'Good luck,' said Amos giving Sienna a parting nod as he began to close the doors.

'Amos…' began Isaac in a small voice, but there was no time for goodbyes.

'Ride fast,' said the stable master as the doors to the coach house closed.

'Isaac! Come on!' cried Sienna.

For a moment, the young man just stood there as the sound of running feet grew closer. Then he took hold of the free horse and stepped up into the saddle.

'Yah!' said Sienna, and both horses sprang forward as four guards and a priest rounded the corner of the street.

Leaning low over the saddle, Isaac glanced back. Even from a distance, he could feel the priest's anger. He could also feel the power rising through the man's body. A fierce ball of searing white flame appeared between his hands and Isaac knew they were dead.

'Sienna!'

'Just ride!' cried Sienna, but *she* did not know what was about to be unleashed.

Isaac felt defensive energy rising in his body then he screamed as the cuffs on his wrists burned into his skin with a searing heat. His power was shackled and he was unable to save them.

Behind them, the priest was just about to unleash his power when there was an almighty crash and one of the coach house doors burst open, smashing into the priest and knocking him to the ground.

Coming back to his knees, the priest shot a furious gaze into the disused coach house where a great bear-of-a-man was trying to calm an agitated horse.

'Oh, my lord,' said the man. 'A thousand apologies! Poor old Starke doesn't know his own strength. He just got spooked by all the commotion outside.'

The priest gave a snarl of fury as he realised the prisoner was gone. Divine Servant Arden had spent a great deal of time with this prisoner and there had even been talk of him being sent to the capital for cleansing.

'Are you all right, my good sir?' said Amos as he emerged from the coach house and began to dust off the priest's cassock.

'Get away from me, you oaf!' cried the priest, and Amos was fortunate that neither the priest nor any of the guards recognised him from his visit to the keep. With further self-recrimination he backed away into the coach house and closed the door, leaving the priest and the guards wondering how they were going to tell Divine Servant Arden that his most valuable prisoner had just escaped.

Sienna and Isaac didn't slow up until they were out of the city and onto the forest road heading north. Only then did Sienna slow down to check if they were being followed.

'Sienna,' said Isaac as she scanned the road for any sign of pursuit. 'Sienna, where are we going?'

'We're going to lie low for a few days,' replied Sienna as they continued on their way. 'And then we're going to see someone who might be able to help?'

'Does he live in the forest?'

'No,' said Sienna. 'He lives in Guile.'

'Is he a magic-user?'

'Kind of.'

'And does this *kind-of-a-magic-user* have a name?'

'Yes,' said Sienna. 'His name is Decimus Fate.'

44

To Never See the Sun

Two days later, Fate and the Tutor were standing in the pleasant surroundings of the Nymphacie water gardens. Concealed by the autumn colour of decorative trees, they watched as a young couple walked along the twisting pathways of the gardens. One was Jane, the young woman that Inganno had ensnared with a love potion; the other was Fidanza, the young man whose memory had been wiped clean by one of Inganno's cruel and powerful potions.

Just a few days earlier, Weasel had reported that a man fitting Fidanza's appearance had been helped by women in green robes after being attacked on a street of ill-repute. Fate happened to know that a religious order, known as the Scions of Abnoba, wore green robes and often frequented such places in the hope of helping some of the 'fallen women' who worked there. So it was reasonable to assume that *they* might have helped Fidanza.

Sure enough, they had found Fidanza in the temple of Abnoba being cared for by the same people who had helped Sienna Blade when she was injured in a fight with the Tutor. After trying to reassure the confused young man, Fate had arranged for him and Jane to meet in the water gardens, the very place where they first met.

Now the two young people looked shy and self-conscious. Fate and the Tutor could see Fidanza's confusion and Jane's efforts to keep her own feelings in check.

'It's sad,' said the Tutor as the young couple stopped to watch the tumbling water of a fountain. 'He really doesn't remember her at all.'

'No,' said Fate. 'But I wouldn't give up hope.'

'You think his memory will return?'

'Perhaps… and perhaps not,' said the sorcerer. 'But a house remains a house even if the plans for building it are lost.'

'You've been spending too much time with the monks of Tan Jit Su,' said the Tutor and Fate laughed.

'Fidanza might not remember that they were engaged,' continued the sorcerer. 'But he's essentially the same person and I wouldn't be surprised if they fell in love all over again.'

'You're really quite the romantic, aren't you?' said the Tutor and Fate arched an eyebrow as they turned to leave.

Having done all they could, the two men returned to Blackfell House where Motina had prepared a lunch of hot soup, meat pies and freshly baked bread.

'There's a letter arrived for you,' said the housekeeper.

'Anyone I know?' asked Fate as he and the Tutor took a seat at the table.

'I've no idea,' said Motina. 'Although the address looks like it was written by a woman's hand.'

Fate glanced at the letter while the Tutor looked down at the food.

'Pies?' he said as Motina reached for a ladle to dish out the soup. 'Are you sure these are safe to eat?'

Fate concealed a grin and there was a hollow 'clock' as Motina turned round with the ladle that just happened to clip the Tutor across the side of his head. The demon hunter flinched as Motina took her seat.

'You don't need to have any if you don't trust me,' she said in an affronted tone.

'I'll take two,' said the Tutor and Motina gave a snort at his attempted charm.

'I assume you've heard about the mysterious death in the Fourth Quarter,' she said, ladling out soup while the Tutor cut some bread.

'Mysterious death?' queried Fate.

'The son of a wealthy widow,' said Motina. 'She died over a year ago and now her son's been found dead in the basement.'

'The basement?' said Fate as he and the Tutor exchanged a look.

'Yes,' continued Motina. 'It's all very mysterious... They say he was found in a room with a metal door that was locked from the inside. Terribly gruesome,' she added. 'The young man's throat was torn out and he was lying in a puddle of tar. Apparently, he was a potion maker with a flair for conjuration.'

'Sounds like he meddled with something dangerous,' said Fate and the three of them shared a smile.

They ate in silence until Fate turned to Motina.

'And did you see Madam de Lorni?' he asked.

'I did.'

'How is she?'

'She's sad, of course,' said the housekeeper. 'But she's better for knowing that Luca is alive.'

'You told her?' exclaimed the Tutor. 'I thought we couldn't risk anyone finding out that Luca was still alive.'

'Madam de Lorni is a gifted actress,' said Fate. 'I was confident that she could play the part of a grieving mother.'

'But she'll have to play that part for *years*.'

'Well, for a year at least,' said Fate. 'Just until the contract on Luca's life expires.'

'You're terrible,' said the Tutor.

'I think he has a soft spot for her,' added Motina.

Looking a little awkward, Fate turned their attention to an object lying in the centre of the kitchen table. It was a slender length of yew wood, the smooth grain a pleasing blend of honey gold and cream.

'Have you used it yet?' he asked.

'I'm frightened to,' replied Motina.

'The realm of Faerie can be unsettling,' said the Tutor. 'But it should be respected, not feared.'

Fate nodded while Motina just stared at the wand.

'Warrior maid indeed,' teased Fate and Motina blushed.

'I can't help it if that's how a Faerie Lord sees me,' she quipped and Fate suddenly became serious.

'He's not the only one who sees you as that,' said the sorcerer. 'I've thought very much the same since you blasted me in the chest with a powerful spell.'

Now it was Motina's turn to appear awkward. Bending down to her soup, she changed the subject.

'Aren't you going to open your letter?' she asked.

Picking up the letter, Fate looked at the red wax seal, an elegant 'A' wound about by a single peacock feather. He didn't recognise the seal, but it all made sense as he opened the letter and began to read. The letter was from Countess Cévaro, but she had used the seal and signed the letter using her maiden family name.

Contessa di Aragona

'Anything interesting?' asked Motina as Fate laid the letter down.

'It's from the countess,' Fate replied. 'The demonic attacks on the serving girl are getting worse.'

'The poor child,' said Motina. 'Is there anything to be done?'

'The count threatened to kill the girl for bringing 'evil' into his house. So, the countess has taken her to Abbess Shimitsu at the Shīku temple.'

'That man's a bast…'

'A wise move,' interrupted Motina. 'I'm sure the abbess will be able to help.'

The housekeeper sounded confident, but the Tutor did not look so sure. If the girl's soul really had been promised to some dark entity, then even the monks of Tan Jit Su would struggle to keep the demonic forces at bay. He and Fate shared a look of concern as Motina changed the subject once more.

'Oh, and there's another thing…' said the housekeeper between mouthfuls of soup. 'Remember the sorcerer that Bohr arrested in Confluence? Well, I now know who it was.'

'Oh?' said Fate, unable to conceal the note of interest in his voice.

'It was Archmage Dahlian.'

'Dahlian!' said Fate, his brows drawing together in a frown.

'Do you know him?' asked the Tutor.

'A little,' said Fate. 'He's a powerful member of the Arcanium. Arresting him is a bold move indeed.'

'Bohr won't stop until he controls the entire world,' said Motina and the Tutor gave a dour nod of agreement.

'You've had dealings with the Emperor's sorcerer?' asked Fate.

'Of course,' said the Tutor. 'It was Bohr who corrupted the demon hunters. He changed them from a force for hunting evil into an arm of the emperor's will.'

'The emperor's just a pawn,' said Fate.

'I know,' said the Tutor. 'The emperor signed my death warrant, but it was Bohr who sent the demon hunters to kill my family.'

'Bohr's influence is growing,' said Fate. 'Even the world of Faerie is paying attention.'

'Maybe you should write to the Arcanium,' said the Tutor. 'Find out if anyone else is under threat.'

'Perhaps,' mused Fate.

'But not today!' said Motina with a note of exasperation. 'Today we're going to rest and give thanks for the lives of two innocent young men.'

Fate's inward gaze made it clear that his thoughts were now focused on Oruthian Bohr and what his ambitions might mean for the world. But the Tutor could sympathise with Motina. Pouring them all a cup of tea he leaned back in his chair.

'So, you told Madam de Lorni about the Butcher of Guile?' he asked in a tone of surprise.

'I didn't tell her all the gory details,' replied Motina.

'Then what did you tell her?' asked the Tutor and even Fate looked up to see how she would answer.

'I didn't call him The Butcher at all,' said Motina. 'I said his name is Samuel Culpepper, and he can never see the sun.'

Fate and the Tutor smiled, but Fate's smile was tempered by the thoughts running through his mind. He was thinking about the only living sorcerer whose power had matched his own; a feral mage who had a plan to break the bonds that kept the human world safe from the terrors of the demonic realm.

Fate was thinking about the emperor's personal sorcerer, a man by the name of Oruthian Bohr.

Epilogue

Bohr

Bound by shackles that negated his magical powers, Archmage Dahlian swept his gaze around the chamber in which he now stood. Thirty feet in diameter, it was like a great bowl sunk into the marble floor of the imperial palace, the sides sweeping up to form three-quarters of a complete sphere. The chamber was lined with blue ceramic tiles that gleamed and shimmered as if the ocean had risen up to contain him. It was impressive and unsettling, and Archmage Dahlian could feel the thrum of the magic running through it.

'Don't worry old friend,' said a deep resonant voice. 'The pain of cleansing is intense, but it will only last a few seconds. Or so I am led to believe.'

Archmage Dahlian looked up into the eyes of Oruthian Bohr; deep green eyes that glittered with flecks of gold. The emperor's personal sorcerer was standing behind a column of stone on which three marble spheres sat in cradles of twisted gold.

'Cleansing?' challenged Dahlian. 'Is that what you're calling it?'

Bohr smiled, the expression accentuating the angular features of his face.

'That's what the priests of the Divine Spirit call it,' he said. 'And I am happy to indulge the whims of my new disciples.'

'Disciples?' said Dahlian. 'I thought you were all servants of the Divine.'

'Indeed we are,' said Bohr. 'But no one can match the power of *my* devotion.'

Bohr looked down as a ball of white flame appeared in his hand. The ball of fire grew hotter and brighter until Dahlian had to shield his eyes and look away.

'No,' said Bohr. 'The priests of the Divine Spirit follow me because I am a living testament to the power of their god.'

'You don't believe that,' said Dahlian. 'All this talk of your conversion… it's all lies.'

'True,' said Bohr with a smile. 'But those lies allow me to reach far beyond the limits imposed by Confluence. With Confluence out of the way, I will be able to go anywhere and do anything.'

'What are you going to do?' asked Dahlian. 'Kill us all?'

The smile faded from Bohr's face and his green eyes glittered with a dangerous light as he looked down into the chamber.

'Let's just take this one mage at a time, shall we?'

With that, he picked up one of the marble spheres from its golden cradle and placed it in the first of three hollows in the stone pillar. Immediately, the sphere of the chamber was completed by a shimmering wall of energy.

Realising he was now trapped, Archmage Dahlian began to struggle against his bonds. He tried to summon his magic and cast a spell, but the bracelets on his wrists flared with magical symbols and he cried out in pain. Feeling a sense of desperation he tried again, but the skin of his arms began to blister and burn as Bohr placed the second sphere into the activation column.

Dahlian gasped, and his eyes went wide as his own magical essence begin to resonate with the energy of the chamber, then he slumped to his knees as he felt that same energy being drawn out of his body. His mouth gaped open as he felt its absence inside of him, a horrible sense of defilement and emptiness as though a part of his mind and soul had been sucked out against his will.

Knowing he was about to die, he looked up as Bohr lifted the third and final sphere. The green eyes of the feral mage were filled with a terrible light, and his grey hair flew up with the waves of energy that were now rising from the recepticule on which he stood.

And now, Dahlian knew that the rumours were true. Oruthian Bohr was draining the power of magic-users and channelling it into himself. For years, Dahlian had fought against Bohr's relentless pursuit of power, and now his own magical powers would strengthen the enemy he had resisted for so long.

What a cruel thought to haunt him at the end.

Through a tormented haze, Dahlian watched as Bohr placed the final sphere into its hollow sconce. He felt a surge of unspeakable agony and his mind was filled with a searing white light. And yet, in the brief moment before death, he caught a glimpse into Bohr's black heart; a writhing knot of fierce talent, ruthless ambition and soul-corrupting madness. A brief moment of connection and then Archmage Dahlian was gone, his flesh vaporised, his magic absorbed by the chamber and channelled into the body of Oruthian Bohr.

Bohr took a breath and breathed in the smell that follows a lightning strike. He opened his eyes and looked down into the empty chamber where the misty plasma of a defeated enemy was slowly fading from the air. He was impressed by the amount of power that an archmage could provide, but in a few weeks' time he would absorb the energy of an even more powerful sorcerer. A feral mage from an obscure city called Dymhaven.

According to the Divine Spirit priests of the city, the young man possessed considerable potential, and that potential energy would soon be his.

With a sense of satisfaction, Bohr replaced the marble spheres in their golden cradles and turned to leave the room, his entire body buzzing with the energy he had just absorbed. He pushed open the doors and the smell of lightning was replaced by the smell of the oil lamps that lined the walls of the corridor.

Waiting in the corridor were two Don'Sha'Vir tasked with guarding the chamber of blue tiles. And standing nervously between the mystical guards was a pale man in the purple robes of a palace advisor.

'What is it?' asked Bohr as the man squirmed beneath his gaze. 'Tell me, or die!' snapped Bohr and the man suddenly found his voice.

'It's the feral mage in Dymhaven,' he blurted out in a rush. 'He's escaped from prison. The Divine Spirit priests are searching for him as we speak.'

For a moment Bohr did not react. Only the tensing of his jaw showed that anything was amiss. But then his lip began to curl, his brows came together and a low growl rose up in his throat. Before anyone else could move, he spun around and grabbed the head of the Don'Sha'Vir to his left, slamming it into the wall of the corridor and suffusing it with a surge of energy that shattered the man's skull and turned his brain into a steaming mass of pulp.

The terrified advisor stumbled back in shock, while the second Don'Sha'Vir merely stood with his hand on the hilt of his curved sword, not quite sure how it should react to what had just occurred. As Bohr removed his hand, the body of the dead Don'Sha'Vir collapsed to the floor, leaving a grizzly mass of carbonised flesh stuck to the wall.

'When?' asked Bohr in a quiet and deadly tone.

'Two nights ago,' said the man.

'Do the priests know where he's gone? Did he head inland or out to sea?'

'Inland, my Lord,' said the advisor. 'They think he's heading for Guile.'

Bohr paused in thought.

'It's a small city in the Seven Vales,' added the advisor. 'The prisoner shouldn't be hard to find.'

'Then find him,' snapped Bohr and the man bowed low, backing away until it was safe to turn and run.

Bohr watched him go.

'*Guile?*' he mused.

He had never given the city much thought, but the same could not be said for the Seven Vales. The region might be considered rustic and insignificant, but it held the keys to his ambition.

Seven Vales and seven ancient trees.

Seven trees that bound the realms together.

While the trees remained strong he could never break the bond between the human world and Faerie. And while that bond remained he could not achieve dominion over all three realms. That was why the trees had to be destroyed. Such trees were considered sacred, such trees had protection. But in the forest town of Twining he had found someone who was willing to take the risk, and any day now, the Black Oak of Twining would fall.

Bohr revelled in the idea, but his thoughts kept returning to Guile.

Wasn't Guile the city where the Kane Twins had recently met their end? He had often wondered who might have the power to kill the notorious twins.

And why would a feral mage flee to the city of Guile?

And was it a coincidence that Guile *just happened* to lie close to the town of Twining?

Suspicion bloomed in the mind of Oruthian Bohr.

Could it possibly be *him*?

For years now he had felt nothing from his old adversary; not even the slightest flicker of power. He had assumed his enemy was dead. But coincidences made him suspicious and Bohr could not shake the feeling, that all this…

Had something to do…

With Fate.

Dear Reader

Thank you for buying Decimus Fate and the Butcher of Guile. If you enjoyed it, I would be incredibly grateful if you could spare a few minutes to leave a short review on Amazon.

And if you have any comments, or you would like to get in touch, then please say hello on:

Twitter: @TheFlanston

Or via my website:

www.peter.flannery.co.uk

Either way it would be great to hear from you and thanks again for buying the book.

With warm regards
Peter

Other Books by Peter A. Flannery

The first book in this new fantasy adventure finds Decimus Fate and the Tutor joining forces to fight enchanted statues and demonic sorcerers as they try to solve the mystery of a deadly disease.

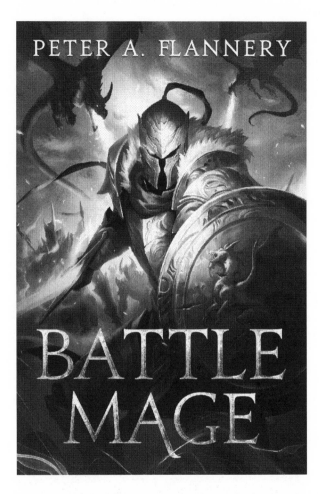

A classic coming-of-age fantasy adventure with great characters, epic battles and super cool dragons.

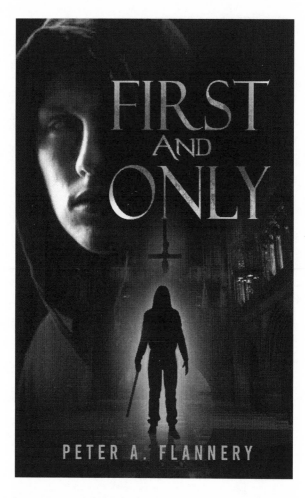

A fast-paced thriller about the world's first genuine
psychic and the delusional killer who stalks him.

Made in the USA
Middletown, DE
19 September 2021